MARGINAL

Also by Tom Carlisle
and available from Titan Books

Blight

MARGINAL

TOM CARLISLE

TITAN BOOKS

Marginal
Print edition ISBN: 9781803360744
E-book edition ISBN: 9781803360751

Published by Titan Books
A division of Titan Publishing Group Ltd
144 Southwark Street, London SE1 0UP
www.titanbooks.com

First edition: October 2024
10 9 8 7 6 5 4 3 2

This is a work of fiction. All of the characters, organizations, and events portrayed in this novel are either products of the author's imagination or are used fictitiously. Any resemblance to actual persons, living or dead (except for satirical purposes), is entirely coincidental.

© Tom Carlisle 2024

Tom Carlisle asserts the moral right to be identified as the author of this work.

No part of this publication may be reproduced, stored in a retrieval system, or transmitted, in any form or by any means without the prior written permission of the publisher, nor be otherwise circulated in any form of binding or cover other than that in which it is published and without a similar condition being imposed on the subsequent purchaser.

A CIP catalogue record for this title is available from the British Library.

Printed and bound by
CPI (UK) Ltd, Croydon, CR0 4YY.

For Mel

I have said to corruption, Thou art my father: to the worm, Thou art my mother.

Job 17:14

PROLOGUE

He was shaken from his reverie by a knock at the door. He ignored it. They knew he had work to do. Knew he needed time to think.

The notecards in front of him, a little stack of books. The ritual, the routine. His mind was ready. He was open. But these days the thread sometimes eluded him. He tried to trace his journey, the paths that had led him here, but everything was a swirl of confusion. They'd all found such blessings in this place, such clarity and focus, but he couldn't shake the sense it was too good to be true. There was always a price to pay.

Another knock at the door. Harder this time, almost frantic.

He made his voice as gruff as he could manage. 'I'm occupied.'

It was Cat. Her voice a little muffled. 'I'm sorry, Bjorn, but—'

She knew better than this. She of all people knew how difficult this could be sometimes.

He rose from his chair, irritated. 'I need this time, Cat,' he said, crossing the room. 'To listen, to reflect. How am I supposed to lead these people if I keep being interrupted?'

'It's Marcus…'

Of course it was Marcus. It was always Marcus these days: he was a tangle of barbed wire, on whom Bjorn kept snagging himself. He sighed, his hand pausing on the door handle, hoping that there might still be a chance to get back to work. 'You can't deal with it yourself? Can't talk it through with Miranda or Elliot?'

Cat's voice was a little shaky. This wasn't like her. 'I just thought that…'

His irritation got the better of him. 'No, you didn't think,' he said. 'If you had you'd have gone elsewhere.'

Cat's voice broke. 'You need to see this,' she said, and when he heard her begin to cry he knew something was truly wrong. He turned the handle.

'What is it – what's happened?'

She was standing in his doorway, head bowed, her hands in her short hair. 'I can't…' she said through her tears. Her voice was tight. He couldn't remember seeing her like this in all the years they'd been here. 'I don't know how to describe it… you need to come.'

He tried to tamp down his own panic. 'Okay,' he said, holding his hands up as though by doing so he might ward off her sorrow. 'Where is he?'

Cat's jaw was clenched. He could see the effort it took for her to speak. 'He's dead, Bjorn.'

He felt it again. The void, reaching for him. Its tendrils stretching out into the world. 'Where?'

'In the vault.'

He forced down the terror, fought to keep his voice calm. 'Something got in there?'

His thoughts were already racing. The System, his life's work, crumbling to pieces. Everything they'd built, destroyed by collapse or flood or fire. It was so fragile, so tenuous.

He heard the coldness in Cat's voice. 'Don't worry,' she said. 'The System's fine.'

He knew he shouldn't rise to the bait, but he couldn't help himself. 'The years I've put into this place…' He regretted it the moment he said it. He was getting lazy. Weak.

'I said it's fine,' said Cat, with something of her usual ferocity. She wiped her eyes, brutally. 'Come on.'

She was already striding away towards the great concrete slab that was the vault, leaving Bjorn to hurry after her. As he did, he surveyed what they'd built here: the patchwork of vegetable gardens dug alongside the bunkhouses, the renovated mess hall looming over them all. It had a stark, utilitarian beauty: a kind of sanctuary from the cruel world. For several years now he had been struck by the thought of losing it. Old age, he supposed.

When he finally reached Cat she was standing at the door to the vault. He could feel the tension radiating off her. He couldn't leave it like this.

God, but this was the part of running this place he hated most.

'If I seemed preoccupied before,' he mumbled, 'thoughtless… I'm sorry.' It was clumsy, inarticulate, but maybe that was better. Cat knew all his rhetorical tricks.

'Okay.' She didn't look at him. The tension hadn't yet dissipated.

'I mean it, Cat. I'm no good at these things. But I'm... I'm trying.'

'I know,' she said. Her voice was without emotion and she stared past him. 'Listen,' she said, 'I can't deal with this now.'

'Of course. But we'll talk properly. Later.' He nodded towards the door. 'Shall we?'

Next to him Cat closed her eyes. 'I can't,' she said. She looked a little green.

'You're not coming?'

'No,' she said firmly, and then, more quietly: 'I... I can't go back in there.'

He felt fear prickle up his spine. 'Will I be able to find him?'

'Oh yeah,' she said, swallowing hard. 'You'll see him.'

And so he opened the door to the vault and followed the familiar route, those steps he could walk in his sleep, until he turned a corner and stumbled across...

The stuff of nightmares.

There was blood everywhere. On the doorframes, on the floor. Splattered across the spines of every book in view, in great curving arcs. Arterial sprays dripping from the ceiling and pooling in corners; scraps of flesh on the shelves, barely recognisable as human. Even when he closed his eyes he knew it by its smell: deep, ferrous, earthy.

At a desk sat a strange, ragged stump: a man, ripped apart at the waist, his spinal column standing up from the ruin. Bjorn recoiled, tripping over his feet in the dim vault, his mind ablaze.

MARGINAL

He groped for the door, wrenched it open, stumbled out into the evening.

'My God, Cat,' he heard himself say. 'My God.'

'I know.' Her voice was choked.

'What could have done that to him…?'

1

THE LANDLINE'S ringing, shrill and insistent in the darkness. Rob's eyes flick to the alarm clock: 3 a.m. At first he assumes it's another telemarketer. That's the price you pay for keeping your number online, however discreetly.

But in his heart of hearts, he doesn't believe it. He's been expecting a midnight phone call for years. That's the only reason he kept a landline: in case Marcus needed to reach him. He throws off the covers, staggers over to the phone.

'Hello? Is that Rob Barton?' A tiny, Germanic lilt to the voice. Even after all these years.

'Speaking.' His heart sinks. He knows that voice. With it comes memories of Craigdhu, and the Pit. The darkness that makes him afraid to close his eyes.

'Gosh. It's been... it's been so many years.' It comes out as genial, as if Bjorn were talking to an old friend. Like there was no distance between them at all.

'Who is this?' Rob's words are hard, curt. He knows who it is, of course. He knew right away. He just needs to hear Bjorn say it.

'It's Bjorn Thrissell.' No trace of anxiety in his voice. 'But my God,' Bjorn murmurs, 'you sound so much like your brother.'

Rob's breath catches in his throat. 'Something's happened to Marcus.'

Bjorn sighs. An old man, regretting the intrusion of reality. 'Yes. Yes, I'm afraid that's right.' Rob's mind is already racing. Marcus, lost in the woods, calling out for help that never arrives. Or worse: Marcus in the Pit, the light in his eyes dimming as his voice plays in an endless loop.

'You bastard.' The words come out before Rob realises.

On the other end of the phone there's silence. For a moment he wonders if Bjorn's hung up on him. Then there's the faint sound of breathing on the end of the line.

'I know you're angry with me,' Bjorn says eventually, his tone flat.

'You don't have the slightest idea what I feel.' He takes a deep breath. 'You've no idea what the past decade has been like. Forever wondering if what I see on the news is your doing.' Bjorn is still silent. 'So go on, then,' says Rob. 'What have you done to him?'

There's a trace of a sigh in Bjorn's voice. 'I assure you, we had nothing to do with—'

'Bullshit.' Rob cuts him off, his grip tightening on the phone. 'If something's happened to Marcus, it's because of you.'

Bjorn's quiet again and Rob feels horribly exposed, wondering if he's walked straight into a trap. When Bjorn's voice comes again, it's low and weary. 'Rob, please,' he says. 'Let me explain.'

But Rob's not listening, not really. He's thinking about how

Marcus spoke to him that night in the woods: like he were a stranger, an enemy to be hunted down.

'Your brother is dead, Rob.'

Of course. Of course he's dead.

'Whatever happened to him, it's on you,' Rob says, his voice heavy with grief and anger. Bjorn doesn't answer. Later Rob will recount the details of their conversation and realise he knows almost nothing about how Marcus died. But in that moment he doesn't even think about Marcus, doesn't even care. All he cares about is hurting Bjorn. 'You hear me?' Rob says into the silence. 'I hold you responsible.'

When Bjorn speaks again his voice is stronger. 'I assure you, it was not my fault.'

This isn't fair. Rob tried so many ways to find out about Marcus over the years, to check in on his brother, and Bjorn shot down every attempt. All that time he'd denied Rob the last chance of a relationship with his own family, and even now he's the one in control.

'Do you have any idea how long I spent trying to reach you?' Rob says, his hand tight on the phone, his voice a whisper. He closes his eyes, pushes back the familiar ache in his chest. As if those years in Craigdhu had altered something fundamental, broken him in a way that couldn't be fixed.

'I got your letters,' says Bjorn. 'The phone calls, the emails. I got them all.'

'And... nothing.' Rob's shaking his head now, not that Bjorn could see it. 'Not a word. Until today, when you call me out of nowhere and tell me Marcus is dead.'

'You deserve to know.'

He'd held on to so much about Bjorn: that shabby old cardigan hanging loosely over his wiry frame, with his grey hair brushing its collar, or his patchwork beard in a constant state of disarray. Most of all, he remembered how Bjorn took Marcus under his wing. Filled his head with ideals, convincing him he was achieving something great.

But Rob had forgotten his smug, superior air: the terrible sense of being granted charity by a person you hate. A laugh escapes his lips, a horrible, manic sound edged with hysteria. 'Surely you didn't really consider keeping it from me?' He waits, but either Bjorn thinks the question is rhetorical or he doesn't deign it worthy of an answer. Typical. 'What happened, then?'

'There was… an incident.' Bjorn swallows hard, the sound distorted and grotesque through the phone's speaker. 'Something attacked Marcus, we think.'

'Attacked him?' He has an image of his brother lying alone in the wilderness, his voice growing ever fainter as his calls for help go unheard. Darkness falling, blood pooling beneath a gash in his side.

'Some sort of animal. He was – mauled.'

'You're kidding.'

'I know it sounds unlikely, but this far north—'

Again comes the anger: driving out any questions, any sorrow for Marcus. 'You're in Scotland, man, not Siberia.' He waits a second or two for Bjorn to snap back, but there's no reply. 'He wasn't attacked by a wolf. So what killed him?'

The faintest hesitation. 'We don't know that.'

'Nothing in the cards, then.' That would definitely get Bjorn's attention. Any mention of the System. It might have been the only thing in the world he actually cared about. Sure enough, when Bjorn speaks again his voice is cold.

'There's no call for that.'

'Believe me, I could say a lot worse.'

Bjorn doesn't bother to disguise his sigh. 'I called to tell you what happened,' he says. 'Now you know.' He takes a breath, apparently collecting himself. 'I'm terribly sorry,' he says with an air of finality. 'He was a good man.'

Despite himself, Rob's stunned. 'That's it?'

'I don't see what else there is to say,' Bjorn says, resigned.

'I want to see the body.'

Bjorn's answer comes immediately. 'Out of the question.'

Rob's laugh is hard and bitter. 'As if you'd dream of stopping me.'

'This is private property. We're well within our rights—'

'How about the police, then? How would you feel about stopping them?'

Bjorn's silent for several seconds.

'I don't like bullies, Rob,' he says more firmly.

'Don't you dare try and take the moral high ground,' Rob snarls back, startled by the aggression in his voice. 'My brother deserves a proper burial.'

'And he'll get one,' says Bjorn. 'Here. In the community to which he gave his life.'

'No.' He can't let this happen. They've taken Marcus's life, taken away Rob's best chance at a family and left him rudderless in the world. They can't take Marcus from him in death.

'I'm sorry?' Bjorn sounds genuinely surprised.

'I'm the last surviving member of his family, so that makes me *de facto* executor of his will, and I won't let him rot up there. I can't.' Rob's voice cracks. 'He deserves to come home. To be laid to rest properly. I need to say goodbye.'

Bjorn's silent for a long time. Rob imagines him seething.

'This is a mistake,' he says finally.

'I'm not thrilled about it either,' Rob says. 'But I'm coming.'

2

He'd never forget his last day in Craigdhu, no matter how hard he tried. Hunched in the darkness, his words playing over and over in an endless loop, until he couldn't tell what was real any more. By the time they were finished with him, his own voice sounded alien.

He remembered stumbling out into the daylight and wondering how long he'd been in there. Hours, days, weeks? Time lost all meaning in there, refracted on itself. The moments became agony, sheer agony.

He'd seen others emerge from the Pit looking broken, like walking shadows. Now he was one of them: sixteen years old and as frail as an old man. Bjorn had always insisted it was a mercy. 'I'm calling them back to who they are,' he'd said when Rob asked him about it. 'They know that, deep down. They just forgot it for a while.'

So that's what it felt like. Once upon a time he'd likened it to being cleansed, purified by the force of his own words. Instead he felt annihilated, torn apart.

His mother didn't have the strength to shun him tonight. He saw her try when he entered the bunkhouse. Saw her turn away from him like she was supposed to. She couldn't bring herself to do it, not this time.

She kept glancing back at him, then trying to occupy herself with something in the kitchen: now putting away cutlery, now drying a mug. Now leaving the room, now setting herself down on the bed. Now taking a deep breath to calm her nerves.

'Oh, God,' he heard her murmur from the other room. He'd not followed her: he knew what was expected of him too. Knew how this was supposed to play out. The others were expected to shun him for the next twenty-four hours. To give him a chance to reflect on who he truly was, that true self to whom he'd been forcibly reintroduced in the darkness. They weren't to look at him, not even when they served him his meals.

Twenty-four hours of agony, of being cut off, and then the immediate re-embrace of the commune as though the exile had never occurred. There was a pattern to it, a ritual whose contours he'd once found strangely comforting.

Her voice came again from the next room. 'Oh, Lord.' He felt it then. She was coming to him. She'd fold him in her arms, pull him close to her, whisper that she'd protect him. That it would be their secret, and that nobody else need know. He could see it as clearly as though it had happened already – and then, without warning, the picture changed.

A slamming door, and the thud of teenage footsteps on a

wooden floor. Marcus stomped past him, not saying a word, his face a steely glower. Strode into their shared bedroom and began talking in a voice that was low and furious. There was something authoritative in it, like he was speaking to a subordinate.

He'd seen some of the older men mentoring Marcus, teaching him how to manage a team and how to take on responsibilities around the camp. But this wasn't that. There was no compassion in his brother's voice.

'Don't indulge him,' Marcus said. 'Don't you dare. He's only just out of that place, and he's vulnerable. You know that. He needs time alone. To ground himself.'

His mother was silent, and he imagined her stunned – wearing a look of disgust at this child of her own body. But when he heard her speak again she sounded cowed, tentative. 'I… I know. I understand. It's… it's hard, that's all.'

'It'll be a damn sight harder for you if you lose him for good, don't you think?' Rob wanted to go to her, to charge in and tell his brother to shut his fucking mouth, but what good would that do? He could yell and scream and the best-case scenario was that Marcus would look straight through him as though he wasn't there. More likely he'd be sent back to the Pit, forced to listen once more to the hateful sound of his own voice, calling him back to the life he'd forgotten. 'You know that's what's at stake here. If the world gets its claws into him, if it distracts him from what he's learned here, he's never coming back.' Silence. 'Say it, woman. I want to hear you say it.'

'Yes,' she said, faintly. 'Yes, I know what's at stake.'

'So what are you going to do about it?'

Silence again. If only he could see his mother's expression, see the way she looked at Marcus. Was she scared? Disgusted? Defiant?

He hated his brother sometimes, but that was normal, wasn't it? Everybody hated their siblings eventually. They knew everything about you, knew how to push your buttons. They were like your doppelganger: you saw yourself in their distorted mirror. What parts of himself did he recognise in Marcus? His drive, charisma, sense of purpose. All of them were in Marcus first, perfected in him. That should have brought them closer, but it only exacerbated his brother's cruelty.

All Rob wanted was for someone – *someone* – to tell him they understood. To say they knew that shunning was the shittiest way to treat a person, and this was no way to build a better world. Write it down, for God's sake. Slip it under his door. Except that was the last thing anyone here could do. Doing so would get them sent to the Pit.

He wanted to cry. Wanted to curl up on his bed and weep. Couldn't even do that in peace. Marcus would be there soon, on the top bunk, listening. Reporting everything back to Bjorn and Cat.

There was nowhere Rob could go to be alone: nowhere, maybe, except the vault. You could lose yourself down there, among the rows of shelves. It was vast, so much bigger than it needed to be. *To make space for all that we'll create*, Bjorn had said when Rob asked about it. It had been a shooting range once, Marcus told him. That was why it was so big. Bjorn had repurposed the space when he came up here, built that maze of desks and shelves and cubbyholes and then encouraged them to let their imagination run free. It felt a bit ridiculous when there were so few of them, but even Rob knew it wasn't a good idea to say that aloud.

'I'll do what's right,' he heard his mother say to Marcus. 'You can trust me.'

Marcus was silent for a long time. 'I hope so,' he said. When he stormed out of their shared bedroom, he didn't even glance at Rob.

His mother woke him in the middle of that night. Standing at his bedside. Her hand on his shoulder, a finger pressed to her lips. In the bunk above him he could hear Marcus snoring gently. In the moonlight her face was all shadows, but he could see the fear in her eyes. She pointed towards the kitchen, and he rose from his bed and padded across the room, horribly conscious of the creaky floor. What would Marcus do if he caught them? Rob had seen his aggression firsthand more times than he cared to remember. He'd never laid hands on his own mother, but it wasn't much of a stretch to imagine Marcus doing so.

She followed him, her footsteps nimble and catlike, lifting his heavy fleece-lined shirt from the end of his bed as she went. He knew what she was going to say the moment she did that. But then he saw the supplies laid out on the table, the knife beside them.

'I can't,' he said, although even as he said it he wasn't quite so sure anymore. Down there in the Pit, he'd felt a kernel of resistance, had grasped something he could hold on to, the memory of a love that went beyond the commune's stultifying confines, and he'd gripped it tightly as his own words swept over him again and again. 'I can't go without you.'

'You have to,' she said. Her voice was a hushed whisper, and she couldn't stop herself glancing over at where Marcus lay in his bunk. 'I can distract them, keep them from finding you, but to do that I've got to be here.' She put a hand against his cheek then, but instead of tenderness in her voice he heard only fear. 'You have to go without me,' she hissed. 'There's no time.'

Through the window of their kitchen he could see the cloudless sky, a bright moon hanging in it. There would be no cover, nowhere to hide until he hit the treeline. If anyone spotted him, he was fucked.

'You can do this,' she said, as though she'd read his thoughts. 'Everyone's asleep. Out the door, head for the gate, and then into the trees. Keep the road on your left, and don't stop until you see the village. When you get there, you call the police. Understand?'

It was all he could do to nod mutely. She took the knife and slipped it into his pocket. 'I hope you don't need this,' she said, 'but if anyone tries to take you back, you stop them.' She held his face. 'You understand me?'

Again he nodded. His mind felt slow, unable to focus, like some part of it was still listening to that recording. She took a foil-wrapped sandwich, and slipped it into his shirt's other pocket. 'Hey,' she said with a new tenderness. 'You need to be brave for me, you hear? It's going to be okay.'

'What should I tell them?'

'Tell them what this place is like. Tell them about the Pit.' She shook her head, a look of helplessness in her eyes. 'I don't know, Rob. The words will come when you need them. Tell them to get me out.'

The woods were a block of thick darkness. He hesitated for a moment at the door of the bunkhouse, feeling the silent pull of his bed behind him. A day of discomfort and he'd be accepted again. Rotas to participate in. Digging the gardens, chopping the carrots, clearing the tables. Boring, but simple. He was walking away from it all. Out there would be foster homes, interviews with social services, and the indignities of trying to join a secondary school. God only knew what he'd tell people if they asked where he'd been all these years. He wasn't sure he'd have the courage to tell them he'd been here – how would he ever begin to explain it?

He could feel his mother's eyes on him. Knew that if he were to turn back, to tell her he couldn't do it, he'd be dooming her too. He owed it to her to get out.

She'd fight for him if he got caught trying to run, wrench him out of the darkness whatever it cost her to do so. He could imagine her, ragged and bloody, throwing open the door of his cell. Looking like the woman she must have been long ago, before she joined the Scriveners, that fiery postgrad who'd thrown her life away to follow Bjorn. He liked to think about what she'd been like in those days, before this place took the best of her, before it forced her into its routines and compelled her to write thousands of words on index cards.

He buttoned his padded shirt up to the neck and made for the treeline. He was nearly at the road when he saw a light click on in their bunkhouse, followed in quick succession by another, and then another. Marcus was awake. It was only a matter of minutes before he woke the others. Rob ducked into the trees, became a shadow. Slowed his pace. Moving cautiously now, his torch off. It was almost impossible – every snap of a twig was amplified, and he was groping his way through the woods like a blind man, praying he wouldn't break his ankle in a rabbit warren or knock himself out on a tree trunk. He couldn't bring himself to stand still – doing so was nauseating, unbearable, so somehow he managed to keep moving. He had to be in motion. Had to be heading away from this place, no matter how slowly.

It took just three minutes before he heard the truck's ignition. It came rolling down the hill with the lights on full beam and Elliot in the driver's seat. Marcus on his other side, leaning out the window like a dog. At the first sight of the beams Rob froze, pressed himself up against a tree trunk in a desperate attempt to remain unnoticed. He was only a few metres away from the road, had resolved to stay close to it to keep from getting lost in the dark. Now he cursed that decision. He was uncomfortably visible, he was sure of it. All they'd have to do was turn their beams on the trees and they'd see some misshapen trunk, something that looked a little too much like a sixteen-year-old playing hide-and-seek, and he'd be done for. But he couldn't possibly move now. If he tried, the sound of cracking twigs would summon them straight to him.

He tried to stay still, tried to make his breathing silent. Tried to feel the ground underfoot, the sensation of the breeze on his face – the way his mother had taught him to when he was anxious.

If he moved, he'd be back in the Pit. Dragged there like a sacrifice by his own brother. Lights were coming closer. Washing over the trees, lengthening the shadows. The truck pulled to a stop. Then Rob heard the handbrake, the sound of a door opening, and finally footsteps. His brother calling for him: behind his left shoulder, he thought, but he didn't dare turn and look. He closed his eyes, praying for a miracle, but when he did all he heard inside his head was the sound of his voice on that fucking tape, repeating all he knew to be true in an endless loop until it no longer even sounded like words anymore.

They searched the woods for ten minutes, although it felt like much longer. Stumbling over one another, alternating between joy and despair. He heard them growing further and further away from him – heard Elliot exclaim in delight that he'd found something, only to groan as it turned out to be a rotting stump. Heard Marcus's calls, at first in a ghastly parody of brotherly love – *come on, man, all is forgiven, you don't need to do this* – then growing progressively more irate as the time drew on.

Don't think I didn't see it in you, you worthless twat. The cowardice. The laziness. I lived with it every fucking night. This place is better off without you, and we both know it. If it wasn't for Mum I'd leave you out here to rot.

And then, somehow, they were heading back for the truck, Marcus muttering *fuck fuck fuck* under his breath. Rob wanted to whoop in delight, but he was shaking so hard he wasn't sure he could utter a sound even if he'd wanted to. Instead he spent the rest of the night groping his way through the trees by moonlight, melting into the woods whenever he heard the sound of a vehicle.

He reached the village as the sun was rising. A little before 7 a.m. Orange light on roof slates. Nobody on the street. He felt horribly exposed on that main road, certain that at any moment Elliot would roar down the hill and haul him into the truck.

He couldn't even form his thoughts into words. Didn't know where to start. Just wandered down the road in a daze, hoping someone would spot him, hoping they'd take the decision out of his hands. Open their door and ask him what he was doing, invite him in to sit and eat with them.

Instead he heard the sound of an engine at his back and leapt out of his skin. Turning, he saw a Range Rover reversing out of a driveway, a burly man leaning out of the window and looking embarrassed. 'Sorry there, pal,' he said. 'Didn't expect anyone around at this time of day.'

Years later Rob would realise how a normal person would have reacted. Would have raised a hand to say, 'no worries,' or maybe asked the guy what the fuck he thought he was doing. In the event, his reaction was probably what saved him. He said nothing, didn't even move out of the drive, just stared slackly back at the guy. The man watched Rob for several seconds over his shoulder, then turned off his engine, stepped out of the car and walked over.

He was shorter than Rob and much stockier, with dark hair cropped closely and a visible bald patch. He had a warm, amiable face, and as he approached Rob he did so without anger. He held his hands up before him as though trying to calm a cornered dog. Rob supposed he must have looked afraid. No doubt he was emaciated, dishevelled, his clothes washed out and his face pale. When he looked at photos of himself from then he hardly recognised the kid looking back at him.

'Are you okay, pal?' the man said. 'I haven't seen you around.' Still Rob couldn't answer. His lips were dry and cracked, and he mostly just wanted to weep. 'Are you here staying with somebody? Are you Lisa's nephew? Gemma's?' The man narrowed his eyes. 'No,' he said. 'No, you're from up on the hill, aren't you? Did something happen?'

It was all Rob could do to nod.

'Come on,' said the man, glancing back along the road as though he too feared Elliot's sudden appearance. 'Let's get you inside and get you some breakfast. You look half-starved.'

And he put his arm around Rob's shoulders and led him inside.

Was he a fool to think it would all be better then, that it could all be fixed? When the man, who was called Andrew, sat him at the kitchen table and called the police, and when he asked again what had happened, was Rob wrong to hope that speaking the words might make a difference? For a while it looked like it might. When the police came and set him in the back of their car and listened patiently to his statement, or when they called Bjorn in for questioning; when they asked Rob about his experience for the second time and he knew they'd relay every one of his questions to Bjorn in that interrogation room; all of this had to be the first step to getting his mother back, he remembered thinking, his best chance to save her from that place. Maybe that was all they'd needed, all along: a higher authority. Somebody with real power.

All that hope. It would feel like folly, later, sitting desolately in one of his foster bedrooms, or in the bleak squalor of a children's home. He should have known Bjorn would be prepared for this. That every one of them would deny any knowledge of his mother, that her personal effects would have disappeared somewhere into the vault's cavernous recesses.

The police searched – oh, how they searched – but he realised as early as that first week that they'd never find her, no matter how much they promised, no matter how hard they told him they'd fight. There was too much information to sift, too many places to hide her. Nobody could have managed it, and Bjorn knew that. He'd built himself an apparatus that made him all but unstoppable.

It was Marcus he hated most. He knew the police would have asked Marcus what happened, and he imagined his brother sitting across from them, denying all knowledge of his own mother. Denying he had a family, denying he'd sent his brother to the Pit. Too many nights Rob had to block out the image of Marcus standing over their mother's body holding a razor, his hands wet with blood. Or else strangling her, the tendons straining on the back of his hands as he pressed them around her neck, watching the flesh turn purple and not caring for even a second. It wouldn't have been a peaceful death, he knew that, not if Marcus had anything to do with it.

3

ONE DAY the bailiffs will come back for Lucy, she knows it. She doesn't know the date, nor the reason, not yet, but it doesn't matter. It's inevitable. She can't keep working this hard forever: she'll make a mistake. An error with her taxes, or an over-commitment, one project too many. There will be a legal battle, a point of paperwork she hasn't considered, something that makes her liable. And all of this will crumble.

It will happen slowly, and then all at once: the first crack in the dam, the first missed deadline, and then the bills piling up. The panic, the terror, the nights with too much booze and too little sleep.

As a girl, that day felt like someone had literally torn the fabric of her world. When she closes her eyes and recalls it, she sees her posters ripped down, her furniture kicked to pieces – locking screws splintered, MDF frames bent out of joint.

And so, she keeps working. Keeps building systems, keeps logging hours, keeps tracking income and expenses. Keeps pushing doors, making connections, networking. She's getting better at finding stable prospects, people who've stayed the course: no small feat in her line of work. They're the big fish, the prizes.

She could have taken another office job, she knows that. But look at how it worked out last time – the agony of a restructure, the months of wondering, the apologetic conversations with her line manager while the HR rep sat in the corner. A kind of slow-motion torture, which she couldn't go through again. It had been a salutary lesson, that much was undeniable: you had to find your own anchor points, no matter that the very ground in which you set them was churning, prone to upheaval. So you set them as firmly as you could, hoped for the best, and always had an escape route.

That's what this job offered: escape routes. If it all started to topple, hopefully she'd have enough connections left to steady herself before the collapse. There were no guarantees, she knew that. This line of work was transient, mercenary, and it made little apology for that fact. But at least it was honest about it.

There were very few people pretending this was something it was not.

To look at Rob you wouldn't know he'd been in a cult. Lucy hadn't, not the first time she'd met him. He'd been advising on a documentary she was putting together about cryptocurrency. Somebody said he was good at explanations and Paul, her producer, set up a meeting. They'd met in a Starbucks, a studiously neutral choice she later realised was almost certainly deliberate.

Paul was right. Rob was good at explaining. She understood crypto pretty well, but he made it clear in the way that an audience needed. She asked him if he'd be happy to be part of the documentary, a quick talking-head piece to camera, and was startled by how forcefully he refused. He went from a mild-mannered bloke in an Oxford shirt to someone positively fierce.

She knew fear when she saw it. There was a story there.

Fortunately, she knew how to get stories out of people. Understood when to push, and when to hang back; when people needed permission, and when they needed to be challenged. Pragmatism, that's what she called it, although more than one person had called it bloody-mindedness. *You're like a dog with a fucking bone*, the subject of her breakout piece on corporate fraud had said once. *You just don't know when to let it go.* It was a good job she didn't, though, at least in his case. A couple of weeks later the whole edifice came crumbling down, and if she'd backed off when she'd been told to she'd have missed the show. Instead, she got a front-row seat to the CEO's ignominious exit, hustled out through a fire escape while babbling to the press about the snake that devoured the world.

She'd met Rob not long after that and told him all about it at their first meeting, a deliberately provocative choice to tease out a reaction. His reaction was more than she could have hoped for. He went white, his eyes widening in disbelief.

'What did you say?' he asked her. 'The snake that devours the world?'

'Yeah,' she said. 'You look like you've heard that before.'

Rob hesitated. For a moment, Lucy thought he might shut down, retreat into that mild-mannered façade. And then, to her surprise, he started talking. Told her about his mother, about the article she'd written on that very topic. How she'd written it in a cult up in the Scottish Highlands. He spoke in halting phrases, like he was weighing each sentence before he allowed himself to speak.

When he stopped talking, Lucy knew she had something here. But she'd seen what happened when she pushed Rob too hard. She needed to be careful. 'Rob,' she said softly. 'I know there's more to this. I understand if you don't feel like you can tell me about it right now. But if you ever do, I'd like to hear it.'

Rob's eyes searched her face. Then, slowly, he nodded. 'Thank you,' he said. 'I'll bear that in mind.'

She kept his number once that project wrapped, knowing full well it might come in handy one day. And, to her surprise, she kept meeting Rob, every couple of weeks. He was unexpectedly good company, perhaps because he was so untainted by the same culture that everyone else had absorbed in their teenage years. He had a whole decade of childhood things to catch up on, and for some reason he seemed to have the idea that she could help with that. Be it Britpop, *The X-Files* or the video games he should have played as a kid, she couldn't deny she found it satisfying to be the expert on something. Occasionally, just occasionally, she thought of him like an alien trying to understand human customs in a desperate attempt to fit in. She didn't tell him.

So when he called her and said he needed to talk, she figured it was probably because he'd discovered that Prince had appeared in an episode of *Animaniacs*.

Apparently it was not.

She's arranged to meet him in a Caffè Nero in the centre of town. He's late. That bothers her, always has. Her time is literally billable. Every minute she sits waiting in this coffee shop is time she could spend writing, networking, researching. Rob ought to have the same mindset. He's a freelancer too, although it seems to work differently if your specialism is computers. Perhaps that's why, more often than not, he'll let his meetings stretch out beyond the allotted time, showing up fifteen minutes late with an apologetic smile and not even offering to buy her a coffee.

She'd mention it to him if she thought it would do any good, but it didn't work the first three times and she couldn't imagine it'd make much of a difference now.

At a rush of cold air she looks up and sees Rob entering the coffee shop. Nine-and-a-half minutes late, and flashing her a dopey, apologetic grin. She glances down at her latte. Already half gone and cooling rapidly. She'll need a refill before long.

He looks flustered, his hair rumpled like he's not had time to drag any product through it, his eyes bleary. When he places his order he presses his fingers to his brow, apparently stifling a headache, and when it arrives he carries it to the table as though terrified he'll break its surface tension.

'I'm late,' he says. 'Again.'

She raises an eyebrow. 'At least you're self-aware.'

'I'm sorry,' he says. 'Something happened.'

'Everything okay?'

Rob rubs his forehead. 'You know I have a brother, right? Up in Scotland?'

'Yeah. Mark?'

'Marcus.' Rob sighs. 'Well, he… uh.' He takes a sip of his coffee, burns his tongue, winces. 'Sorry. I don't talk about this much.'

'It's all right,' she says. She tries not to glance at the clock in the corner of her screen. 'Take your time.'

'Yeah. Thanks.' He takes a deep breath, stares down at his coffee for a long time. Speaks to her, eventually, with his head down. 'So, uh… Marcus. Marcus died.'

'You're kidding.' She knows enough about Rob's history to know his family never came back from that cult. 'Shit. That's awful. Do you know what happened? Was it sudden?'

'Nope. He was… mauled. Apparently. Whatever that means.' He holds his hands up. 'I don't really know anything. I got a call from Bjorn last night, out of the blue, and he told me. First time I've heard from him in nearly a decade.'

'Shit.' She reaches across the table to take his hand. 'Shit, Rob. I'm really sorry.'

'Thanks.' He takes another sip of his coffee. He looks bewildered, like a lost little boy. She can't blame him: he's all alone in the world now. 'I told Bjorn I'd go and get the body. Not that I want to, but I… I owe it to Marcus to give him a proper farewell. To try and remember what he was like before Bjorn got to him. I'll spend the rest of my life hating him otherwise.'

She wishes she still had some coffee left. His grief is raw, disquieting: it's like he's shed a layer of skin. 'Bjorn took so much away from you,' she says. 'How do you deal with it?'

Rob gives a half-hearted shrug. 'Therapy, mostly. Work.'

This is bullshit. She's been a journalist long enough to know that. But it doesn't really feel like the moment to press it. 'Doesn't it make you want to scream, though? The injustice of it all? I swear, if it was me…' She catches herself. 'Sorry. It's not about me.'

'No, it's okay.' He sniffs. 'It's not like there's much I could do about it. I tried, once upon a time. Didn't do a thing.'

'You're kidding. I never knew that.'

'Yeah. I was so certain they'd find her and bring the whole thing down.' He gives a bleak chuckle, then goes back to playing with his teaspoon. 'I was young.'

'That's fucked up.'

'Yeah.'

He's silent for a long time. Shoulders slumped, rings under his eyes. He looks beaten already. Maybe that's what makes her say it.

'I could help you,' she says. 'Bring him down.'

Instantly his expression hardens, as though a whole different person comes out. He lifts his eyes and stares at her, apparently trying to determine if this is for real. 'You're serious.'

'There's a story here that could cause Bjorn some issues. If you're willing to let me tell it.'

Rob reaches for a sugar packet. Turns it over and over, taps it against the table. She can tell he's conflicted, and she can't blame him, not really. He's spent so many years trying to build a life outside of that place – why would he want to open the door to it again?

The more she thinks about it, the more it excites her. A true-crime podcast about a cult, with a personal angle. It could be the next *Serial*. She hates to seem mercenary: she feels sorry for Rob, really she does. Still, this is the sort of story careers are made on.

She stays quiet, trying not to come on too strong, but she can see Rob's wavering. That brief flash of anger seems to be fading, sinking back down under his usual melancholy fug.

'No,' he says finally. 'Thank you for offering. It really means a lot. It's just… I tried to bring him down once. And nothing came of it.' He sighs. 'I just want to say goodbye.'

She nods slowly, watching the opportunity slip away from her, thinking *shit shit shit*. How exactly is she going to salvage this?

'Listen,' she says. 'I'm not the police. They've got procedures to follow, evidence thresholds. I'm better than them. I know how to bring somebody like Bjorn down. Know exactly what to look for.'

He shakes his head, his eyes hollow. 'I just want it to be over,' he says.

And then she says something she's not proud of. 'It's never going to be over, not while he's still out there.'

Something of that steeliness comes back into his eyes, and it makes her wonder what he was like at sixteen.

'My therapist would hate you,' he says after a moment.

That's all the answer she needs. She presses her advantage. 'When do you leave?'

'Tomorrow morning at seven.' He studies her face. 'Alone.'

'No,' she says. 'Don't do this alone. Imagine going up there solo. Walking back into the lion's den. Nothing good can come from that.' She taps the table for emphasis. 'Let me do this for you. As a friend.'

Rob gives a heavy sigh. 'You really think you can make life difficult for him?' he says, and she can hear a tiny note of hope in his voice now.

'I'm certain of it.'

4

LUCY KEEPS essentials ready in a drawer for when she needs to move quickly. Underwear, socks. Lightweight trousers, thermal vests, hiking fleeces that retain warmth. Drab colours – muted olives and blues – so she doesn't stand out from the boys. Never make yourself the centre of attention. She learned that lesson early: massaging bruised male egos took up time and energy she'd rather not waste. Better to be there in the background, quietly making things happen.

She shoves the kit into the bottom of her rucksack. In the side pocket she slots in a laptop charger – one of two, they're easily lost – and two spare batteries. A backup phone and charging cable. Paracetamol, anti-inflammatories (tablet and gel form), support bandages. She's not needed them for a while, but you never know. Then her notebook and the little stack of paperbacks she grabbed on the way back home this afternoon. *The Unicorn's Shadow: The Rise and Fall of Silicon Valley's Brightest Star.* On its cover a geometric unicorn, its eye a menacing red dot like HAL 9000. *Charisma and Control: A Comprehensive Guide to the History and Psychology of Cults.* You had to think broadly, try to find the angles.

At the top of her bag there's space for her laptop, zipped up carefully in its shock-resistant case, and another charger. But that could go in later. It's still early.

Rob's flat is in a new development, the sort of place that advertises itself as *luxurious*, meaning *solitary*. Bachelor pads, mostly. Close to the bars but with little real community. She's never been inside, but she can imagine the interior well enough. Gleaming minimalism. Everything tucked away in its place. Low sofas set around a coffee table. She couldn't live like that: there's no chance for sprawl, its only personality one bought off the shelf.

Rob's going to do most of the driving: she'll leave her car downstairs in the garage. She rummages in the rucksack at her feet and removes her notebook. A simple, wire-bound model, in the type she'd used for years. A5, not A4. The bigger ones got tangled in a bag, the binding bent out of shape, and then the pages wouldn't lie flat.

The last page in her notebook is filled with a rough plan, covered in arrows to mark where she'd rearranged sections and marked by hurried, scribbled crossings-out. Rob outlined his own plan for this project over coffee, and it wouldn't work. There wasn't the depth to it, the level of engagement: he'd never be able to make people care.

That's where she comes in. She's already booked them an

MARGINAL

interview, something to provide much needed context. She's keeping it quiet for now, though. If everything goes to plan, Rob won't know about it until they pull up at Micah's door.

She's arranged for them to meet Micah at his home, a Scottish town about an hour away from the commune. Judging by his online profile, he seems to be some kind of evangelist for the Scriveners: he was thrilled when Lucy contacted him. Rob won't like it, she knows that, but he'll have to make his peace with it soon enough, at least if he wants this done properly.

She slips her notebook back into her rucksack and sets off towards the entranceway, where a row of call buttons sits beneath a glass overhang. The place is soulless, more like an office block than a residential one, and she half expects to find a receptionist in the foyer. Through the glass a tastefully bland hallway stretches off towards a couple of lifts. A stack of mailboxes on the wall, recessed spotlights on the ceiling. Maybe living in the equivalent of a budget hotel makes Rob feel safe.

She tries to keep her voice neutral when Rob answers the buzzer. These days she's good at keeping the judgement out of her voice. She's learned that the hard way too.

'Hey,' she says, with an effort at sounding casual. 'You ready for me?'

'Just need another minute or two,' he says. 'Come on up.'

Irritation prickles across her spine. She was here on time, like they agreed. She'd been early, in fact. Hung back in the car until 7 a.m. so as not to hurry him. And still he insists on keeping her waiting.

But of course she says none of this.

'Cheers,' she says instead as the buzzer sounds. And then she makes her way inside.

Rob's flat is at the end of a corridor on the third floor. Lucy can't help wondering if the interior will be everything she expected: a bachelor's paradise, gleaming and minimalist. She taps with a knuckle on the faceless door. There's the sound of scuffling footsteps and the door opens a crack. Rob peers out at her. He looks like he's just woken up: his T-shirt is crumpled and he wears a battered pair of tracksuit bottoms that are fraying at the knee.

'Sorry to keep you waiting,' he says, taking a step back so she can enter. It's not the pristine space she expected. He's made little effort to put his stamp on it: every wall is the same shade of magnolia, although from what she can see he's tried to offset it with the pop-culture ornaments that sit on top of his bookcases and coffee table. 'Do you want a coffee?'

'I'd rather get on the road,' she says. 'It's a long drive.'

He runs a hand over his face, sniffs. He looks tired: his skin is crinkled with lines and there's dull smudges beneath his eyes. 'Yeah,' he says. 'Let me get one, though, okay? Just to get me going.' He's already heading back into the kitchen-diner.

When Lucy enters the room he's jabbing at an espresso machine, and although his lips are moving she can't hear him over the sound of grinding beans.

She feels uncomfortably exposed. 'How do you feel about me getting some audio on the way up?' she says. 'Set the scene.'

Rob goes through the motions of preparing coffee, his eyes never straying from his hands. 'Whatever you think,' he says over his shoulder.

She takes a step back, hands fidgeting with the strap of her rucksack. Rob's still faffing around in the kitchen. She wants to sit down, but something makes her hesitate. She shifts her weight from one foot to the other, unable to get comfortable. She feels suddenly off her game: uncomfortably aware of how she's in Rob's space, and forcing her way into the life he's so painstakingly built since leaving Craigdhu.

'You're sure you don't want one?' he calls over.

'No.' She sees Rob frown and remembers her manners. 'Thank you.' She shakes her head. 'I thought you'd be—'

Rob raises an eyebrow. 'Better prepared?' He's walking back towards her now, an insulated mug clasped in his hands.

'Well, yeah.'

'I've been trying not to think about it. Too many memories.' He sniffs. 'I just can't work it out. How the hell he died, I mean.' He takes a slug of his coffee, winces. 'I've barely slept.'

Now she feels like a bitch. 'Of course,' she says. 'But you can leave that to me, okay? You focus on laying your brother to rest. I'll make sure we get enough to bring down Bjorn.'

He gives a low chuckle. 'Marcus would have hated that phrasing.'

'Yeah?'

'Yeah. He was a big believer in struggle. Thought it was character forming. He wasn't an easy person to be around.'

All of a sudden she wishes she had her voice recorder.

'You want to talk about it?' she says. 'Why he stayed up there?'

'No,' says Rob grimly. 'Not really.'

'Okay, then.' She holds her hands up. 'Let's get going.'

5

LUCY'S SCRIPT: INITIAL NOTES

Up here, in the wilds of Scotland, there's not much in the way of crime. There's not enough people, for one thing. It's astonishingly remote. The crimes you do expect to encounter are almost inevitably inspired by Agatha Christie: Highland lairds murdered at dinner parties, dead bodies found lying on the heather. The village of Craigdhu is home to a set of artisans who pursue their craft with a passion that borders on obsession, creating works of art (and wheels of cheese) that are shipped out to discerning buyers across the UK.

But the story I'm about to tell you is one you're probably not expecting. Because up here, about as far from civilisation as you might get, you'll find something extraordinary: a cult. Living in an abandoned military base are a group of about two dozen people, some of them ex-lawyers and business managers, who have given up everything to pursue knowledge.

In the late 90s, their leader – a man called

Bjorn Thrissell - wrote a productivity book that was quite astonishingly unsuccessful. So unsuccessful, in fact, that his publishers outright refused to print it, calling it esoteric, dangerous and 'almost impossible to market'.

And yet, somehow, the manuscript got out. And it found an unexpectedly devoted following in the early days of internet forums. Such a devoted following, actually, that some of those first fans sought Bjorn out. They were the founding members of what came to be called the Scriveners, and many of them are still living in a commune with Bjorn today.

But I talked about a crime. It's not just that Thrissell convinced people to give up their homes and life savings and join him here - which is unusual, but hardly illegal. No, what's much worse are the stories of people who've lived up there, who've shared their experiences of what they encountered at Thrissell's hands. Like Rob Barton, whose mother took him up to Scotland as a child. She was among those founding members, her and her two sons.

At the age of sixteen, Rob ran away, and the story he told when he escaped was nothing short of astounding. He described how committed the group were to pursuing what Thrissell called 'the Immortal Spirit', a daily practice that consumed six hours of each member's day.

Sessions began with two hours of isolated reading, in which members would read through a wide range of texts until something resonated, at which point they'd document what they discerned to be the Spirit's leading. This was then typically followed by an hour and a half of documenting and reflecting on these insights, and yet *another* hour and a half of cross-referencing and synthesising them with previous discoveries. The final hour

MARGINAL

was reserved for deep meditation, allowing the Scriveners to contemplate and internalise what they'd learned.

All of which sounds broadly harmless, if a little eccentric: a kind of informal academia. And perhaps that's how it might have remained had Rob not also mentioned his mother, who disappeared soon after his escape and of whom the police could find no trace.

You'll hear of how the police were eventually unable to act against Bjorn, citing a 'lack of evidence of criminal intent'. You'll hear about how Rob was left to pick up the pieces in foster care, his mother and brother having been shut out of his life by Bjorn Thrissell and the system he built. And you'll hear of the years he spent trying to rebuild his world.

Until now. Because now, in death, Rob's brother has been snatched away once and for all. And Rob's had it with letting Bjorn destroy what matters to him. He's going to fetch his brother's body from Scotland, and confront Thrissell at the very heart of his web. And he's allowed us to follow him as he does it.

Welcome to **[NAME]**

6

He's still not sure therapy is doing him any good. It's given him some tools, but his therapist can't understand what he went through up there. She can't know what it felt like to commune with the Immortal Spirit, or what it felt like in the Pit.

Recently she told him she wasn't sure those terms were helpful. 'Using them keeps Craigdhu alive in your mind,' she said. 'You're free of that place. Stay free.'

He wants to believe all that. It makes sense on a rational level. He can see the ways Bjorn and the others got inside his head. Exactly like he saw it all those years ago, when he first stumbled across those message boards.

But he can't make himself feel it, not deep down. No matter how many times he goes through the CBT exercises, no matter how many hours he spends meditating, no matter how many pills he takes. The hunger is still there, the disquiet. The Searching, that's how he liked to think of it. The desire to know more, the sense of something waiting to be born.

MARGINAL

Those are Bjorn's words, his therapist says. He's still speaking in Bjorn's voice. Doesn't he want to leave that behind?

Yes, he tells her. Of course I do. But even now he can't be sure if that's true.

Like today. He can't bring himself to start the car. Just sits there, staring off into space. He can feel Lucy watching him. Can feel her judging him. She's not even tried to hide her doubts. Not that he can blame her. She's got a job to do, and he looks flaky, unstable. Even he can see that.

He needs to get going. Turn the key. Press the clutch. But his thoughts are all tangled and twisted around each other, knotty and impenetrable. All of them leading back to the commune, to the vault, to this cancer that ate away at everything good in his life, that hollowed out his mum and his brother and…

No. No, he's been down this road before, and it leads nowhere good.

He still hasn't moved. He can see Lucy's trying not to comment. Trying not to meet his eye. He motions towards the glove compartment. 'Find us a CD, would you?' he says, trying to sound casual. She looks glad of the distraction. It's old music in there, mostly: Catatonia, Garbage, The Cranberries, everything he'd missed during his years in—

Shit. Maybe he's not ready for this after all. He thought he'd processed what happened up there, but he's beginning to feel like he's just bounced off the surface. There's a knot of barbed wire where his personality should be, and he's never even begun to unravel it – wouldn't even know how to.

'You're freaking out,' says Lucy, rummaging through the glove compartment. 'Not a great start.' She bends forwards, fumbling for something in her rucksack. Emerges holding a voice recorder. 'You want to talk about it? And if so, you reckon you could do it on tape?'

He laughs then, without expecting it. Thank God for Lucy: she's always been good at pulling him out of himself.

He glances over at the recorder. 'Listen, Lucy,' he says. 'It's not a good place. I swear. It gets inside of you—'

Now she straightens up, looks at him. Her eyes wider, a gleam in them that feels almost malicious. 'Tell me about it.'

He stares into his lap, not knowing where to start. 'How much do you know about Bjorn?' he says eventually.

'I've done my homework,' says Lucy. 'But tell me about him anyway. In your own words.'

Rob chews his lip, sighs. 'He'd never call himself a cult leader. I guess you know that much, but if not, you should. He'll tell you that all of those people up there, they can come and go at will. No one's going to chase them down if they leave, no one's going to murder them.' He rolls his eyes. 'Allegedly. He'd like you to think they choose to stay.'

'And they stay because of him.'

'Yeah. Him, and what he's trying to create.' He stares down at his hands in his lap. He's digging one thumbnail hard into his palm and hadn't even realised. 'They're true believers. They think he's building a new world.'

Lucy frowns. 'With a note-taking system?'

'Uh-huh.'

'I found bits of his book online,' she says. 'Some wonky scans of it. Gave me a headache.'

Rob gives her a grim smile. 'They still haven't gotten around to typing it up, then? They were talking about doing that ten years ago.'

'It must be deliberate.'

'I think so. Bjorn doesn't want all this to be common knowledge, not anymore. He likes having his chosen few squirrelled away up there.'

Lucy leans forwards. 'But you've read it all, presumably.'

Rob looks out the window. 'Yeah, I've read it. Cover to cover. I can still recite parts of it from memory. People used to show up at camp with hand-stapled photocopies they bought from the back of a magazine. These great sheaves of dog-eared paper.'

He can see Lucy trying to take it all in, knows what she's thinking. She understood that Rob had grown up in a commune, spent his formative years detached from the world. She'd just never imagined it being so prosaic. Nobody ever did.

'You're going to need to fill me in on something,' she says. 'Just so I've got it in your words. They did all that because they wanted to… to take better notes?'

He feels the familiar gleam of satisfaction that comes from being the only one to know the truth. He hates how much he likes it. 'You'd not be asking that question if you'd spent longer with the book,' he says. 'It's like… something possessed Bjorn when he wrote it. It's got a power beyond itself. It's patchy, and repetitive, and confusing, but after you've read it, it… resonates.' Even now he can't quite shake off his admiration for the thing. 'I don't think even he knew what he'd written. He never meant to start a movement. But the book: it got inside of people. It grew without him even trying. And soon enough they showed up looking for him.'

He can't decipher Lucy's expression: maybe she's appalled, maybe thrilled. 'Do you have a copy?' she says. 'With you?'

'Fuck no,' says Rob. 'It's caused me enough misery.'

It all fell apart for Rob when he wrote that blog post. At sixteen he'd thought it was no big deal. Sure, he should have cleared it with the others. Maybe that was careless. And maybe he gave away a little too much about life in the camp. The rituals, the rhythms. But he'd spent so many years doing what he was told. He needed some kind of outlet. It wasn't like he could talk to Marcus, or Cat, not without getting himself marked as a potential dissenter.

God, they were all such hypocrites. They claimed they wanted you to question: to challenge received wisdom, to pursue the Immortal Spirit wherever it led. But the moment the Immortal Spirit led you somewhere they didn't like then you knew about it. The coldness, the silence. Working at your tasks without a single person speaking to you. And the scrutiny. Your room searched, your notes read. He wasn't sure if they thought they were being subtle, but if so then they weren't much good at it. He'd seen their fingerprints, the dog-eared pages, the scattered papers beneath his bed.

He wasn't even sure who they'd asked to do it. For all he knew, it was his mother. He doubted it, though. There was something about how she spoke to him that indicated she was still proud of him. They hadn't broken that yet, though they'd probably tried. With their sense of community, the claim they were a shared family. All searching for the Spirit's leading. Scanning the word to try and discern it. You didn't need a father or mother to help you do that. You were all united in your shared goal. There were teachers who could help you out, guides, mentors, but nothing said they had to be your parents. Maybe it was better if they weren't. They could be more objective, more clear-sighted.

Now he thought about it, he supposed Miranda was right when she told him not to write the thing. Because that was what started it all, wasn't it? That was how he found the message boards. That was how he made friends outside of this place, albeit friends with anonymous online handles: otherside_14; the_sharpest_lives. He should have known they'd ask about where he lived sooner or later. Should have realised that not everyone lived like this.

Hadn't Bjorn said it enough times? They were a chosen people, set apart, blessed with a noble inheritance? No matter that some days it felt like a curse, like dragging a dead horse along with you. He reckoned he wasn't the only person here to feel that way, although that could have been the world talking. They didn't understand what was important, didn't understand what was happening here. But they would one day, Bjorn said. When the new world came into being. Then they'd see the power of what he'd built here.

When his friends sent him the article – '10 Signs You Might Be in a Cult' – he laughed it off. It wasn't a cult, they all knew that. It was a commune, a group of people working together with a shared goal. They had control over who they interacted with, what they read, even whether they stayed. They chose to stay because there was something powerful about being bonded together in this way. Sharing their resources, supporting one another in pursuit of the truth. There were other members, living out in the world, who chose not to come here. Believers in the System, who'd gone out as witnesses to its power. Rob hadn't met any of them, but he'd no reason to doubt their existence. Bjorn had mentioned them often enough.

There was an answer for every allegation in the article, so he could tell his new friends why they were mistaken. Except doing so seemed to confirm their suspicions, rather than dispelling them. Apparently he should feel doubts, should be allowed to ask questions. Apparently his certainty was a sign of indoctrination.

Everything they said to him was well-meaning, polite in a way that seemed at first disarming and then borderline aggressive.

wot if u told him abt us
y aren't u allowd to leave
how do u know hes not lying to u

He began to question himself. Started asking if they were truly his friends or, like Bjorn had mentioned, the resistance that arose against any truly new thing. The old world trying, in all its bewilderment, to strangle the new before it gathered strength.

Maybe the other Scriveners knew something was up long before Rob went to talk to Bjorn. Maybe they'd spotted him looking exhausted, spending hours at the computers and producing almost nothing. He'd wonder about that, later, when he thought back on it. How many of those conversations over dinner were attempts to pump him for information, to ascertain exactly who he was talking to beyond this little corner of the world. What sounded pastoral was just another test to pass.

Watch your body language. Watch your answers. Don't lose control. Don't let them see you break.

In the end he went to Bjorn directly. Knocked on the man's door, knees trembling, and asked if he could come in and speak for a while.

'Of course,' said Bjorn, and then ushered Rob inside. His cabin was as spartan as the others, unleavened by personal effects. A bed, neatly made. A desk, covered in books, papers and a smattering of notecards. A single lamp casting a pool of light over them. 'Have a seat,' he said to Rob, and Rob picked the chair furthest away from the desk. It was a stiff, uncomfortable thing, the seat covered with a cushion that had seen better days. Bjorn seated himself on the chair closest to the desk and shuffled it round to face Rob. 'So,' he said, leaning forwards, his fingers interlaced. 'What is it you wanted to discuss?'

Maybe it was Bjorn's soft, soothing voice in that moment, or something about his demeanour that suggested the father Rob at best remembered vaguely, but Rob let his guard down. Let himself believe it was safe to tell this man about his doubts, about the impossibility of reconciling his experience with what he'd read online and the yawning chasm that had opened up between what he wanted to believe and what he felt when he sat at his desk. Bjorn listened to everything without moving or interrupting, his face placid, and when Rob was finally done he sat back in his chair and sighed.

That was when Rob knew he was in trouble: the sigh. A weary, disappointed noise, the sound of somebody weighing up how best to respond to a problem. Rob understood then that he was the problem, even began trying to retract his idiotic statements, babbling that he'd misspoken and it truly wasn't as bad as he was making out, but Bjorn silenced him by holding up a hand. His gaze remained placid and unruffled, almost paternal, as he spoke gently to Rob.

'I know these things feel natural,' he said. 'Even welcome. And I know it feels as though you should pursue them. Truly, I do.' He held Rob's gaze, as though determined to ensure Rob was taking all this in. 'So I appreciate this may not be easy to hear… but you have been listening to lies.'

Rob knew he shouldn't say anything more, knew that if he did so there would be consequences – even worse than the ones he was already facing. He still believed, then, that he might be able to fix this, although in the years to come he'd realise that his fate was likely sealed long before he ever opened his mouth.

'I take no joy in this, Rob,' said Bjorn, leaning forwards again. 'What you have to do now will be difficult. But you will not have to undertake it alone. That's why we're here. To lift you up. To support you when you're weak. To help you recall the things you already know to be true.'

Bjorn was silent. Apparently he'd done his work now: the sentence was clear. But Rob hadn't been dismissed. Didn't dare move without permission. So he waited. Five seconds. Ten seconds. Still Bjorn didn't speak, holding Rob's gaze with that infuriating stare. 'I'm sorry,' said Rob finally, when the agony became too great, 'but I don't understand.'

'Exactly!' said Bjorn with force. 'You don't understand. I couldn't have put it better myself. But never fear. You will understand soon. It may take merely hours, it may take days, but trust me when I say it is worth the effort.' Again he stared at Rob, a strange light in his eyes, as though he could see something in Rob that Rob himself was unaware of – some future self, trying to emerge.

'You're sending me to the Pit.' Rob's heart sank into his chest. All these years he'd avoided it: he must have known this day would come eventually.

'No,' said Bjorn with a smile, and Rob's heart leapt despite himself. 'You're going willingly.' He rose, and crossed over to Rob's chair, and laid a hand on his shoulder. 'Thank you, Rob,' he said, 'for telling me all this. And for your commitment to what we're doing here.' He touched Rob's elbow, motioning for him to stand. 'Now, let's focus on helping you get well.'

It would occur to him, years later, that he could have run. There and then. But he didn't. He let Bjorn lead him to that squat concrete room that used to be a weapons locker, and watched him close and bolt the door with him inside it. The darkness was all-consuming. He couldn't even see his hands in front of his face.

The space was tiny: if he stood against the back wall and stretched out his arms, he could touch the front of the room, feel the outline of the door. He would become all too familiar with its contours in the next twenty-four hours. In total the room was about thirty paces long – he figured that out pretty quickly, too – with a ceiling too high to touch.

Somewhere up there were a set of speakers. Two, he thought, but possibly more. It certainly sounded like more: as though he were being assailed by a chorus of voices who were determined not to be ignored, and who surrounded him on all sides.

He didn't recognise his own voice at first. When it began speaking from up there on the ceiling it sounded so earnest, so youthful, so naïve. He couldn't remember when he'd recorded it. He thought perhaps he'd been twelve. He recalled his mum asking him to prepare for it, and then sitting in the vault writing out his thoughts about how the System worked and how it could transform the world. His mother had looked it over in their room when it was done, scratching out first sentences and then whole paragraphs before rewriting others.

'You can't say that,' she'd muttered, pencil in hand. 'And

that's not what you meant. No, that won't do at all.' A growing anxiety in her voice as she worked, her pencil notes becoming more vicious. The end result barely sounded like him. Not that he said anything. 'This is what you meant, isn't it, darling?' she'd said when it was done, and of course he'd nodded, because he wanted the task to be over, but when he came to memorise the pages he could hear the disconnect. He hadn't protested, had sat in front of a microphone and recorded the thing like he was told to, and then mostly forgot about it.

Only now, hearing his younger self reading the words, did it all come flooding back – but four years on, he found he could no longer recall which were his own thoughts and which had been scripted by his mother.

He'd have plenty of time to puzzle over that question in those first few, dreadful hours, as the words washed over him again and again. 'The System is a tool for transformation,' he heard himself say, 'maybe the greatest tool of all. It is the doorway to a new world, and it is the chisel by which that new world will be moulded.' Again he heard the words, 'The System sets us free. The System shows us the truth. The System reveals the things we cannot understand alone.'

By the tenth time, he was slumped back against the wall of the Pit, trying to remember what his bedroom looked like, trying to recall his brother's face. He could do neither. By the twentieth time, he felt like his head might explode. By the thirtieth, he wanted to weep. He'd no idea how long each repetition ran for, no way of tracing how long he'd been there in the dark. He felt it as an eternity. In the months afterwards he'd hear those words in his dreams, and even as an adult, certain phrases would evoke a visceral response he couldn't altogether control. His chest would tighten, he'd begin to sweat. More than once he'd become so nauseous in a coffee shop that he'd ended up leaving the building. His therapist suggested he might have overheard something his subconscious considered a threat.

'I want to be free,' he heard his younger self say. 'I want to be wise. I want to be transformed.' By the time Bjorn opened the door, Rob no longer knew what he wanted. He barely knew his own name.

Bjorn's smile was kind, his manner gentle. He opened the door just a crack, apparently hoping to spare Rob the pain of the light. He needn't have bothered. When he entered the room, Rob was on the floor, his back pressed against the wall, his head between his knees.

'Rob?' he said in a whisper. 'May I come in?'

Rob tried to speak, but no words came out.

'Rob?'

'Please...' Rob managed to croak. His voice was still going in the background, a thousand times clearer and more forceful than what left his mouth, and he'd barely the strength to make himself heard over it.

Bjorn entered the room and knelt down before him. 'I know this is difficult,' he said. 'I hope you know that we do it out of love.' He waited for Rob to raise his eyes. 'Rob? You do know that, don't you?'

He should have screamed that this was nothing of the sort. Should have told Bjorn to fuck off, should have told him he wanted nothing to do with what he was building here. He'd wonder, later, why he didn't do that. But in that instant, all he wanted was to make it stop. To stop the endless repetition, and walk out into the light. To sleep, and to eat, and to see his mother.

'We do this because the alternative is worse,' Bjorn continued. 'So much worse. The alternative is losing yourself.' His face shone with a strange light. He looked rapturous, ecstatic. 'You are the inheritor of a sacred gift. You are the forerunner, the pioneer, the pilgrim on the shores of a new world. You know this. You knew it when you first spoke those words, and you only forgot it for a time. But no more. Now you are restored.'

And then Bjorn hugged him. A fierce embrace, shocking in its suddenness, so heartfelt and unexpected that it made Rob want to weep tears of joy. 'My boy,' he heard Bjorn say in his ear. 'Welcome back.'

He couldn't recall, in that moment, why he'd ever wanted to leave.

And perhaps it might all have been okay if he'd left the doubts down there in the dark, but when he came back into the light they came back too. He was able to push them down for a while – it helped that he knew his own words well enough now that he could recite them without thinking.

He couldn't go back to the message boards, even if he wanted to. There were eyes on him now. Bjorn, Elliot, Cat. Marcus. His mother. He had to show he'd found revelation, that he was at peace.

'I'll find it,' he wanted to tell them. 'Just give me some time. I'll get back again.'

There was no time. There was no hinterland between faith and doubt. Either he believed it all, or he was on the road to hell. His life became a performance, a charade. He knew what they were asking, really asking, when they set themselves down next to him at dinner and asked, oh so amiably, *so Rob, how's it going?* They wanted him to be bright, earnest, to be the kid he'd been a year ago. But he was just so tired, and they just kept asking, and wasn't it inevitable that one day he'd break down and ask them please, for the love of God, to shut the fuck up?

After that they sent him back to the Pit again. For longer this time, although he wasn't entirely sure how long. He lost count after the seventy-fifth repetition. This time Bjorn didn't embrace him. This time people started avoiding him like he was contagious, watching their words around him. It was subtle, sure, a couple of steps away from him, a couple of inches further down the bench at dinner, but it was hard to ignore once he spotted it.

That was when the anxiety started. When he began running over his conversations long after they'd concluded, checking for anything unclear, anything poorly worded. Scratching out apologies on notecards and slipping them under people's doors. They didn't much like that – more than one person knocked on their bunkhouse door and asked his mother what the hell her son thought he was doing. After the second such confrontation, she told him he needed to be careful: and he was a good son, he could see the fear and exhaustion in her eyes, the tension in her jaw and the hollows in her cheeks, so he did what he was told. He watched his words, carefully, oh so carefully, never speaking until he was sure it was safe to do so. When he opened his mouth, the others viewed him like a creature that had crawled out of the earth, and he understood why, with his croak of a voice and his chapped lips and his eyes so pleading and uncomprehending.

It was Marcus who got him sent to the Pit that final time. Marcus who told Bjorn that Rob had stopped doing his studies, hadn't produced a single insight in weeks and was lost in his own mind. This time Rob tried to fight Bjorn off, tried to stop him as he dragged Rob away by the arm into the darkness, but no amount of flailing and screaming could loosen Bjorn's grip, and pretty soon Marcus came along to help him too.

'I'm sorry, Rob,' Marcus whispered. 'It won't always be this hard. I promise. Sooner or later it'll all make sense.'

This time he didn't bother counting. All he knew was that he had to get out.

7

NOTES FROM *The Scrivener's Code: Deciphering the Language of Change That's Written Between the Lines*

COMMUNING WITH THE TEXT

It begins with a notecard. A record of something: a true experience.

Perhaps you've yet to experience the mysticism of communing with a text. How you immerse yourself in it, and it speaks to you. A word, a phrase, a sentence will seem to leap out.

This is not by chance. It is the Immortal Spirit speaking through the text. It is something of eternity reaching out.

The Hebrews called it *Midhrāsh*. The Christians called it *Lectio Divina*. But this can't be confined by any one faith tradition. Each simply recognised something intrinsic to human experience.

There is a new world seeking to be born, and you are its vessels. There is a new creation speaking through the world,

MARGINAL

one that only the chosen few can recognise. It will break the structures of all that came before, like new wine bursting forth from old wineskins.

Many will fear it. They will try to discredit it, to say it is nothing new, and that all it can hope to do is retell the same, tired stories. They are too mired in the world to comprehend what is happening. Something is speaking through the text, and if we would only listen – truly listen – we might find it burning with a divine light, one that burns hotter than the fires of the sun.

How can you access this power?

Far easier than you might believe.

Set a book before you. Anything you have to hand. The content doesn't matter: we are interested in what lies beyond, what is *waiting to be born*. That will loose itself regardless of the text. It is deeper than author intention, and truer than rhetoric. It is the true purpose of language, the one that spoke the very world into motion.

With the book set before you, begin to read. Start at the beginning, or in the middle, it doesn't matter. What you're searching for is *resonance*. The sense you get of a book speaking directly to you. This happens with the oddest of texts. The passage in an engineering textbook that hums with a power you can barely define, and suffuses you with melancholy and terror. The descriptive section in your mother's recipe book that has stuck with you since you first read it three decades ago.

It is not the book that speaks, nor the author. It is something deeper.

It is the call of a new world waiting to be born.

Few among us will hear the murmur of the Immortal Spirit. Those chosen few have a rare gift: they can look through this mundane existence to see the world as it truly is.

This is not an easy life. How easily you can find yourself cast into the outer darkness, once the din of common existence begins to fade. And yet in the dark, you can hear the whispers of the Spirit: words that enrich your soul, and lead you away from this fickle generation.

Not many can bear such a life; not many dare risk such introspection. And yet those who can have become the great visionaries of our time: William Blake, Carl Jung, Madame Blavatsky. How bleak our world would be, had they not sought the Spirit in the wilderness — and yet while we welcome the gifts they gave us, we neglect the cost. The loneliness, the silence, the struggle.

You will know if you have heard the call. Perhaps you have felt yourself being pulled beyond the confines of the life you have always known, alienated from friends and family, drawn to something greater. Perhaps you have felt yourself thirsting after truth, as you watch the hollow promises of politicians and activists and evangelists alike blowing away like ash in the wind.

When I first heard that call, I ran from it. The System frightened me. I felt its strange power, but I was a young man back then, with academic pursuits, hobbies, friendships, none of which I wanted to discard. And so, after those first, tentative forays into the text, I stepped back from it, fearful of losing myself. I dove instead in the rituals of domestic life: family dinners, homework and the odd drunken night with friends.

And yet the more I tried to cling to that life, the more persistently I heard the call. It felt as though the very act of resistance encouraged it, until it became impossible to ignore. Within a matter of months I became overwhelmed: miserable, preoccupied, lost.

Revelation came from the most unexpected place: Saturday morning, in a crowded marketplace. I had taken to walking in an attempt to free myself from the infernal clamour of my thoughts, and had stumbled into the town square without even noticing. It was a shabby affair, bric-a-brac stalls and amateurish paintings, and I drifted by most of it without really seeing a thing.

Until, by a stall selling antique books, I felt a worn volume call out to me. James Hutchison Stirling, *The Secret of Hegel*. There was nothing about it to draw my eye: it was bound in faded leather, battered and scuffed. I simply could not tear my eyes away from it. It seemed to resonate with a barely suppressed force.

I reached up to it, set it on the table, and began to read. The world around me dimmed, the noise faded, and I read these words:

'In the commonest objects of the universe, man recognises the symbols of his own existence.'

I knew, then, that this was the revelation I'd been seeking. I heard again the leading of the Spirit, its promise to speak through the text. It was a fleeting moment – it vanished almost as soon as it had come – but the sensation stuck with me long afterwards. That burning sense of wonder. I knew I had neglected the call, and I could ignore it no longer.

I meditated on Stirling's words for hours, allowing them to consume me. The phrase echoed through my mind, reverberating with truth. I turned it over and over, exploring every facet of it, every implication, until it became a part of me, woven into my being. I must have seemed obsessed, but I don't regret a single moment.

From then on, I poured every ounce of my being into the System. I saw the world anew, as if a veil had been lifted from my eyes. My friends and family became like shadows, their concerns suddenly trivial. The loneliness I'd once feared became a cherished friend, and every hour I spent alone a further chance to pursue the Immortal Spirit.

8

Rob's asleep, snoring slightly with his head against the door panel, when Lucy pulls up outside a red-brick house in the suburbs outside Edinburgh. It's almost suspiciously generic, the world's most standard two-up, two-down.

But the second she kills the engine, Rob wakes, and she sees that hardness in him surface again. She's instantly on the defensive. She needs this.

'Where are we?' he says. 'Are you lost? Why are we stopping?'

She forces herself to take a breath. Turns to him. 'Listen. You're not going to like this.'

Rob's jaw tenses. 'Oh no,' he says. 'Whatever you've got planned, no.'

'If you really want to bring him down…'

'I want to get my brother's body back, Lucy. That's what I want.'

She ignores him. 'I have to tell this story in a way that makes sense,' she says. 'And that means I have to get context. I'm sorry.'

He hesitates for just a second, and she wonders if he's thawing. 'This couldn't have waited?'

'Maybe. But it's a hell of a drive up here, and I wanted to see his face.'

'And *he* is?'

'His name's Micah Dunkeld. He's part of the Scriveners. Quite a vocal member, actually.'

Rob's voice is cold. 'One of the missionaries.'

'Yeah. Yeah, that's right.' She can see the hurt in his eyes. 'Look, you've every right to be pissed off that I didn't tell you in advance. I don't mind going in alone.'

'No,' he says. 'No, I'm not sure that's a good idea.'

She can't help feeling a little pissed off. 'I'm a big girl, Rob. I can cope.'

'That's what they want you to think,' he says sourly. 'You need someone in there who'll help cut through the bullshit. That's me.'

When they step out of the car there's birds singing in the trees, the faint smell of flowers in the air. Rob stands a few steps behind her, like he's worried Micah's very presence might be infectious. She presses the doorbell and tries her best to appear composed.

Moments later, the door opens and Micah stands before them. He's tall and fit: late thirties, dressed in a simple but well-fitting button-down shirt and slacks, with a mop of black hair and a healthy glow to his skin. He looks like a computer programmer.

He looks them over, a smile prickling at the corner of his mouth. 'Hey,' he says. 'I'm Micah. I'm so thrilled you're here.'

She feels Rob tense behind her. 'Lucy Hawthorne,' says Lucy, offering her hand. 'It's a pleasure.'

'It's honestly amazing to meet you.' There's something a little puppyish about him, and she can't help but feel flattered. It's rare to meet a fan. 'I loved *Balance Sheet Bullies*.' He glances over at Rob and gives a double-take. 'And you're – my God, are you Marcus's brother?'

'Uh-huh.' Behind her, she can hear Rob trying to stay calm.

'No shit. You look just like him.' He shakes his head, awed. 'We've not spoken much, you know – the odd video call – but all the same, I had no idea he had a brother.'

'It's been a while since we last spoke.'

Micah pauses, taken aback. His eyes narrow. 'Huh. Is that so?'

They're still on the doorstep, and that makes Lucy nervous. Time to move this along. 'Do you mind if we come inside?'

'Sure,' says Micah, taking a step back. 'Where are my manners?' The interior décor matches the exterior. Clean, organised and completely unremarkable. Something about that rankles at her. It feels… institutional. 'Would you mind taking off your shoes?' says Micah with an apologetic smile. 'It's a rented house, you know. Landlord just put the carpet in.' He nods through to a small lounge on their right. 'We're in here,' he says. 'I'll stick the kettle on.'

Rob sits down heavily on a sofa that Lucy recognises as an Ikea purchase, while she rummages around in her rucksack for her notebook and microphones. The carpet's soft and plush beneath her feet, and from somewhere nearby there's the sound of distant laughter from a playground. The whole scene feels surreal.

She can hear Micah bustling around in the kitchen. The whistle of the kettle, the clink of teaspoons. Rob looks grim. He's breathing deeply, obviously trying to keep himself from freaking out. She doesn't have long to fix this, at least if she's hoping to get anything usable from today.

'Hey. Listen to me,' says Lucy, and Rob manages to lift his head at least. 'It's okay, you hear me? You know these people, know what they're like. Know their tricks. So you're prepared, right? No surprises.' She gives him what she hopes is an encouraging smile. 'And I'm here with you.'

'That's what I'm worried about,' he says, swallowing hard. 'I know how easy it is to get sucked in.'

She's not seen him like this before. He looks like he might actually run for it. She's starting to wonder if she's misjudged this.

'If we need to pull the plug, just give me a sign.'

'Okay.' She can hear him relax. 'What should I do?'

But before they have a chance to figure out a signal Micah's back with a tray of hot drinks. All the mugs bear the same pattern of horizontal grey stripes. Another Ikea purchase, she thinks. She owns a set. They're what you buy if you're trying to convince people you're a functioning adult.

'Tea,' Micah says, handing Lucy one. He sets a mug down for Rob on the coffee table, and Rob just stares at it. Out of the corner of her eye, she can see Rob watching her drink with obvious discomfort. Micah sets himself down on an armchair and slaps his knees. 'So listen,' he says, 'what do you want to know? I guess you've read my books, or else you'd not have driven all this way.'

'I'd like to know what first drew you to the Scriveners, if that's okay? In your own words?' She nods to the recorder. 'I assume you're okay with me recording this?'

'Aye, sure, sure.' He rubs his chin. 'Well, where to start. I suppose what appealed to me was that sense of building something truly new.' He thinks for a moment or two. 'Did you ever read Mark Fisher? *Capitalist Realism*? He talks about how capitalism cannibalises itself. Keeps on feeding off itself, over and over again. That's why fashion runs on a thirty-year cycle. There's something sterile about it, something... static. And what Bjorn created, well, it's not that.' He gives a little chuckle.

'Go on,' says Lucy, trying to ignore Rob's deep frown. 'Tell me more.'

Micah's a little disconcerted by Rob. Turning his head away to escape that glare. He drums his fingers on his knee, thinks. 'Do you believe in God?' he says to Lucy.

Lucy freezes, blindsided. Her instinct is to try and answer, and then she remembers herself, remembers what she's meant to be doing. This is an interview. He can't do this. 'You... you're not supposed to speak to me,' she says gently. 'I'm sorry if I didn't make that clear. I need you to speak to the audience. As though I'm not here.'

'Of course,' says Micah, giving an affable shrug. 'I'm sorry.'

'No worries,' she says with a breeziness she doesn't entirely feel. 'Let's go again.'

He takes a deep breath, preparing himself. 'I don't know if you believe in God,' he says a little theatrically. 'I certainly didn't. I couldn't get my head around the idea that there's some guy up in heaven who's directing our lives. But when I started using the System, I'll tell you… it made me think again. Not that I believe in God, not even now. You don't have to. All you have to believe is that there's a force out there somewhere, an innate goodness underneath things, that wants everything to work out for the best.' He nods to Lucy. 'I bet even you believe that,' he says with a smile. 'And when you use the System, you connect with that. I don't know exactly how. Maybe it's that you pick up on something in the ether, and you're tuning into your subconscious mind… or maybe it is something mystical. I don't know. They gave it a name, Bjorn's first followers. *The Immortal Spirit*, they called it. It's all very grand. But that's what the System comes down to: letting yourself be a vessel for a new world to come into being. Letting yourself move beyond your conscious mind to your deepest longings, and then joining with others who want to do the same.' He glanced over at Lucy, gave her an embarrassed little grimace. 'How's that?'

But Rob gets in there first. 'It's bullshit,' he says viciously. He's leaning forwards in his chair, glowering at Micah.

'I'm sorry?' says Micah, looking genuinely baffled.

'Don't pretend I'm the first person you've heard that from,' says Rob, incredulous. 'You know as well as I do that it's bullshit.'

'Well – I mean – I'm afraid I can't quite agree there.'

'Come on, man,' says Rob. 'Come on. All that shit about the Immortal Spirit? At best what you're doing is freewriting. You want to pretend this is something new, but it's not. It's shallow, and it's fake.'

Micah's voice is strained. 'I'm sorry you feel like that,' he says, somehow managing to stay polite. Lucy feels bad for him: she's brought this guy into his house who's now openly attacking him. 'But you've seen the vault, Rob. You know how much Bjorn has produced up there. You can't deny that it's an achievement.'

'Just because he's got a whole library full of bullshit doesn't stop it being bullshit.'

Micah's quiet, then thoughtful. 'I suppose I don't see what makes you so defensive,' he says. 'I mean, really, what harm is it doing? It's providing people with a sense of purpose, a focus… and it's brought about so much good in the world already.'

There's something manic in Rob's voice now. 'You don't see the harm?' he says. 'How many people have given up their life savings to this thing, Micah?'

This is safer ground, Lucy can tell. Micah looks positively relaxed, and she knows he's heard this question before. 'They've done so willingly,' he says. 'Done so to pursue a life of purpose.'

'I suppose you don't know what Bjorn does to people who try to leave,' says Rob through a clenched jaw. Micah's silent, his expression hard to read. 'I'll tell you if you want. I was one of them. He locked me inside a cell and made me listen to my own words on a loop until I was re-educated. Fucking *hours* in solitary confinement. No light, no food. And when I made a break for it, they chased me down. I'm certain he killed my mother. Not that I can prove it.' He glares at Micah, daring him to respond.

Micah's expression is gentle, sober. 'I'm so sorry that was your experience.'

'You— you what?' Rob looks appalled. 'My *experience?* It's fact, man. I could show you the police report.'

'Seems to me that if the police believed you they'd have shut the whole thing down,' says Micah, raising an eyebrow. 'And yet…'

'Listen,' says Rob through a clenched jaw. 'I'm not the one who has to answer for myself here. It's Bjorn who needs to defend himself, and what he's built up there.' He glares at Micah. 'Marcus is dead, you know. I'm sorry to be the one who had to tell you.'

Micah's smile falters.

'No,' says Micah. 'No, that can't be true.' He glances over at Lucy, who tries her best to look impartial. 'Surely not. When did this happen? How?'

'Couple of days ago,' Rob says. 'Something up there killed him. Bjorn called to let me know. A wild animal, apparently. I'm on my way to get his body.'

There's a tremor in Micah's voice now, and he's visibly upset. 'I… I had no idea,' he murmurs, putting a hand to his forehead. 'This is awful. He was… an inspiration.' He pinches the bridge of his nose, and takes a deep breath, as though forcing himself to stay present. 'You can't pin this on Bjorn, though,' he says, head still bowed. 'You said this was an animal attack. That's nothing to do with him.'

Rob lets out a noise that's halfway between a laugh and a growl. 'And there was me thinking you were searching for truth.'

This hits home. Micah's head snaps upright, and when he speaks again there's real anger in his voice. 'How dare you,' he says. 'I ought to tell you to get the fuck out of my house.' He shakes his head. 'You're not looking for the truth, Rob, you're lashing out. I understand if you want to lay the blame at someone's door, but that's all it is.'

Rob scoffs. 'Right. So as soon the truth becomes inconvenient for Bjorn Thrissell, this becomes about my mental state?'

Micah takes a deep breath, tries to regain composure. 'Look,' he says. 'I'm sorry for your loss. Really I am. Marcus was... he was a good man. But using his death as a weapon against Bjorn... it's the wrong decision. Surely you can see that.' He sniffs. 'Sometimes awful things just happen, Rob. You know that as well as I do.'

Rob's eyes widen. 'Oh, fuck this,' he says, rising from the sofa. 'I don't know what I expected.' He's halfway out of the door when he stops, delivers his parting shot. 'I'll get to the bottom of this,' he snarls, 'make no mistake. I'll find out what happened to him up there. And if Bjorn is responsible... there'll be a reckoning.'

And then he's gone, and with him Lucy's best chance to get any more decent content.

'I'm so sorry,' she says to Micah. 'I should have warned you. I thought he'd be able to cope.'

Micah seems barely to hear her. 'It's not easy to be an apostate,' he says, half to himself. 'Trying to block out the memory of what you know to be true. That's all Bjorn was ever trying to do, you know. To spare him that pain.'

Her skin prickles. God, she wishes she could stay. She's barely scratched the surface here. But she needs Rob. He's her ticket into that camp, and she's not at all sure that if she leaves him in the car much longer that he'll go through with this.

'Thanks again for the tea,' she says, making for the door. 'I'll be in touch.'

When she steps outside, the car is still there, thank God. Rob's in the driver's seat, his head bowed, his hands gripping the steering wheel so tightly his knuckles have whitened.

'Hey,' she says as she gets in, and she's got a whole speech prepared about how sorry she is, but she doesn't get a chance to say any of it. He turns to her, his eyes furious.

'Don't you dare make Bjorn look like a viable option,' he hisses. 'Don't you dare. I want you to make him pay. Like you promised.'

It takes all her strength to keep from smiling.

9

EXTRACT FROM WHISPERSHELL NETWORK

COMMUNICATION CHANNEL OPENED - 08:46 12-04-1996

Message from Brigadier Ian McLeod, Head of Scottish Defence Science & Technology (SDS&T):

Sir, we have received reports of individuals squatting at Site 248. Please advise on how to proceed

Message from Major-General Alistair Cavendish, Assistant Chief Of The Defence Staff (Special Programmes):

Please send details of occupants and estimated risk level

Message from Brigadier Ian McLeod, Head of Scottish Defence Science & Technology (SDS&T):

Occupants number no more than six. All under forty. No military connection discernible. Observation shows occupants fulfilling basic needs, conducting light renovation and apparently studying

Message from Major-General Alistair Cavendish, Assistant Chief Of The Defence Staff (Special Programmes):

Please confirm Site 248 has been thoroughly cleansed and no trace remains of former activity. Confirm all samples and documentation have been destroyed following the failure of Project Nexus

Message from Brigadier Ian McLeod, Head of Scottish Defence Science & Technology (SDS&T):

Site 248 has been thoroughly cleansed as per Protocol 45D/1. All Nexus specimens have been either removed or destroyed prior to leaving. No evidence that current occupants are aware of the site's former designation

Message from Major-General Alistair Cavendish, Assistant Chief Of The Defence Staff (Special Programmes):

Advise no further action to avoid drawing attention to Site 248 and its former designation. Maintain oversight role. Monitor the activities of occupants and intervene only where needed

COMMUNICATION CHANNEL CLOSED - 09:32 12-04-1996

10

LUCY'S SCRIPT: INITIAL NOTES

So I know the question you're probably asking yourself, and honestly it's the same question I asked myself when I first heard about this: what's the danger? Why should I be worried about a bunch of people taking notes in a makeshift library?

Well, here's why: apophenia. A phenomenon where people get so invested in a text they start to see things that aren't there, spotting patterns in random data, or making connections where none exist.

You could make a pretty good case that the twentieth century, with its embrace of deconstruction, has created a fertile ground for apophenia. When the meaning of a text is neither stable nor fixed, you end up in a kind of interpretative free-for-all.

For some people, that's unbearable. They need something to cling on to. So they pick an interpretation, and make it their Rosetta Stone: it informs everything else they read. Before long, they're seeing hidden messages wherever they look, and they're convinced they alone have gained access to a higher truth.

That's where things can start to get dangerous, because when you believe that you have a monopoly on meaning, when you're convinced that your interpretation is the only valid one, it's a short step from there to fanaticism.

Just look at what happened in the town of Eldersfield, back in 2013, where a group of people - who claimed, incidentally, to be acting on divine inspiration - tried to sabotage a water treatment plant.

They'd convinced themselves the government was manipulating the water supply, and decided it was their sacred duty to stop it. They spent months meeting in secret, plotting out their approach, and when the time came they broke into the facility at night and tried to shut off the water supply.

They were discovered by a security guard before they could put their plan into action, but that's not the interesting part. What's interesting is what the police found when they looked into the conspirators' backgrounds: all of them were highly educated, with no less than five master's degrees between them (in philosophy, literature and computer science) - and up until a few months before the planned attack, they all had extraordinary careers.

Every one of them had left their job in disgrace, having become paranoid and distrustful of authority. They'd become convinced that there were hidden messages everywhere. Police found a mountain of notecards in their houses, filled with cryptic writing and bearing a striking resemblance to those used by the Scriveners.

You won't be surprised, I suspect, to know that Bjorn denied all knowledge of the group. He was at pains to emphasise that the Scrivener's Code was a peaceful philosophy, and that what the group had done showed they couldn't possibly have understood what he was saying.

But you have to wonder, don't you? Whether Bjorn, in his quest to unlock the secrets of the universe, has unleashed something he can no longer control. Whether the very philosophy he intended to bring meaning and purpose to people's lives has taken on a life of its own.

And if that's true, then the Scriveners could potentially be in every nation on Earth. The next time you see a military uprising, or a terrorist attack, or an inexplicable political decision, it could be them.

Or then again, maybe not.

What we do know is what Rob has shared about his time there. We know about the torture – because torture is what it is. We know about the isolation and the mental anguish. The rituals, the self-mutilation and the despair.

Does that in itself make the System a force for evil? Is that enough evidence?

That's for you to decide. But I think you'll agree it's a question worth asking.

11

BEFORE LONG the motorways turn into A roads and then B roads, and then roads without names. When she cracks the window Lucy can smell peat and pine. She can't shake the feeling of being watched, although by what she's unsure. The land itself feels hostile, as though people aren't supposed to live this far out.

There are few farms up here, no houses, not even any birdsong: only the occasional battered-looking sheep. She wonders how they manage when it rains. There's no shelter, and the wind comes right off the sea. Not hard to imagine them being swept away.

The road goes on, and on, and on, climbing gently over miles of empty highland, hardly a trace of civilisation, only rocks and trees. Maybe that suits Bjorn. Finally, they reach a T-junction at the base of a mountain, the road to the right peeling off into a valley and another to the left sloping uphill towards a small settlement.

It's a beautiful day – the sky a strange, eerie blue, the only trace of clouds a set of faint wisps far above. Even so, the village doesn't look like much. The houses are solid and squat, their windows small, built to survive. It's nestled at the base of a mountain, and the light from the sun seems barely to reach it.

She can imagine what she'll see when they get closer: weathered stones, worn-out faces. A hard life in a place like this. As the car climbs upwards, struggling a little with the gradient, she gets no satisfaction from discovering she's right. The village extends a couple of hundred metres along the main road, the buildings huddled together as though for warmth. She spots a garage, a fish and chip shop, a pub with a mock-Tudor frontage. A cricket pitch, roughly carved from a field in the outskirts. There can't be more than a hundred people living here.

'Can we stop briefly?' she says. 'Take a look around?'

Rob frowns. 'I'd rather not,' he says without taking his eyes off the road. 'We've come this far. I want to get it over with now.'

'Sure. Sure. I just— we need some background, I mean. Something to contextualise your story.'

'We can stop afterwards. I promise.' That hardness is back in him. 'Trust me, Lucy. They're no friends of Bjorn down there.'

'Do you still know anyone there?'

'Nah. One of the men helped me after I ran away, but he left pretty soon after. Didn't like the thought of being so close to Bjorn.'

They're passing through the village now, the road before them rising in a steep curve. She catches a glimpse of faces at the windows. Wondering, no doubt, who's stupid enough to go up to the commune.

'God. Did they threaten him?'

'Nope. That would have given the police grounds for a warrant. They didn't do a thing to him. But knowing they were up on the hill, after what I told him... it freaked him out, I think.'

'What do people even do around here?' she says, once the village is in their rear-view mirror. 'There can't be much work.'

She can hear the engine struggling, watches Rob shift into a lower gear. 'It's all the quarry,' he says. 'Slate mining, and a few basic services to support it. A pub, a shop. It's a weird place.'

'Man. You're really up at the edge of the world here, aren't you?'

He gives a harsh laugh, just audible over the struggling engine. 'You could say that again.' Their speed is dropping, the little needle on the speedometer ticking steadily down. 40 mph, 35 mph, 30 mph. 'I still can't believe I let you talk me into this.'

She puts a hand against the glove compartment as the road becomes even steeper. The speedometer hovers at 20 mph. She feels suddenly claustrophobic. To her left is a dense tapestry of ancient woodland. In the rear-view mirror the disappearing Craigdhu looks like a model village, its whitewashed houses huddling together for warmth. It might even look idyllic if not for Craigdhu Quarry across the valley, jagged and raw as a fresh wound.

'You're sure you're okay with this?'

'I'm certain,' says Rob firmly. 'That place took everything I had.' He's not looking at her, and she's glad of it: there's real anger in his voice. 'You were right, Lucy. I needed this. I should have done it years ago.'

Before Lucy can fully take this in, they've crested the hill, and the camp unfolds before them. It's surrounded by a mesh perimeter fence that stretches out about the length of a football field, and as they pass through a set of heavy metal gates she can see figures in practical, hard-wearing clothes moving about the site, loading sweet potatoes into crates. There can't be more than two dozen of them, but there's a palpable sense of industry.

There's a patchwork of rectangular vegetable gardens dotted around the site, their vibrant greens standing out right away. All that greenery stands in stark contrast against the buildings. Her eye's drawn to the largest of them, a two-storey building painted a flat grey.

'What's that?' she says, nodding over to it.

'It's the mess hall,' says Rob, with a hint of contempt. 'It's where we gathered for meals, meetings... just about anything, really.'

In front of it sits a firepit bordered by rough wooden benches, and then the bunkhouses: single-storey stone buildings with small windows set deep into them. Dotted among them sit a couple of equally austere smaller dwellings, which look like single-occupancy houses. Along the back of the camp stretches another huge building roughly the size and shape of a swimming pool.

The place looks like it's been deliberately stripped of its character. It's not at all what she expected. She'd expected Bjorn's followers to be esoteric, ramshackle. Flamboyant, perhaps. It bothers her. She'd thought she understood him. Now she's not so sure.

Next to her Rob's leaning forwards, as though trying to better take it all in. His face is hard, and it looks like he's stifling a grimace.

'You okay?' she says, and he nods.

'It's hardly changed at all,' he says, steering the car up a gravel track to where a couple of battered-looking pickup trucks are parked. Figures begin to emerge from the bunkhouses and mess hall. Rob takes a deep breath, sits back in his seat with his face turned to heaven and his eyes closed.

'Hey,' she says again, laying a hand on the back of his seat. 'Tell me you're okay, Rob.'

'I'm okay,' he says after a second or two, his voice flat. 'Just give me a second.'

Outside the figures are getting closer. They're led by a tall woman in a vast woollen jumper, her brown hair sharply parted. Behind her follows a man in a hiking fleece who looks to be in his late thirties, with reddish hair and a thick beard, and a younger man with a buzzcut who's all angles – long limbs beneath a shabby black denim jacket.

She takes a steadying breath, opens the door and steps out. Raises a hand in greeting. *God, it's cold up here*, thinks Lucy. The air is chill and crisp. If only she hadn't left her coat in the car – it's hard to look confident when you're visibly shivering.

'Hey,' she says.

The woman approaches, offers her hand. 'Hey,' she says, smiling broadly. 'Welcome.' She's older than Lucy had first thought, early fifties perhaps. An air of youth about her, a grace and muscularity that suggested she kept herself in shape.

Lucy wonders if she's a recent recruit, or if she'd been here in Rob's day.

'I'm Lucy. Rob's… uh… friend.'

'Cat.' She nods over her shoulder. 'This is Kristian, with the beard, and Pyotr. You'll meet everyone else soon. They're so looking forward to seeing Rob again.' She glances at the car with an expression of concern. 'Is he not getting out?'

'Yeah. I think he's just… composing himself.'

'We're thrilled he's back.'

Lucy's taken aback by their hospitality. Surely it has to be deliberate: they can't have forgotten the circumstances under which Rob had left. 'I'm not sure I'd use those words when he gets out.'

'He's always been welcome here,' says Cat, her smile widening. 'He ought to know that.'

Lucy feels uncomfortably exposed, and she glances around her, searching for safe conversational ground. 'So, this is a lot less rustic than I expected.'

'You should have seen it when we arrived. It was ex-military, totally abandoned. Really quite a state. We've worked hard to get it looking like this. I'll give you a tour in a bit.'

'Have you all been here since the beginning?'

Now Kristian speaks up. 'No,' he says. His voice is low, with a trace of a Slavic accent. 'Pyotr and I only came a few years ago.'

'Mm-hmm,' says Cat brightly. 'We're not a big operation, but people still manage to find their way up here every now and again.'

'Sure. I met Micah Dunkeld on the way up. He's one of your evangelists, right?'

Cat raises her eyebrows. 'That's exactly right,' she says. 'Yes, Micah's one of our, uh, evangelists, although I don't much like the term personally. How did you two come to cross paths?'

'Listen,' Lucy says. 'You ought to know why I'm here.'

Cat's smile falters slightly. 'I thought you were Rob's partner. His... significant other.'

'No,' says Lucy. 'Actually, I'm not. I'm here in a journalistic capacity. To try and help Rob articulate what he experienced up here.'

She can feel the atmosphere shift. 'Huh,' says Cat, a smile still plastered across her face but seeming less believable by the second. She reaches beneath her sweater and unclips a walkie-talkie from her belt. 'If you'll excuse me for just a second. We might need to clear that with Bjorn.' She clicks a button. *Crk-crk.* 'Bjorn?'

Kristian is staring at Lucy with a disconcerting intensity. The corner of his mouth is twisted into something like a smile, but there's no lightness in it. 'We've had some issues with journalists in the past.'

'Sure,' she says. 'I understand Bjorn got a bit of a rough ride in the press when *The Scrivener's Code* came out.'

'That's one way to put it,' mutters Pyotr from behind Kristian.

Well, at least this is more familiar territory. She's dealt with angry subjects before, and is well-practised in de-escalation. 'Listen, I want you to know that we don't have any agenda here. Or I don't. I just want to tell the story.'

'If you say so,' says Kristian, running a hand through his beard as he considers this. 'You'll understand if I have my doubts.'

'What he's trying to say is that there's no such thing as a neutral observer,' says Pyotr. 'You've already decided on the story you want to tell.'

Lucy bristles. Not because he's wrong – he's not – but because of how expertly Pyotr's cut through Lucy's corporate playbook. She needed that corporate playbook. Without that, things can get uncomfortable out in the field.

'Okay. That's fair. But I want you to know...' she thinks for a moment, trying to find a set of words that aren't entirely worn out. 'I want you to know that you get some control over this too. That your voice is important, not just Rob's.'

Cat's still talking on the walkie-talkie. Lucy tries to follow her conversation, without success: she's too busy managing Pyotr. The last thing she hears is, 'Okay, I think we need you.'

From behind Lucy comes the sound of a car door opening. She turns to see Rob mouthing 'Sorry'. He looks rattled and tired. She gives a silent prayer that he doesn't lose his shit again.

'Rob!' says Cat, plastering a smile back on her face. She opens her arms as though planning to embrace him, and then thinks better of it. 'It's so good to see you. I'm not sure I'd have recognised you.'

Rob's face is stony, and Lucy can see the effort it takes him not to rise to the bait. 'That's because I've had some proper food since you last saw me, Cat. And I've not been locked up in a cupboard.'

A slight hesitation in Cat then. She hides it well, the faintest twitch in her cheek, but Lucy can tell. 'Okay,' she says, with admirable calm. 'I'm just sorry we couldn't get you back here under happier circumstances.'

Rob stares at her as though she's mad. 'In case you don't remember, I didn't exactly leave under the happiest circumstances either.'

Cat nods, feigning remorse. 'I know,' she says. 'And I'm so sorry about that. It didn't have to be that way. Truly. I think even Bjorn regrets how it happened.'

'Oh, how big of him.' He looks over at Kristian and Pyotr. 'Do your newbies know about how Bjorn lied to the police? How he forced my own brother to gaslight me?'

'Okay,' says Cat again, acknowledging this statement with a nod. 'I hear that. But you know as well as I do that there's always multiple sides to a story. We all did what we thought was best at the time.'

There's something like disgust in Rob's expression, a vague and ill-defined contempt: his mouth has fallen open and he looks a little unhinged. 'That was the last time I ever saw my mother, you realise that?' He's shaking his head. 'I never even got to attend her funeral.'

'I know,' says Cat, bowing her head. 'And I'm truly sorry for that. We tried to find you. You were between foster homes.' The tears in her eyes are oddly convincing. 'Oh, Rob. If only we'd been able to help you back then… you were hurting so much.'

But Rob is clearly unconvinced. 'Oh no. No, don't you do this. You can pretend that the life I lived here with you was idyllic if you want, but I know what I remember.'

'I'm sure,' says Cat, dabbing at her eyes. 'And I understand. I do. But memories can lie to us so easily…' She gives him a tiny, embarrassed shrug. 'That's the beauty of the System, I suppose.'

Lucy can see the effort it costs Rob not to yell. 'Enough,' he says firmly. 'I don't want to hear that again. God knows I've heard it plenty. Now where's Bjorn?'

'You don't have to take this from him, Cat,' says Pyotr, cutting in. He takes a step forwards towards Rob, covering the distance between them with a single large stride. 'God, the arrogance. You think just because you're in pain that gives you the right to lash out?'

And then suddenly everyone's shouting – Rob, Cat, Pyotr – and Cat's using her height and strength to hold the younger man back, doing her best to stop him grabbing Rob's jacket. She looks Pyotr dead in the eye, staring him down like he's a wild animal, and then lifts her hands and shoves him hard in the chest. He staggers backwards, and before he can come back for another swing Cat steps between the two men, her arms outstretched to keep them apart. 'Enough!' she shouts, her voice cutting through the chaos. There's no sense of theatre in her voice now: this strength comes from necessity, and from her position here. She speaks to Pyotr. 'You're being reckless.'

Pyotr glares at her, but at least for now he's not moving. 'I've met people like him before. They won't stop until they've burned everything to the ground.'

'I said, enough,' Cat says, still more fiercely, and now Pyotr seems to get the message, even if he doesn't look happy. 'I don't care what he says. That's not relevant, do you hear?'

'People like him have never understood what Bjorn's doing up here,' says Pyotr viciously, biting his lip. 'Never.'

Rob closes his eyes, takes a breath. 'Look,' he says, sounding pained. 'Believe it or not, I don't want a fight. I came here for Marcus. To say a proper goodbye.'

Pyotr starts to speak, but Kristian holds up a hand to quiet him. Lucy's surprised at how gentle he can be, despite his huge frame. 'Listen, Rob,' he says. 'We're not your enemies. We're just trying to do our work. Take Marcus's body, by all means.' He heaves a sigh. 'It's not like he needs to be buried up here. But don't make this about revenge. We didn't kill him.' His eyes flick towards Cat, as though concerned he's overstepped the mark.

But Rob's not looking at Kristian now, doesn't seem to have heard a word he's said. He's staring past Kristian, and when Lucy follows his gaze she sees why.

Bjorn.

He wears a shapeless grey cardigan, his hair shaggy and grey, his beard unkempt: he looks like Bill Oddie on a bad day. Lucy puts a hand on Rob's shoulder. A reminder that she's there. A reminder not to do anything stupid.

Then Bjorn looks her in the eye, and in it she can see something that frightens her. People follow this man, no matter how unimpressive he seems. They think of him as a visionary. Think he has something to offer them, that he can change their lives. People like Rob's mum. She'd believed in Bjorn enough to drag her boys all the way to the edge of the world.

Now Rob was the only one left. It made you wonder.

12

BJORN STANDS a short distance from the car, watching them with his arms folded. Some of the intensity seems to have gone from his gaze since Rob last saw him, although perhaps that's because he's not looking directly at Rob – it's like he's looking through him, to a point an inch or two beyond his left shoulder.

Rob takes a breath. Feels the bracing, clear air of the commune, the familiar salt-tang on the wind, the scrubby grass beneath the car. His heart's pounding. He's spent years imagining what he'll say if he sees Bjorn again, but now he's here, every beautifully constructed retort has left his mind.

Next to him, Lucy's hands rest flat on her thighs with an affected casualness. After maybe thirty seconds, she nods over to where Bjorn's standing, waiting for them. 'Don't you think we ought to go and say hello?'

Rob swallows. 'I'm not sure I can.'

'You can.' She says it matter-of-factly, without anger, and something inside him bristles: she doesn't know what it's like, can't understand what it means to be back here.

'I'm trying,' he says. 'I really am.'

She nods. 'I know,' she says, and then after a moment's pause: 'But you're giving him all the power.'

He closes his eyes, moves without thinking, and before he knows it, he's walking towards Bjorn as though compelled by some force outside of himself. His jaw is clenched like he's bracing for a punch. Then, somehow, he finds himself in front of Bjorn, trying to be strong, trying not to look him directly in the eye.

'Welcome back,' says Bjorn, not offering his hand.

Rob glances around. 'It's not changed much.'

Is there something snide in Bjorn's half-smile? 'Maybe not on the outside.'

'Where's Marcus?' he says. He can hear Lucy's footsteps behind him, knows she'll want to prolong this conversation, but now he's here he just wants to see his brother. Anything to stabilise this roiling world.

Now Bjorn hesitates, just for a moment: there's a tiny catch in his throat, and his fingers worry at the sleeve of his fleece. 'I think we ought to sit down for a moment or two before—'

'I don't want to be here a moment longer than I have to be,' Rob says, more forcefully than he intended. Lucy touches him lightly on the elbow, as though in warning, but he doesn't turn. Bjorn glances over at her, apparently surprised that Rob's brought a companion, but he continues speaking in his same, sombre tone.

'You need to be… appropriately prepared,' Bjorn says, with the hint of a sigh.

He should have known. Bjorn was never going to make it easy for him. Even now he wants to control things. No matter that Marcus is dead, or that this place killed him, or that Rob wasn't with him for his final moments: Bjorn wants to stage-manage the viewing of the corpse too. Rob can't contain his irritation. 'What the fuck, Bjorn? What are you hiding?'

Again, Lucy's steadying hand on his elbow. 'What happened to him?' she says, her voice calm, her very presence radiating stability. There's that questioning look in Bjorn's eyes again: *Who is this?*

Rob nods over his shoulder, not wanting to let Bjorn off the hook for longer than a moment or two. 'This is Lucy,' he says. 'She's a journalist. I asked her along to document what you're doing here.' He raises his eyebrows, feeling a faint ripple of triumph: Bjorn wasn't expecting this.

'Yes, Cat told me as much.' Bjorn frowns. 'I'm not sure what you're hoping to achieve by this, but you'll understand my concerns.'

'Well, I'm afraid this isn't your story,' says Rob. 'It's mine.'

Bjorn puts a hand to his head. 'I'm sorry,' he says, sounding weary. 'Both for what happened to Marcus, and your mother. Truly I am. But I only ever intended this place for good. If you've come here to conduct some kind of smear campaign, then why should I give you my blessing?'

'And how do you think that'll play down the road, or with the papers?' says Rob, with a nasty smile. 'If I tell them your secretive cult is keeping me from retrieving my brother's body?'

Bjorn closes his eyes. At his sides, his hands are clenching and unclenching. 'If you'll give me a moment,' he says tightly. He reaches into the satchel at his side and removes a small wooden box. Flicks it open to reveal a set of notecards. He rifles through them, picks one out apparently at random. Reads it over, and nods. 'Hmm,' he says, seeming to relax. 'Very well.'

'Sorry to ask,' says Lucy, 'but what was that all about?'

Bjorn lets out a resigned sigh, like he's explained this so many times before he can answer without thinking. 'I never act without seeking guidance,' he says. 'It's a matter of principle.'

Lucy glances at Rob and he rolls his eyes. 'Can I see what it said?' she asks.

'Of course,' says Bjorn, handing it to her. It's a small pink notecard, the type Lucy remembered using to revise for her GCSEs, and it leaves a faint, gritty residue on her fingers. On it is written, in surprisingly neat handwriting:

> 20160910/A/1: 'From the dimly lighted passages of the court, the last sediment of the human stew that had been boiling there all day was straining off.' And so it is for us. The world in all its frenzy is determined to pursue its individual follies. All of them will burn away in time. Such is the nature of things. What remains will be only the pure, the true. Refined by fire.

'And that's... guidance?' she says, handing it back and brushing her hands clean.

'It is.'

'It seems awfully random.'

'It is,' cuts in Rob.

'It is *not*,' says Bjorn firmly. 'Although I understand why it might seem that way to an outsider.' He speaks to Lucy. 'I believe in the leading of the Immortal Spirit, who speaks through the word, and through whom a new world will come into being. The text is her vessel: I am her obedient servant.'

'If it sounds ludicrous,' says Rob, 'that's because it is. It's nonsense.'

But Bjorn's still watching Lucy. 'I'm not sure your friend is so convinced of that,' he says. 'But listen – if it's right to let you record in here, then it's right. You should go and talk to Cat, she'll tell you what you need to know about the place.'

'That's it?' says Rob, sounding almost disappointed. 'What about Marcus?'

'Of course,' says Bjorn. 'Forgive me. That's why you're here, isn't it.' He looks a little dazed, as though still trying to take in this new direction. 'Your brother is in the vault. Because of the state of his body, we've not yet managed to remove it for examination.'

'You've not called the police?'

'No,' says Bjorn with distaste. 'They don't understand how we do things up here. Never have, not really.'

Rob's eyes widen. 'We have to do that. Right away.'

Bjorn sighs deeply. 'I'm begging you not to,' he says. 'You simply can't. Not yet. The damage they could do to us is… unimaginable.'

'You mean the vault.'

'That's right. You weren't here last time, but it was dreadful. An awful time.'

He sees Lucy frown. 'How many people have died up here, Bjorn?' she says. 'Over the years. I know it's at least two.'

'You mean Rob's mother.' He glances over at Rob. 'If you only knew how her death has haunted me.' He rubs his neck, spackled with a faint razor burn. 'Nora undertook a trial. One that we expected would make her stronger, that would sharpen her focus. Unfortunately, it was a trial she wasn't strong enough to survive.'

'Oh no,' Rob says through clenched teeth. 'No. Don't you dare. You made my own brother lie to the police. You hid her away when they came looking for her.'

Bjorn puts a hand to his head. 'She knew what she signed up for,' he says. 'She committed to it. Welcomed it, even. We were calling her back to herself. As we did you.'

'She died in the Pit, didn't she?' Rob says. 'Because that's what you do to people who have questions. Shut them away until they see the error of their ways.'

'No,' says Bjorn firmly. 'That's not fair. There's more to it than that, and you know it.' He puts a hand to his head. 'That was a dreadful time, Rob, although you weren't around to see it. We did what we thought best. For everyone. Were we wrong? Perhaps. But don't pretend we're evil.'

'Deny it all you like,' says Rob. 'That doesn't let you off the hook.'

'I won't discuss this on record,' says Bjorn, speaking to Lucy now. 'I simply won't. If you want to have a civil conversation about this, that we can. But I won't let myself be dragged through the mud by people who have no interest in understanding what we do here.' He doesn't look at Rob. He doesn't need to.

'So you won't tell us more about what happened to Nora?' says Lucy, her heart sinking. 'Even if it meant helping people understand the truth of what happened?'

Bjorn eyes her warily. 'Speaking off the record?'

'Yes, if you like.'

'She was undergoing a process of…' He hesitates, weighing his words. '… of restoration. It was intense, yes, but believe me when I say she consented to it. We had no reason to think it would end the way it did.'

Rob scoffs. 'I don't think you understand what consent even means.'

Bjorn's jaw clenches. 'I appreciate this might be difficult for you to hear as her son, Rob, but I saw a different side of your mother. I remember the day she came here. The *passion* she had back then, her hunger for knowledge.'

'People change,' Rob shoots back. 'That doesn't seem to be something you've ever been able to grasp.'

'We were calling her back to herself!' says Bjorn, his face reddening. 'We were helping her remember what truly mattered to her, what had always mattered.' He shakes his head. 'We were like a second family to your mother. We loved her. All of us did.'

'That's not love.'

Bjorn turns to Lucy. 'I can't do this,' he says. 'I simply can't continue this conversation. Not when Rob's so determined to take what I have to say and twist it against me. I've seen it before, and it's nothing but destructive.' There's a muscle twitching in his cheek, and his whole body seems to be calling him elsewhere. 'I was willing to give you the benefit of the doubt, you know,' he says. 'Times have changed, and I thought journalistic standards might have too. But it's clear I can't trust you to report on our community fairly. Not with him here.'

Lucy starts to protest. 'But we'll be objective,' she says. 'We just want to hear—'

'I'm sorry,' says Bjorn sharply, 'but I must insist you leave. Both of you. We're done here.'

And with that he turns abruptly and stalks off towards one of the low buildings.

13

She's starting to worry now. At the thought of a week of lost work. A blemish on her CV, and a hole in her finances. And behind it all, bailiffs. The door kicked in, her laptop carried off. Shattered wood and torn paper.

No. She can't let this fall apart. She's been waiting for this opportunity ever since she first met Rob. Whatever it takes, she's going to tell this story.

She turns to Rob, talking to him without really seeing him. Knowing, just knowing, that she can save this.

'Give me a second,' she says. 'Let me see if I can talk him round.'

Rob shakes his head. 'Good luck,' he mutters. 'You're braver than I am.'

She doesn't turn back, doesn't even acknowledge him. Instead she speeds up, breaking into a light jog. Thank God she brought her trainers. Bjorn's heading for one of the low cabins, his head bowed. He looks old and tired, not the charismatic figure Lucy expected him to be.

His hand is on the door when Lucy reaches him. Perhaps he heard her footsteps and this is a sign he wanted to talk, but she's not so sure. He'd been lost in thought, dead to the world, and she wonders if he even registered that the sun was shining.

'Hey,' she says, deliberately casual. 'Do you have a moment?'

He turns and registers who's addressing him. Purses his lips. 'I thought I made myself clear,' he says, raising an eyebrow. Blinking hard against the sunlight. 'What do you want?'

'Look,' she says. 'I apologise for how the conversation went. I'm... I'm not sure Rob ever processed losing his mother like that.' She doesn't meet Bjorn's eye, senses it's best not to. She's got her pitch all lined up; she'll let herself feel dirty later. 'But my intentions are pure,' she says, trying to sound as earnest as possible. 'All I want is to understand. That's all I've ever wanted. It's the reason I became a journalist.'

She can't read his expression. He's listening, his head tilted to one side, but there's something inscrutable about his eyes behind those circular glasses.

'And how do I know you won't twist my words?'

Lucy takes a deep breath. Nearly there. 'I'm not here to push an agenda,' she says. 'I'm here to listen, to learn, and to report the facts. As objectively as I can manage.' She keeps her body language as open as possible, tries not to acknowledge the anxiety buzzing in her skull. 'Give me a chance to tell your story.'

Bjorn's silent for a moment, thinking. 'Rob won't like that.'

'Leave Rob to me. I'll talk to him, help him understand that confrontation won't get him the answers he needs. But I need your help. Need you to vouch for me, you know? To ensure your people are willing to open up to me.'

Bjorn pinches the bridge of his nose. 'I'd never have agreed to this if not for the Spirit,' he says. 'God only knows why, but it seems like letting you in here is for the best.' He shakes his head, pats his satchel. 'I can't reason it out. If you make us look good, then people come out here looking for us. If you make us look bad, then they vilify us. Again.' He turns back to his door. 'Still, I suppose that discomfort is proof we're doing something right here,' he says gloomily. 'That we'll follow the Spirit's leading, no matter how unpalatable.'

She can't help herself. In his face she sees the terror she knows so well. A life smashed into smithereens by faceless men. 'Wait,' she says, and again he pauses with his hand on the key. 'Look, I don't want this to destroy you. I couldn't live with myself if I did.'

'And Rob?'

'Forget Rob,' she says, and she means it. 'For now, anyway.' Bjorn half-turns, taken aback. 'I didn't get into this business to ruin people's lives. I can't bear that thought. You have to let me help. At least help me understand. Help people understand that what you're doing here isn't... evil.'

Bjorn laughs, a short harsh bark of a laugh. 'Evil?' he says. 'Come on, now. Tell me you don't believe that.'

She's no fool. She knows an opening when she sees one. 'The way Rob tells it...'

Bjorn folds his arms. 'Huh.' Thinks for another few seconds. 'Fancy that.' He sighs. 'Just so I'm clear. When this is all over, you're happy if I have the final say over the audio?'

She knows exactly what Rob would have told her: *Don't let him control you.* But she's got a plan. She's the one in control here. As usual.

'I wish I could promise you that,' she says. Cool and professional, without a trace of anxiety. 'I retain editorial control. You must know that.'

'Ha,' says Bjorn, with what looks like genuine amusement. 'When you get over to the vault, look up "control", why don't you? You might be surprised by what you find.' He studies her for a moment. Disappointed, perhaps, that she didn't press further. 'Very well,' he says, sticking his hands into his pockets. 'All the same I'd like to listen to it, when it's done. To know what you're saying about us.'

'Of course.'

He pauses, weighing something up. She can see the effort it's cost him to give up control, the anxiety it causes. Or maybe she'd only seen it because Rob told her to look.

'One more thing, Lucy.'

'Yes?'

'I've met plenty of others like you. Journalists, I mean. That won't come as any surprise.' There's some steel in his glare. 'You'll have to work hard to convince me you're any different from all the rest.'

'Noted.'

When she turns, Rob is still standing with his back pressed up against the car. He looks paranoid, twitchy. Checking the horizon like he's afraid of being ambushed. She's not sure where he expects it to come from: the camp is a vast expanse of flat ground, bordered by wire fences. He'd see anyone coming long before they reached him.

He's been watching her the entire time, obviously. Makes a token effort to look like he hasn't, glancing around from side to side, but he's not fooling anyone.

'So you convinced him to let us stay around,' he says when she's finally close enough. She'd kept him waiting. Strolling back to him, hoping to make him squirm.

'Mm-hmm,' she says, her tone neutral. 'He was more open than I expected.'

Rob's eyes narrow. 'He was?'

'He wants to protect the reputation of this place,' she says. 'He saw pretty quickly that it was in his best interests to tell his side of this story.'

'Tell me what he said.'

Lucy tells him. He can't hide his wariness, and it makes her want to scream.

'I don't like this,' he says.

'You're looking for red flags.'

He looks at her with something like incredulity. 'You're fucking right I am,' he says. He's glaring at her now, in full speechifying mode. 'And you should take note. All these people were taken in by him. Cat, Micah, Pyotr. They're not idiots. They had jobs out there in the real world. Lives.'

Oh no. She's not backing down that easily. 'I'm just saying that maybe you're seeing what you expect to see.'

'Oh, come off it. You've been here ten minutes and already you're an expert.'

She takes a breath. 'I'm not saying that, Rob. I'm not. But this is a good thing.'

'I hope you're right.' Rob scowls down at his feet. That's practically a victory today.

'Look, we need to get some audio. I'd like to go and set up an interview room.' She's already moving round the car, searching for the mics.

'It's a power play, you know,' says Rob, following her round, 'stopping me from seeing Marcus's body until later. It's about controlling the timeline.'

She pauses, remembers why they're there. 'Yeah,' she says. 'Yeah, I can see that.' She pauses with her hand on the boot, makes an effort to meet Rob's eye. 'Do you want me there? Or shall I mic you up beforehand?'

Rob doesn't reply. She can't read his expression.

'Look. Go by yourself if you want.' She says it against her better judgement, hoping he'll push back, but he remains silent. 'I'll wait outside.'

She can see unease cross his face. 'Nope,' he says. 'I'd rather not leave you on your own in this place, you know.'

'I'm a big girl,' she says, straining for lightness.

But he doesn't smile. 'This isn't a joke, Lucy. These people are really dangerous.'

'I know, Rob,' she sighs. 'I get it.'

'Do you?'

She hesitates. 'I guess... I guess I can see what you said about them,' she says. She's making it up as she goes along, and it doesn't feel good. 'Coercion, control. How the ideology gets into your head.' He doesn't believe her. It's written all over his face. 'But I've not seen anything much to say they're dangerous yet. I don't feel… I don't feel scared.'

'Don't you see?' says Rob. 'That's the problem. Nobody is ever scared of them. They look harmless. And then before you know it you're in a solitary confinement room, or you're being shunned by literally everyone you know. And you try and reason with them, and that's when it hits you: there's no arguing.' He shakes his head. 'If you're not scared yet,' he says, 'maybe you're not looking closely enough.'

14

In the common room of his teenage foster home there'd been a jigsaw puzzle. The box said it was 1,000 pieces. Someone had left it half-completed when he arrived, and there'd been something oddly satisfying about trying to fill in the gaps. Whenever he walked past, on the way to the kitchen to make tea, he'd stop and slot in another piece or two. By the end of his first week in the halfway house he'd completed the whole thing.

The image was of a serene countryside landscape: lily pond, herons, and cows standing on a distant, sun-dappled hillside. It was comforting, the kind of idyllic scene that you knew didn't actually exist, but you could hope to stumble across, nonetheless. Five minutes after he finished it, he swept it off the table and started it again. He was now on his fourth attempt.

'You know, I think that puzzle might be older than me,' he heard someone call over. Rob looked up to see Gary, another resident, grinning from the couch. 'I'd swear you've done it a dozen times.'

Rob gave a half-hearted chuckle. 'Helps me think,' he replied, slotting in another piece. 'Keeps my hands busy, you know?'

Gary nodded. 'No news about your mom yet, then?'

Helen appeared in the doorway before Rob could answer him. 'Rob?' she said, in the compassionate tone that he mostly heard when there were visitors. 'Mr Holloway's here.'

Rob's stomach lurched as DI Holloway entered the room. He'd spent more time with Holloway than he'd have liked over the past two months: knew every detail about him, from the frayed edge of his jacket cuffs to his penchant for paisley ties. 'Hi, Rob,' he said briskly, and then to Helen: 'Can Rob and I talk privately?'

Helen led them down the hall to a familiar, small room reserved for serious conversations. It was uncomfortably similar to the police station: plain white walls, battered old table with four hard plastic chairs. Rob sat forwards, elbows on the table, head in his hands. 'I'm guessing this isn't good news.'

Holloway's voice was gruff but kind. 'Look, Rob,' he said, 'I know this is awful for you. I do. And I want you to know we're doing everything in our power to find your mum.' Rob nodded mutely. He'd heard this all before. Holloway sighed and continued, 'I gave you my word that I'd be honest with you. So I owe it to you to say that we haven't found anything. We've searched high and low in that place and… nothing.'

Rob looked up at him, startled by how hollow he felt. 'You searched everywhere?'

'We did,' said Holloway, leaning back in his chair. He ran a hand over his stubble. 'Believe me, lad, we checked everything.

I spoke to Bjorn myself, grilled him for hours. He didn't change his story. Claimed your mum left years ago.' He raised a sardonic eyebrow. 'Not that he's got any records of that, although he's got plenty of others.'

'Of course he'd say that.'

'Aye, I thought the same,' said Holloway. 'So I spoke to the others, one by one. Went through every single one of them, and they all corroborated Bjorn's story. They were good, too. Sounded authentic, not like they'd rehearsed it.' He rested his hands on the table, palms open, as though laying bare everything he'd been able to find. There was something bleak about it: like he was saying, *I'm giving you all I've got here. I know it's not enough.*

'There's got to be some trace of her there,' Rob said, desperately. 'Did you check the vault? The Pit?' he glanced up at Holloway. 'There must have been DNA. Something that would hold up in court.'

Holloway's eyes were tired, a tiredness that ran deep. 'Yep,' he said, 'we found traces of DNA in the Pit, like you said. But it doesn't prove anything, Rob.'

'It has to!'

'It doesn't, lad,' he said, his expression a mixture of frustration and resignation. 'Without a sample from your mother to compare it to, we can't prove she was there. And even if we could prove it, Bjorn and the others would just claim she left voluntarily. It's our word against theirs.' He leaned forwards now, his eyes locked on Rob's. 'I know this isn't what you want to hear, but cults like this are hard to bring down. They're good at covering their tracks. They're full of loyal followers, who say whatever they're told to say, and more often than not they've got deep pockets as well.'

Rob felt a surge of anger. 'You're saying they can just get away with it? People like Bjorn can do whatever they want, and no one can stop them?'

Holloway's jaw tightened. 'I'm not saying that,' he said. 'If we get something more on him…'

But Rob could see the truth in Holloway's face. 'But you're giving up, right?'

'I don't think that's fair…' Holloway said, but even as he was speaking his voice tailed off. 'Ah, fuck it.' He rubbed his temple. 'Rob, if I had limitless resources, I'd set people up to watch that place day and night. I'm with you, okay. There's something ugly there.' He took a long breath. 'But unless something new turns up I can't keep searching. We've got other cases piling up with more leads, and my DCI's saying that I don't have the evidence to take Bjorn to court. It's out of my hands.' He studied Rob for a long moment. 'I'm sorry, kid. I really am.'

There were tears pricking at the corners of Rob's eyes and he hated himself for it. 'That's it?' he said, his voice cracking. 'She's just gone?'

Holloway closed his eyes. 'The moment I get another reason to investigate that place, I'll be up here like a shot. I'll get him.'

'Next time,' Rob said, gripping the side of the table so hard it cut into his hand. 'When somebody else disappears. Or when someone loses their mind and gets a knife.'

Holloway sat back in his chair and studied Rob for a long time.

Rob could see him trying to decide on the right course of action. As if such a thing existed. Finally, he landed on something he was happy with. 'Look,' he said, 'you're not the first person I've seen who's had something awful happen to you, right?'

Rob felt a flash of anger, but before he could snap back, Holloway silenced him with a glare. 'I know that isn't very comforting. But I'm telling you for a reason.' He held Rob's gaze, determined to ensure he was listening. 'I can see you're in pain. And I'd understand if you wanted to soak in that pain for a while. But don't do that, you hear? Missing person cases like this, they consume people. If you're not careful, you'll never get past this.' He shook his head. 'You have to find a way to move on. Not right away, not necessarily, but before long.'

'Move on? How the hell am I supposed to move on?'

Holloway gave a one-armed shrug. 'I'm not sure I'm qualified to speak to that,' he said. 'I'd find something to occupy your mind, for a start. Something more useful than a jigsaw. Find a trade, learn to play the guitar… something.' He looked down at the table. 'I'm not trying to be glib, Rob. You've got to figure it out for yourself.'

'That's your answer?' said Rob, feeling anger burn inside him. 'Learn to play the guitar?'

'Maybe that wasn't the best example,' said Holloway with a grimace. 'All I'm saying is, don't let him win. And don't spend the rest of your life wondering either. You spend too long thinking about something like this and you'll lose your mind. I've seen it happen before.'

15

EXTRACT: Notes from Bjorn's slip box

20160910/A: `Mr Carton, who had so long sat looking at the ceiling of the court, changed neither his place nor his attitude, even in this excitement.' An invitation to stillness. In such moments lies true wisdom. The challenge is remaining still when all around you is clamour and chaos.

20160910/A/1: `From the dimly lighted passages of the court, the last sediment of the human stew that had been boiling there all day was straining off.' And so it is for us. The world in all its frenzy is determined to pursue its individual follies. All of them will burn away in time. Such is the nature of things. What remains will be only the pure, the true. Refined by fire.

20160910/D: `The friends of the acquitted prisoner had dispersed, under the impression – which he himself had originated – that he would not be released that night.´ Emphasising the danger of the present moment, and the need for deception. There are those who would seek to direct us to their own ends. They are the ones to fear. A blessing on misdirection: not all here are friends.

20160910/G: `The corner has been mentioned as a wonderful corner for echoes; it had begun to echo so resoundingly to the tread of coming feet, that it seemed as though the very mention of that weary pacing to and fro had set it going.´ A truly powerful word. This speaks to the power of the vault... of sitting in those walls and hearing all that has gone before, which resounds throughout history. We do not work in isolation; we stand on the shoulders of giants. And through that alchemy, a new world is born.

20160910/G/1: `Not only would the echoes die away, as though the steps had gone; but, echoes of other steps that never came would be heard in their stead, and would die away for good when they seemed close at hand.´ Mystifying, but nonetheless resonant. A warning, perhaps, to not assume what we hope for will come to pass... or, more ominous still, a reminder of how easy it may be to miss the coming of the Spirit.

16

Lucy wastes no time getting to work. She's seen how unstable Rob's been since they set off, knows how easy it would be for this whole project to fall apart. She owes it to herself to get as much material as she can before that happens.

She and Rob meet Cat outside the large meeting hall that Rob calls the mess hall.

Cat runs a hand through her closely cropped grey hair. She's several inches taller than Lucy. 'You're lucky Bjorn agreed to this,' she says. Not unfriendly, just factual.

'I know. I assume you weren't keen.'

There's the hint of a smile at the corner of Cat's lips. 'You're sharp,' she says drily.

'This isn't my first rodeo.'

Cat raises an eyebrow. Surprise? Amusement? Lucy can't tell, can't read the older woman at all. Despite herself, she feels unexpectedly flustered.

'Look,' says Cat, 'I want you to get this right. Want people to understand what we're doing here, what we're about. If you're going to tell that story properly, then you need to at least know who does what.'

'That's good of you,' says Lucy, and she means it. 'I appreciate it.'

Whatever smile had been pulling at Cat's lips disappears so quickly that Lucy wonders if she imagined it. 'I'm not doing it as a favour to you,' Cat says. 'It's in my best interest. If you want to tell people about this place then I'd like you to at least be accurate.' Her brow furrows. 'There's a lot of good here.' She ignores the look Rob gives her. 'I'd like people to see that.'

'I'll be balanced,' says Lucy, but the moment the words leave her lips she's appalled by how trite they are. Ordinarily she'd have a proper pitch to hand. She's better than this. 'Like I say, I've been doing this a while.'

'Balanced? Sure you will.'

Lucy decides not to pick that fight. 'Okay. So who do I need to speak to?'

In a gleaming kitchen at the back of the mess hall she meets Elliot, a tall, rangy-looking man who looks like he's stepped out of a 1970s folk band, although apparently he doesn't play guitar. The kitchen is a hive of activity, with preparations for lunch underway. Elliot's team of helpers are chopping up and roasting trays of root vegetables for soup. There's Danny, an ex-con in his late forties whose tattoos are starting to fade and who's starting to run to fat, whom she talks to while he's knocking back the bread that's been proving.

Amy, a brisk, business-like woman whose blonde hair is cut into a no-nonsense bob, tells Lucy about her old life as an office manager, and how little time she got to pursue her real passions. 'I'm living a kind of dream here,' she says. 'I can't remember the last time I sat at a computer, and just look at my muscles.'

She holds out her left bicep and asks Lucy to touch it. It's impressive, although Lucy doesn't want to look like she's having too much fun, not with Rob brooding in the corner. They try their best to bring him into the conversation, but mostly he just leans against the counter sipping on a black coffee. It's probably for the best: she's getting better interviews without him cutting in. Not that she can get anyone to talk about Marcus: they're sad, sure, but from what they've heard it sounds like there's nothing to be concerned about. *People die*, she's heard more than one person say. *Let's not get too sentimental about it.*

'He was a good man,' Danny says. 'But he was a stress-head too. It's not good for your heart.' Next to him, Margaret, who's in her sixties and whose wild curls are fading to grey, nods along. She used to be a nurse.

In the gardens they meet Hazel and her team, who are digging up yet more root vegetables: turnips, sweet potatoes, carrots. The vegetable patches are huge, planted with seasonal veg and tended with a scientific rigour. Hazel talks her through the fertilisers they use, the pesticides, how they manage the microclimate up here. She's hoping for a proper greenhouse soon to replace her weather-beaten polytunnel.

'They're quite the little unit,' Hazel says. 'I've got them working like a well-oiled machine.' Lucy's struck by how disparate a group they are. Tommy's in his early twenties, prickly and artistic; Jenny used to be a psychotherapist, and looks worn ragged; Henrik has written a couple of books, although he doesn't like to talk about it; Beatrice and Josef brought their two kids up here. That last one gets Rob's attention, but despite his best efforts to sway them they tell him Harry and Maddy (who are now teenagers) have always been happy here, they've talked about the future, they're even hoping to go to university.

'You can't find trauma where it doesn't exist,' they say. 'It's a good life up here.'

'We'll see,' Rob mutters darkly to Lucy as they head to their next interview. 'Whose parents really know what they were thinking at fifteen anyway?'

She makes a mental note to be careful there. What she can't understand is how everyone's taken Marcus's death in their stride. She'd expected that with the vault closed off, she'd find the beating heart ripped out of this place. Instead, it seems to run itself, a little self-sustaining entity. She ought to talk to Bjorn about that, if she can.

In a server room, Kristian and Pyotr talk to her about IT infrastructure, which leaves her numb. It's the happiest she's seen Rob all week, though, so while the audio is useless she lets it run anyway. He needs a break, a chance to regroup. They're circling the vault now, drawing closer and closer to Marcus, and she's still not sure how he's going to take it.

On and on it goes. She'd never realised how many jobs there were in a cult: there's even a little office space carved out on the upper floor of the mess hall, with desks and computers, swivel chairs and a water cooler. Ken used to be an accountant, so manages the group's finances. Miranda is an operations manager, which mostly means that she sorts out maintenance and food deliveries, although medical supplies are handled elsewhere. Cat is the resident doctor, working out of a little infirmary at the back of the mess hall with Reynaud and Margaret on hand. And Adam, a battered looking twentysomething in a plaid shirt, works in sanitation: he doesn't want to talk about it.

'It's quite a developed operation,' she tells Cat when they're done with introductions. 'I was expecting something a little more—'

Now Cat breaks into a genuine, droll smile. 'Ramshackle?'

'Yeah.'

Cat nods over towards a battered vehicle, parked alongside the perimeter fence that overlooks the village. 'You know, we had high ideals when we first came up here,' she says wryly. 'Thought we were artists. Turns out our skills didn't quite fit the vision.'

When Lucy moves closer she can make out a derelict jeep which some enterprising soul has attempted to transform into an art exhibit. She's seen better. The chassis is covered in a patchwork of scavenged metal plates, haphazardly welded together. It's a mass of clashing colours and textures: some dented and rusty, others bright and new. Although there are wildflowers jammed into the gaps, their cheerful colours battling against the rust, the overwhelming sensation is one of decay.

The headlights sport mismatched bulbs, one a sickly yellow, the other a garish blue, while the windshield is covered in an amateurish painting of a sunset, its bright reds and oranges making her think of a primary school display. Behind it sits the mesh perimeter fence, which has split at the join between two panels, revealing jagged metal teeth.

'Points for effort,' Lucy says, snapping a photo and thinking: *this story tells itself.*

'It's a death trap,' Cat says. 'Thank God we don't have little kids running round anymore, so at least I don't have to worry about tetanus like I used to. I've been badgering Bjorn to get rid of it for years, but he doesn't like bringing in outside help if he can avoid it. Never has.' She shakes her head. 'We're not so naïve these days, you know? We've got good people coming through here all the time. They've helped us get established.'

'You mean you've used them,' mutters Rob.

'That's not fair,' says Cat, raising an eyebrow, 'and you know it. People choose to come here, and they choose when to go.'

'It's not a fair choice. You've rigged it against them.'

'Come on, Rob,' says Cat, rolling her eyes. 'Show me a system that isn't rigged. Bjorn built this place on a set of principles. We've always been open about them. People know what they're getting into.'

'I didn't.'

Cat's silent for a moment or two, leaning against the side of the vault with her eyes closed. She almost looks remorseful. 'No,' she says. 'No, I suppose not.'

Lucy knows she ought to let this play out, but she can't help thinking about the shape of this thing. She needs Cat to tell her about the vault, in her own words: the more detail the better.

She forces herself to move this along, and hates herself a little for it when she sees the look on Rob's face.

'So this is the vault,' she says, nodding to the vast concrete building.

'Mm-hmm. It used to be a firing range,' says Cat, and Lucy can hear in her voice that she's happy to be back on steadier ground. 'The military built all this and then left it to rot. Too difficult to get supplies up here. I don't think they even bothered locking the gates when they left. We're a long way from anywhere.'

The vault is a massive rectangular building with no windows, stretching out the length of a swimming pool. Its exterior is a grubby white colour that reminds her irrevocably of a leisure centre in her hometown. She can't believe how unspectacular it is. 'You said they abandoned it?' she asks. 'That doesn't sound like the army.'

'You'd have to ask Bjorn about that,' says Cat. 'You're not the only one to wonder about it. I think a lot of people do when they first come up here. But ask yourself this: if the army had a big issue with us being here, wouldn't they have turfed us out by now?'

'I suppose so.' She imagines a military command centre getting news of the squatters. Planning meetings where they discussed the possibility of another Waco. 'Didn't anyone ever come to talk to you?'

'Sure. Once upon a time.' Cat shrugs. 'Bjorn convinced them that what we're doing up here is a charitable endeavour.

Self-sustaining, creative, in the public interest. Told them it'd be cheaper to let us maintain it than for it to go to ruin. We still pay some ground rent, though.'

'You do? How do you cover that?'

'With donations,' mutters Rob.

Cat purses her lips, ignores him. 'People are very generous.'

'People give to this place?'

'There's no need to sound so surprised,' says Cat. 'There's people working out there, in the world, who really believe in this place. Even if Rob doesn't.'

'That's what worries me,' Rob says. 'More than once I could have sworn you were having me followed.'

'Come on, Rob,' says Cat. 'It's not really our style, is it.'

'You're not great on aftercare, though, are you? Can't imagine you helped Alex get back on his feet after he lost his mind.' His tone is vicious. 'Thomas, Elena, Michael... do you actually know what happened to them when they left? If they're even still alive?'

'Ask yourself this,' says Cat after a moment's pause. 'What if we had reached out to you? Wouldn't you just have seen it as a threat?'

Lucy holds her tongue, tries to get this back on track. She can't let Rob derail them now. 'I'm just surprised you've got so much outside support,' she says, acting like she hasn't heard a thing. 'I was led to believe this was something... monastic. Inward-looking.'

Cat puts a hand to the door. 'We need to get you in to talk to Bjorn,' she says, 'as he'll set you straight on that soon enough.

MARGINAL

This is the engine room, the heart of the body, but it's not about this place or this group. It's about a new world, a total break from what's gone before.' She rolls her eyes. 'I'm monologuing,' she says. 'It's a bad habit.'

'No, please go on.' Lucy tries not to look too keen. The more she can get people to say in their own words, the better.

Cat chews on the inside of her cheek and for a second she looks oddly skeletal. 'A lot of our donations come from the people who've chosen to live up here,' she says. 'They've given up inheritances, life savings, even houses to be here. But that's not our only source of income, you understand. You'd be amazed at the level of support we have out there.'

Lucy wonders if Cat knows how difficult the Scriveners are to find. How labyrinthine their website feels, with its arcane PDF scans and untrustworthy .zip files, its dreadful font choices and amateurish layout, like somebody's hobby project. Cat seems like she exists in a different world, one in which she's at ground zero for a revolution that changes human history. Maybe Lenin felt the same.

'Anyway,' says Cat. 'I'm getting distracted. You wanted to see the vault – here we are.' She turns the door handle and it swings open into a room filled with floor-to-ceiling bookshelves. 'You're lucky to see this. We've shut people out for a few days, after what happened. I won't show you all of it, though, not after what happened to Marcus.'

'Come on, Cat,' says Rob, lingering at the doorway. 'You've no good reason to keep it from me, regardless of what Bjorn says. I need to know.'

Cat looks a little white. 'Take it from me,' she says. 'You don't want that scene inside your head.' There's a plea in her eyes and Lucy can't make out why. 'You need the chance to say a proper goodbye, to lay him to rest. Seeing where he died won't help.'

'You make it sound like we were close,' Rob mutters.

'All the more reason why you need to say a proper goodbye,' says Cat wearily. 'To remember him as he was, the good and the bad.' Rob scoffs at that, and Cat gives him a half-hearted shrug. 'There was good in there. I promise.' She turns back to Lucy. 'So. This tour. I can show you where Marcus died if you really want to see it, but… well, it's a lot to take in.'

She steps inside, and Lucy follows. Before her stands a bookcase taken up entirely by an old-fashioned card catalogue, organised in a set of wooden boxes. 'That's a lot of notes,' Lucy says. 'Rob always told me that was the heart of what you did up here.'

Cat and Rob's eyes meet, and they exchange a rare smile. 'This is the index,' she says. 'This is how you navigate around the archives.'

'You're joking. There must be a thousand cards on these shelves alone.'

'Mm-hmm,' says Cat, pulling open a drawer. 'We've been here over twenty years. You'd be amazed at the amount of knowledge we've accumulated.' She lifts out a card and hands it to Lucy. On it is a set of nouns in alphabetical order – *facsimile, fact, faction, factorial, factory, factotum* – each followed by a collection of alphanumeric codes. Each entry appears to have been written in a different hand, many of them in differently coloured pens, and the battered state of the card suggests it's been added to over a significant time period.

'So if I wanted to see your entries on *factotum*, I'd need to find...' Lucy checked the card, '*20061014C?*'

'Mm-hmm,' says Cat.

'And that's where exactly?'

'Follow me,' says Cat. She glances back at the card one more time before placing it back into its drawer, then turns left. When she reaches the end of the bookcase containing the index, Cat turns right, revealing another bookcase set at a right angle to the first. Lucy follows her. Before them now is a makeshift corridor – the edge of the building on their left, a bookcase to the right. Lucy is beginning to wish she'd brought a spool of string. The dim lights make the building seem disconcertingly claustrophobic, as though she's inside some great tunnel system.

Ahead of her Cat is striding on, with Rob in train, and Lucy has no desire to be left behind in here. She passes a desk on her left, with a chair pushed neatly underneath and an Ikea lamp atop it, and she's struck by how blandly similar it looks to Micah's house – as though Bjorn's trying to replicate an aesthetic as well as a philosophy. She doesn't dare stop, though. Cat turns right again, then left, and Lucy hurries on after her through the shelves. When she turns the last corner she finds Cat standing before a card catalogue, riffling through its contents.

'This place is... not what I expected.'

'Mm?' says Cat, glancing up. 'Oh, you get used to it. I know it like the back of my hand now. I'll bet Rob's the same.'

'Sometimes I still dream about it,' he says grimly. 'Assuming it's the same layout?'

'How come it's such a labyrinth?' asks Lucy. 'Is it to deter intruders?'

'No,' says Cat, 'although that's an added bonus.' Lucy doesn't like her smile: it's all teeth. 'It's Bjorn's idea,' she continues. 'Connections don't happen in a linear fashion. You have to search for them. Designing it like this makes that process tangible.'

'It's hardly intuitive.'

'It's like anything. Once you understand it, you don't even think about it. It becomes part of you: as close to you as your own thoughts. I can read a reference and find my way to it with my eyes closed.'

Part of Lucy wants to test this assertion, if only for the pleasure of seeing Cat walk into a wall. 'So all of this is index cards? All interlinked?'

'Not all of it. There's also the works we've produced. Longer pieces. Essays, articles, theses. Some of them published, but many produced purely to help people realise their own thoughts at length. Those are indexed, stored and referenced too.'

'God,' Lucy murmurs. 'It's never-ending.'

'Exactly,' says Cat, nodding. 'You see what I mean by the engine room. Everything we create feeds that body of knowledge, and that body of knowledge feeds what we create. Over time, themes emerge. In a different era you might have called them prophecies. Images of a new world, or our own world viewed through a cracked mirror. Thus a new humanity begins to take shape.'

'That's rather grandiose,' says Lucy.

'It is,' says Rob. 'If you look for the changes this place has brought about, you'll be hard pressed to find them. All it does is ruin lives.'

'Just because we don't shout about them doesn't mean they didn't happen,' says Cat icily. 'Sometimes it's better to work in the margins. That's where real change happens.'

'Doesn't that ever bother you?' says Lucy, trying to keep Cat talking. 'The gap between your rhetoric and the reality?'

'I understand why you'd think of it like that,' says Cat. 'You haven't experienced it for yourself. Not yet. But you'll see. I'm sure of it. Once you've encountered the Immortal Spirit, there's no turning back.' There's something a little eerie in Cat's face now, a fanaticism Lucy hasn't seen there before. It feels like Cat's speaking words that don't belong to her, like something is using her as a mouthpiece.

'And Marcus…?'

Cat breaks from her reverie. 'What?'

'Marcus died in here, right? Was he all alone when it happened?'

'He was.' Cat looks suddenly uncomfortable. 'Come to think of it, I'd rather not be in here much longer. I'm sure you understand.' She turns, and makes to retrace her steps. 'Come on,' she says. 'I'd hate for you to get lost.'

But Lucy remains in place. 'Is that normal?' she says. 'To be in here alone? Aren't there dozens of people in here at any one time? I mean, surely there must be, to produce all… all of this.'

'It's not abnormal,' says Rob. 'Not for some people.'

Cat's foot taps impatiently on the floor. 'He was working in the middle of the night,' she says. There's a heaviness in her voice. 'I don't think he'd been sleeping well for some time.' She gives a little shudder. 'It could have happened to any of us.'

There's something bizarre about Cat's demeanour. Lucy has the distinct sense that Cat has somehow become a stranger to herself, walled off a part of herself where she can't reach it. Lucy can see that desire written across Cat's face, her conscious attempt to assume a placid, unruffled manner despite the storm raging beneath.

She can't leave it unchallenged, she knows that. She'd hate herself forever for missing an opportunity like this. 'I don't believe you,' she says.

'I'm sorry?' Cat's still looking towards the exit, all the better to avoid Lucy's insistent gaze.

'You heard me. I reckon you think he was… different. That it was his fault.'

Cat wheels round. 'You don't know what the hell you're talking about,' she snarled. 'You can't go throwing around assertions like that, especially when Rob's here. That's his fucking brother you're talking about.'

Lucy looks her up and down – unafraid, despite Cat's stature and obvious strength, and motivated as much by curiosity as by journalistic instinct. 'Were you afraid of him?' she says. 'Because Rob was. Was there something in what he'd written that frightened you?'

'I'm warning you,' says Cat, taking a step towards her.

'You're not going to hit me,' says Lucy. 'Go on, what was it? What did he do to you?'

Cat's jaw is clenched, her fingernails digging into her palms. 'I won't discuss this with you.'

'Really?' She's close now, Lucy knows it. This isn't the time to build intimacy: this is the time to challenge Cat directly. 'Who else are you going to discuss it with, then? Bjorn? Kristian? Nah, I didn't think so. Which I guess means you're just going to swallow this, and brood on it for the rest of your life. Worked out pretty well for Rob, didn't it?'

Cat's actually shaking now, trembling all over as anger courses through her body. Lucy lets her rage, watching a smile prick at Rob's lips from the corner of her eye. She's seen this before. The fire will burn itself out soon enough.

And then – yep – it's gone. Cat's standing against a bookshelf, head thrown back against it, face lifted to the sky. 'He wasn't a good man,' she says, her eyes still closed. 'Not deep down.'

'Go on.'

Cat sighs. 'I don't know what you want from me,' she says. 'You must know nothing good can come from talking about this.'

'I want to know what you mean. What was wrong with him, Cat? What did he do?'

'We're idealists,' says Cat. Rob is nodding fiercely. 'Most of us, anyway. We want things to be better, and we believe that's still possible. That's what all of this is about, deep down. But Marcus wasn't like that. Not really. He could say all the right things, and he was articulate enough that he could make people believe them. He didn't, though. Believe them. For him the System was always about power. Control.' She leans forwards, looks around at the maze of shelves. 'You can find his notecards in here. It's not hard. You'd see it right away, once you knew what to look for. There was something rotten in him.'

'Presumably you weren't the only one to feel like this.'

'No, I guess not.' She glances over at Rob. 'You were scared of him too.'

Rob looks a little nauseous. 'He cared more about this place than he did his own family.'

'You're right. And what's more, we praised him for it.' Cat seems to realise that Lucy wants more from her. 'What is it?' she says. 'Why are you staring at me like that?'

'I'm trying to determine whether somebody could have killed him. If they had the motive, and means.'

'No.' Cat's voice becomes firm. 'No, that's not what happened here at all.'

'How can you be so certain?'

'Come and see for yourself,' she says, walking past Lucy and back into the labyrinth. Lucy hurries after her, with Rob at her heels, turning this way and that, every new alcove and card catalogue seeming like they'd passed it before. She begins to wonder if Cat's leading her in circles, trying to exaggerate the vault's dimensions for the sake of mystique. And then, after an impossibly long time, Cat stops without warning. She doubles back, swallows hard. 'Do you want to tell me that a man did that?' she says in a choked voice, gesturing over her shoulder to the mass of blood. 'And if so, do you want to tell me how?'

17

THE AIR is thick with the smell of blood: a little stale, perhaps, and mingled with the vault's back notes of vanillin and mould, but undeniable. His heart's hammering against his ribs as Cat leads them through the stacks. Rob thinks back to Marcus as he last remembered him, the night he fled. The look of contempt on his brother's face, as though Marcus were furious that Rob would dare compromise his status here.

'I'm sorry,' says Cat, and for a moment it looks like she might even lay a hand on his shoulder, although she thinks better of it. 'I wish there was a better way to do this.'

It's worse than he could have imagined. The lower half of his brother's body is still intact, seated at its desk, the stark white of a spinal column emerging from the ruin of his legs. Around the desk is an explosion of blood, the arcs and splatters carving out ornate shapes on the walls. At first Rob's brain can't make any sense of it. There's no indication of a struggle here, no shattered desks or books thrown to the floor.

It's like Marcus just exploded.

Cat is breathing heavily through her nose. Steadying breaths, like she's about to vomit. Her eyes are closed, her head pressed against one of the bookcases. 'I'm sorry,' she murmurs again, and now Rob can't tell if she's talking to him or Marcus. 'God, I can't do this.' She turns away, her hand held to her throat.

Rob steels himself, forces himself to look. The desk is covered in tacky blood, save for a few overlapping rectangles which are totally clear. Something has been removed: whatever Marcus was working on. Which meant that somewhere in all these shelves were a set of blood-stained notecards that Bjorn couldn't bear to throw away.

His skin prickles, and he's conscious of the silence in here: nothing but their muffled footsteps, and his all-too-rapid breathing, and the dim sound of air-conditioning…

He closes his eyes, tries to think of happy memories with his brother, but all he can recall is Marcus's sullen face, his pugilist's scowl. There's a fresh rage swelling up inside Rob, at this place that had warped them both so far out of shape. Neither of them had to end up this way. This was Bjorn's doing, all of it.

He's seen this place destroy so many people. He thinks of Thomas, scratching frantically at the walls of his room with nails broken and bloody, muttering about visions. He thinks of Julia, lost in the depths of her own mind, her body swaying gently as she chanted in a language no one could understand. He thinks of Alex, who spent all those weeks poring over Lovecraft, until that night they found him wandering the site in a daze, blood under his fingernails, his eye sockets empty holes.

MARGINAL

It was never going to end well for Marcus, he knew that. But he could never have imagined it ending up like this.

'Dear God,' he says, putting the heel of his wrist to his forehead. 'Dear God, dear God, dear God…'

18

Beneath the table, something moves. It darts across the floor, almost too quickly to process, less a creature glimpsed than the sensation of movement itself. Lucy jumps back, terror coursing through her veins, then catches herself. It's a mouse. Of course it's a mouse. What the fuck else could it be?

Maybe it was whatever killed Marcus, something whispers inside of her, and she pushes it down. *Shut up*, she wants to say. *Marcus exploded.*

She drops to her knees, trying to spot it amid the gloom. When she finally does, it takes her a moment to register what she's seeing. It looks like no mouse she's ever seen. There's a great spray of spikes emerging from its spine and it appears to have six legs; it doesn't scurry so much as *scuttle*. At first she can't believe it's real. It must be a trick of the light, or her tired brain. But no – it's real, every hideous bit of it.

'Rob,' she says. 'Rob, are you seeing this?'

But Rob has his head in his hands. 'Dear God,' he's muttering. 'Dear God, dear God, dear God.' He's hyperventilating, and the sound of his panic is enough to send the mouse disappearing behind a bookshelf. Lucy mutters a curse, sets off in search of it. Even just seeing it again would be confirmation she's not losing her mind.

What she finds is altogether more unexpected. In the gap between the shelves and wall there's not just one rodent body but half a dozen, in various stages of disarray. Their ribs exposed in great jagged barbs, their necks bulbous with tumours, their spines twisted upright into something disturbingly human. She crouches down, getting as close to them as she dares: they're pretty desiccated, and must have been here for some time. But something else bothers her, too. There's something unsettlingly deliberate about the pattern of their mutation, be it the placement of their eyes or the curve and twist of their spines. It's like an unseen force has been studying their bodies, experimenting with how it can best weaponise them.

Her mind reels. Something did this to them. Something intelligent, perhaps. And if it could do this to mice…

A chill runs down her spine. *Marcus. What if…*

No. She can't let herself think this way. She tries to think about the story she's uncovered here, how it could catapult her into the big leagues, but her mind keeps filling up with images of her own body, twisted grimly out of shape, and she'd give anything to be able to blot them out. Behind her she can hear Rob's ragged breathing, an anchor to the present moment. It's an unwelcome reminder that, for all she knows, whatever created these abominations is in here with them right now.

Beneath the bookshelf she can make out the lines of a square hatch in the floor. She almost can't bear to look, is certain that down there she'll find the desiccated body of Rob's mother, and everyone else Bjorn has destroyed as he built this place. She has to know, though.

'Rob,' she calls, tamping down her panic. 'Hey. Give me a hand over here.'

He makes his way over to her, a little shaky on his feet. Even in the gloom he looks pale, and she wonders if he might faint. 'What's this?' she asks.

He shrugs. 'Maintenance hatch?' he says. 'What does it matter?'

'Look at this.' She shows him the mice. 'What do you think could have done this to them?'

'Shit,' says Rob, bending down for a closer look. 'I've never seen anything like that.'

'Me neither,' says Lucy. 'And that's what makes me wonder if it's connected to your brother. Give me a hand shifting this, will you?'

The bookcase is heavy, made from solid old wood and filled with several thousand notecards. Even with the two of them pushing they struggle to get it shifted. At the sound of movement, Cat comes to see what's going on. She doesn't look thrilled to see them rearranging the vault.

'You're going to put this back, right?'

'What's down here, Cat?' asks Lucy.

Cat frowns. 'It's a storage room, I think,' she says. 'The military used to keep targets down there, spare parts, WD-40. I wouldn't get too excited, it's just a set of lockers. I guess we could use it if we need, one day, but we're not short of space.'

'All the same, I'd like to have a look. Given the circumstances.'

'Alright,' Cat says. 'I suppose it can't hurt.'

When they open the hatch the first thing that strikes her is the stench. It's a godawful smell, the scent of something that's been rotting away for years with no way for the air to escape. It's so potent that, as one, they recoil, covering their mouths with their shirts to keep from retching.

Lucy is the first to peer down into the hole. It's pitch black down there, the only light sources up in the vault itself, and even as her eyes adjust she can't make out much. It's like Cat said: a set of lockers, a desk, an ancient computer. But the floor is strewn with something else too, cocoons or chrysalids from the looks of them. She flicks on the torch on her phone and points it into the hole. 'Fuck me.'

They're corpses, every one of them. There must be a hundred dead rodents down there, in various stages of destruction – but whatever took hold of them has mutated them well beyond their original form. Half a dozen of them look vaguely humanoid, which is to say they look as if the rodent's skin had been stretched far beyond its capacity over a human's frame. Even in the torchlight Lucy can see exposed muscle, and a host of tumorous growth.

Others are a mass of exposed organs. A stomach, taut and bloated, and two hearts alongside one another. The dark maroon of a liver, sprouting into what resembles rose petals; a tangled, white mess of intestines; all the components of a body multiplying so rapidly that the shell couldn't contain them.

Ribs so pointed they look like medieval torture equipment, but surely no creature could have that many ribs – two dozen, at least.

'Dear God,' says Cat. 'There's so many of them.'

'Tell me you didn't know about this,' says Rob. 'Please tell me Bjorn didn't know.'

'I… I've never seen this before,' says Cat. She looks like she might vomit, and Lucy can't blame her.

Then it strikes her, far too late. Whatever did this could be airborne. She glances over to Rob and Cat, wondering if they've realised it yet. Not that it matters: they've already been exposed.

Lucy takes a deep breath. Tries to think objectively. If she's going to end up like those monstrosities, then the least she can do is document it. She has a journalistic duty.

'If he doesn't know about it yet, then we need to tell him,' Lucy says. 'Right now. Get on the walkie-talkie and let him know.'

Crk-crk. 'No reception.'

Right. Okay. 'Give me a second,' says Lucy, frantically snapping photographs and cursing as the flash shines through the vault. 'Now let's get the fuck out of here.'

Cat looks shaken, unsteady. 'I ought to tell him on my own,' she says. 'We need to put our heads together, hatch a plan.'

'Absolutely not,' says Rob. 'We need to be a part of this.'

'Really, Rob?' Cat's tone is withering. 'How do you think that's going to go down?' She shakes her head. 'I know Bjorn. Know how to handle him. You can trust me.'

Rob flinches at the use of that word: *trust*. 'She can come too, if she wants,' says Cat, nodding to Lucy. And that's when she sees another flicker of distrust cross Rob's face: the thought that maybe, just maybe, Lucy isn't on his side anymore.

But they're a long way beyond taking sides now. She hopes he can see that.

19

THE BOURNEMOUTH ECHO
18 October 2010

Scholars Under Siege: Academics Targeted in Terror Campaign

Bournemouth University academics have been the targets of a series of unsettling incidents, prompting a police investigation into the 'Tygers of Wrath'

POLICE are investigating a series of bizarre and increasingly dangerous incidents against academics at Bournemouth University. The perpetrators, a group calling themselves the 'Tygers of Wrath', are apparently motivated by the belief that certain academics are disseminating harmful ideas.

The group first gained notoriety last month when they disrupted a lecture by philosophy professor Dr James Linden, releasing dozens of live snakes into the auditorium. Since then, the Tygers of Wrath have claimed responsibility for a string of disturbing incidents, including the vandalism of faculty offices with cryptic graffiti and the delivery of threatening packages containing dead animals.

In recent weeks, the group's focus seems to have shifted to Dr Thomas Barrett, an English literature professor known for his work on the Romantic poets. Dr Barrett has received numerous threatening letters, some containing detailed references to the works of William Blake, particularly his famous poem, 'The Tyger'.

'The level of harassment and intimidation directed at Dr Barrett is deeply concerning,' said Detective Inspector Sarah Hughes, who is leading the investigation. 'We're treating these threats with the utmost seriousness and are working to ensure his safety.'

In response to the escalating threats against Dr Barrett, police have increased patrols around his home and office. The most recent incident, in which a member of the Tygers of Wrath was caught attempting to break into Dr Barrett's car, has led to heightened security measures and round-the-clock protection for the professor.

A search of the suspect's residence uncovered a trove of notes, journals and other materials that provide disturbing insight into the Tygers of Wrath and their beliefs. Among the items found were numerous references to the works of William Blake, as well as extensive interpretations and analyses of his poetry. The sheer volume and depth of the materials suggest a deep engagement with Blake's work, particularly his more esoteric and mystical writings.

In a statement given by DI Hughes, she told the press: 'The materials we've uncovered suggest an obsessive, almost fanatical, interest in Blake's more mystical and prophetic works, particularly those dealing with themes of revolution and transformation.'

Experts on fringe religious movements have suggested that the Tygers of Wrath may be an offshoot or splinter group of a much larger organisation.

'We've seen a remarkable number of sects fixating on the work of Blake in Bournemouth recently,' said Dr Elizabeth Samuels, a sociologist who studies marginal religious movements. 'This suggests there's some kind of link. Possibly this is part of a broader agenda, perhaps aimed at undermining or destabilising academic institutions.'

In 2009, a group known as The Eternal Flame claimed responsibility for a series of arson attacks on industrial sites across the country. The group's manifesto cited Blake's concept of 'dark Satanic Mills' as justification for their actions, arguing for the destruction of these sites to purge society of its corrupting influences.

In a similar vein, a group of artists and musicians known as The Beulah Collective has lately gained notoriety for their provocative, Blake-themed performances in Bournemouth's public spaces. These performances, which often involve nudity and other controversial elements, have led to clashes with local authorities and accusations of public indecency. The collective has defended their actions, claiming their art is a means of challenging societal norms and awakening the public to the transformative power of Blake's ideas.

20

Outside the vault Cat tries the walkie-talkie again. *Crk-crk*. This time she reaches Bjorn.

'We need to talk,' she says. 'Privately.'

Lucy hears Bjorn sigh into the receiver. 'Can you come to me?' he says.

Cat turns to Rob. 'I'd like you to sit this one out,' she says. 'Nothing personal, but I can't face you and Bjorn squabbling right now.'

'Come on, Cat,' he says, glowering at her. 'I'm done with letting him push me around.'

'But he's not pushing you around, is he?' Cat says. Her arms are folded, her posture untroubled. 'We're three adults, having a reasoned conversation about the best course of action.'

'I've heard that before,' says Rob.

'Look,' says Cat. 'Just go and get yourself a cup of coffee in the mess hall. Clear your head. You know that's the right call.'

Rob shoots Lucy a look as though to say: *Are you okay?* She nods. Secretly she's quite glad that Cat brought it up. She's getting tired of their squabbling too. When he's gone, Cat leads her over to one of the squat concrete buildings. Through the window she can see a neatly made bed, a desk, a little stack of notecards. It's pretty spartan.

'This is where Bjorn lives?'

'Mm-hmm. He needs the space to himself. To help him think.'

'Lucky man.'

'He's got a lot of responsibility,' Cat says absent-mindedly, chewing on her lip. 'Do you think Rob will be okay? After all that?'

'I don't know. I really don't. He's pretty cut up.'

'Huh. Maybe you ought to have stayed with him.'

'No. We need to tell Bjorn what we saw. It's better with two of us there.'

Bjorn's approaching them now, striding across the site. 'What's so important?'

'You need to see this,' says Cat.

'Inside,' hisses Lucy. There are eyes on them, she's sure of it. Maybe it's just Rob's paranoia seeping into her, but she doesn't want to be overheard, not yet.

Bjorn unlocks the door and steps inside. There's only two chairs, and so Cat's forced to sit on the bed. If Lucy were feeling generous she'd say it looks monastic in here, but really it looks like a student bedroom, and not an especially nice one either. Judging from Cat's discomfort, it's her first time on Bjorn's bed. That answers one question, at least.

Lucy starts talking the moment the door is closed. 'There's

something growing underneath the vault,' she says, handing him the phone. 'Look.'

Bjorn's eyes widen. 'Dear God,' he says. 'What are those things?'

'They're mice,' says Cat, 'or at least they were once.'

His voice falters. 'But... what could have done this?' he says. He's still peering at the image, aghast.

'That's what we're wondering too.'

Cat looks grave. 'Whatever it is, it can spread to rodents. We need to be sure it can't spread to humans too.'

Bjorn's face pales. 'Is that a risk?'

Lucy and Cat exchange a look. 'We can't rule it out,' Lucy says. 'And if it is...' She closes her eyes. 'We've got to get everyone out of here, right away. And we need the authorities – Public Health Scotland, the military, whoever it is that handles things like this.' *Things like this*. She hears herself say it and it seems hysterically funny: as though there's a precedent for what's happening up here. She bites her lip to keep from letting out a wild giggle.

Bjorn runs a hand through his hair. 'But the vault. Everything we've built...'

Cat stands up, puts a hand on Bjorn's shoulder. 'If this thing gets out, there might not be anyone left to read our notes,' she says. 'I'm serious. We have to deal with this. There's no other option.'

Bjorn's staring down at the photos on Lucy's phone, looking nauseous. 'They'll destroy us,' he says in a tone of despair. 'Once they see this, they'll burn it all to the ground.'

'You don't know that,' says Cat. 'That's an assumption, nothing more.'

'Look at it, Cat!' Bjorn shouts, holding the phone up. 'Just look at it!'

Cat's shaking her head. 'I don't see that we have any other choice.'

'You're damn right,' says Lucy. She can't believe it's even a matter for debate.

But Bjorn's jaw is set. 'No,' he says with force. 'There's only one way to make this decision.' He reaches into his satchel and takes out the wooden box.

Lucy sees Cat grimace, sees her whole body slump. 'Bjorn,' she says, 'we're beyond that.'

There is real anger in Bjorn's voice now. 'You're wrong, Cat. This is when we need it most. We'd be fools to abandon our principles at our time of greatest crisis.'

'And what if it gives you an answer you don't like? What then?'

'Then we submit,' he says. 'Who are we to question the Immortal Spirit? Who are we to pretend to understand its ways?'

'Bjorn, no,' says Cat. 'Come on.'

'I thought better of you,' he says, his head bowed. 'I really thought you believed.'

'I do believe!' Cat yells.

'No,' he says. 'Not now. But you will.' He nods to Lucy. 'You'll want to come with me.' And before she realises what she's doing, she's following him out of the door and watching him lock it behind him.

MARGINAL

Her last sight of Cat is a furious face at the tiny window, followed by a fist at the glass. Bjorn opens his slip box, rifles through the cards and selects one. Peers down at it, his brow furrowed.

'Oh,' he says. 'Very well.'

He hands it to her. Again she's struck by the strange, powdery sensation it leaves on her fingers:

> 20160915/A: 'There is so much inviting us! — what are we to take? What will nourish us in growth towards perfection?' We are, I believe, entering a new phase of growth. Becoming more and more like the people we were called to be. We must pursue whatever will help us in that goal, and cut off all that is dead. There is no other way.

'You'll have to excuse me, dear,' he says, patting her clumsily on the shoulder. 'I think I need a little more time with my thoughts.'

21

They waste no time taking Cat to the Pit. She doesn't go quietly: Josef, Danny, Ken and Adam try their best to drag her across the site, and she fights them the whole way. Her voice is a mixture of fury and desperation. 'Let me go!' she shouts, her words echoing across the site. 'You can't do this to me, I've done nothing wrong!'

Rob knows they're supposed to act like they can't hear her, go about their business, but who could ignore her anguished cries – whether she's accusing Bjorn of making a mistake, or begging the others to let her go?

'I swear you'll regret doing this,' she yells, her voice growing hoarse. 'Just listen to what I have to say, for fuck's sake. This is important.'

He'd gone willingly to the Pit that first time. He'd thought it was part of his restoration, a necessary step on his journey. He'd been young back then. Cat knows better than he did.

Rob's standing in the door of the mess hall, so he catches a glimpse of her face as they pass him. He's startled by how ragged she looks: her eyes wide and panicked, her hair dishevelled. She holds Rob's gaze for a moment, and it occurs to him that this might be the first time he's ever seen her out of control. It's not a good feeling.

Cat's voice drops as they approach the small, windowless building. Rob thinks she's probably trying to negotiate, to talk some sense into them. He wonders whether she's telling them about the contagion, about what she saw in the vault. If so, it doesn't make any difference: Danny shoves her roughly inside, slamming the heavy door behind her and locking it. Josef heads off, presumably in search of Cat's tapes: the thought of her sitting there in the dark, with only her own voice for company, makes Rob so dizzy he can't bear to look at the Pit any more.

He turns back to the mess hall, where Bjorn is sitting calmly at one of the tables, sipping his coffee and shuffling through his notecards. He looks disconcertingly content, and Rob's not the only one to notice – although of course the others are trying their best not to show it.

He stumbles into the kitchen on autopilot, searching for a cup of coffee to calm his nerves. He still finds it disconcerting how professional it looks in here now, all gleaming metal and hanging implements. Bjorn must have hired an outsider to do it: this place had been very much a DIY operation all those years ago.

Unfortunately he's got company. Amy and Margaret are over by the stove, planning out the next week's meals. They both glance up as he enters, give him a vague smile.

'I was just trying to get a cup of coffee,' he said. His therapist always said he became flippant when he was stressed. 'Think you can help me with that?'

Amy nods. 'I think we can probably manage that.'

'Thanks.' He leans back against one of the counters, closes his eyes to still his racing mind. It's an error: all he sees is that scene of visceral pain. His brother's lower half still seated at his desk, the great inexplicable violence of it all.

He'd always known there was something corrupt about this place. He'd felt it, somehow, beneath the ground. Who knew how long it had been growing? Perhaps it was there all along, ever since Bjorn first found this site.

If he stays here, will it destroy him too? The thought makes him shudder. What if he's already been infected by whatever killed those creatures in the vault?

'Please,' Cat had said to him in the vault. 'Please don't tell the others. Not yet. Not until Bjorn and I have hatched a plan.'

'Using your notecards?' he'd shot back. 'You're outsourcing the fate of these people to chance?'

'It's not chance, Rob. It's more than that.'

He'd not been able to hold back his cynicism. 'Keep telling yourself that.'

Cat had studied him, her gaze cool and level. 'Are you trying to start a panic here?' she said. 'Is that what you want? Because if you tell people about this, that's what's going to happen. And people will *die* if you do that. Not just the folks up here, either. Whatever's doing this, it could spread.'

Amy walks over to one of the cupboards. Fetches him a mug

and a jar of instant coffee. He's grateful for the distraction: his head's a mess of anxiety.

From nowhere he's assailed by memories he's not thought about in years. Marcus, just past puberty, bitching about how there were no girls here. Sneaking into the kitchens with him to steal food. Wrestling on their bunks, as Marcus tried to teach him how to fight. He'd squashed all of them down for so long, but now the weight feels unbearable. He can't breathe.

Margaret's watching him with concern. 'Everything okay, Rob?'

'Yeah,' he chokes. Amy's set a black coffee next to him, and a bottle of milk.

'It's a terrible thing, to lose a brother,' says Margaret, compassionate as anything. 'It's okay to grieve.'

He can't believe they're so credulous, so in thrall to Bjorn... and yet, in that moment, all he wants to do is fall into Margaret's arms and weep. He knows it's ludicrous. Knows that's how they'll get him again, if he's not careful: what looks like compassion is just a façade. All the same...

He pours milk into his coffee and stirs it round, grateful for something to do. Takes a long sip, trying to centre himself. But then the words come out without him quite meaning to say them.

'Do you ever wonder if there's something Bjorn's not telling you?' he hears himself say. 'If he's keeping things from you?'

Amy slams the kitchen drawer. 'Not this again,' she says. 'We've done this all before, Rob. It's over.'

He holds his hands up, helpless. 'It's just... he's got so much power. Over information. Over decisions. Doesn't it make you worry?'

'No!' says Amy. 'We are all part of this, Rob. Every one of us. We've got our part to play here, and so has Bjorn. Don't you fret about us, okay?'

He thinks about those deformed mice, thinks about the blood staining into those card catalogues. Thinks: *If only you knew.*

He could destroy them so easily. Could tell them what he'd seen and watch them tear themselves apart. But he can't bring himself to do it. Cat's got inside his head again, like she always could.

'It really doesn't bother you? Not knowing what happened to Marcus?'

'No,' says Margaret. 'We've made our peace with that. It's how this place runs.'

'Exactly,' says Amy. 'He'll tell us when the time's right.'

He can feel his heart pounding in his temples. 'God, I wish I could be so... so placid.' He sips his coffee. 'I mean it.'

'It's not being *placid*,' says Amy, spitting the word. 'It's called trust. And I'll tell you this, it's a better way of life. I remember what it's like, not knowing what to believe.' She fixes him with a hard stare, as though to leave him with no doubt that she's talking about him. 'You can't just hate your life in this world,' she says. 'Hatred's not enough. You have to pick something to follow. Let it show you the way.'

Rob frowns. 'And what if he's leading you to something dreadful?'

'Aye, but he's not, though, is he?' says Amy with a derisive snort. 'That's you speaking. We've all seen what he's creating, what it all adds up to. Just look around you.'

If only you knew, Rob thinks again.

22

He's got a whole speech planned for when he next sees Lucy, knows exactly what he'll say, but when he starts speaking what comes out is barely coherent. There's the scent of blood and fear in the air, and he's suddenly nauseous, dizzy.

'Lucy,' he hears himself say. 'What the fuck, man... what the fuck.' He's shaking his head, his own gestures strange and exaggerated. 'We have to get out of here, man. Right now. There's something very fucking wrong in this place.'

She stares him down, coolly, levelly. There's something frightening about that gaze. It couldn't be real. 'I need you to stop,' she says, her brow furrowed. 'Take a breath. Before we do anything reckless.'

'Reckless? Fucking reckless?' He tries to catch his breath, but his throat is tight and his heart's hammering in his chest. 'Those things, Lucy. What the fuck were they?'

She moves towards him, her voice more gentle. 'I need you to take a breath,' she says, softly, as though she's trying to calm down a madman. 'For both of our sakes.' She rubs her temple.

'I'm still figuring this out. Those creatures in the vault… they were mice. Once. And then, I guess they weren't.' There's a faint tremor in her voice now. 'We tried to tell Bjorn what happened down there. Or at least Cat did.'

'I never thought he'd turn on Cat. Never.' He takes a deep breath. 'We've got to get out of here, Lucy.'

Her eyes are closed, her head bowed. 'Afraid not,' she says grimly. 'I think we're stuck here, at least for now.'

'You're joking.'

She's not smiling. 'It's hardly the time for jokes, is it.' She looks him straight in the eye. 'Come on, man, you know this. You must have thought about this.'

He'd done no such thing. His brain's a swirl of panic, everything in him screaming to get out of this place, get as far away from Bjorn as possible. Back to the safety of his flat, the familiarity of his routines. Maybe he could forget this place ever existed. He almost managed it once.

Lucy's still thinking. 'Whatever did that to them,' she says, chewing on her lip, 'it did it to them from the inside. It was *in* them.'

He feels a plummeting sensation in his gut. 'So you're wondering who else it's inside.'

'Exactly,' she says.

He knows what she's thinking before she says it, and somewhere in his mind he'd swear he hears a malevolent voice muttering *you knew this was going to happen* – and with it the violent, escalating terror, wrapping itself around his throat, his lungs, his guts. Whatever this thing is, it can't be in them. It just can't.

'No. No fucking way.'

Lucy's face is grave. 'We have to know, Rob.'

'We know already,' he hears himself yell, although the moment he says it he can tell it's just the panic speaking. 'We only just arrived. There's no way we're… infected.'

And then it hits him. He grew up here, spent his formative years here. What if he's been infected for the past decade? What if this contagion has been lying dormant that whole time?

'But you…' Lucy seems to read this thoughts. 'You've never noticed anything, right? If there was something inside of you, surely you'd have to know.'

He shakes his head, trying to calm his racing heart. 'No, nothing. But whatever's doing this, we don't know a goddamn thing about it. How it spreads, how long it takes to infect you, or even what infection looks like.'

'Even if we did,' says Lucy with a shrug, 'I don't see how it makes things much easier. What would we do with the infected? Quarantine them? Until we can get somebody up here to check them out?'

He laughs despite himself. 'You really think Bjorn's going to let outsiders up here? Medical professionals, government officials?'

'I'm not sure he's got any choice.'

'Do you want to be the one to tell him?'

She chews on the inside of her cheek. 'They're going to come up here whether he likes it or not, Rob,' she says finally. 'And if they figure out what's going on, do you really think they'll let Bjorn stop them wiping it off the map?'

She's right. Of course she's right. But the reality of it sends another flare of panic through him. He can't die up here. He just can't. He imagines his obituary, how the papers would make sense of his life. They'll think he's returned to the fold.

'Jesus, Lucy. We can't let that happen.' He swallows his panic. 'We can get out of this alive. I'm sure of it.'

His agitation must be showing. Lucy's using her soothing voice again, her hand on his shoulder. 'We don't know anything about this thing,' she says. 'Not really. And until we do, we're on the same side as Bjorn and the rest.'

'No fucking way.' It comes out of his mouth by pure reflex.

Lucy takes a long breath, and he sees her jaw tense. 'I won't let you leave here, Rob,' she says decisively. 'Not if you have that thing inside of you.'

'How do you propose to stop me?'

'I'll have Bjorn stop you. If that's what it takes.'

He can feel his hands trembling at his sides. His mind's racing. He could still run. Make a break for it, sneak out at night. She'd not be able to stop him.

But then his life will be over. He'll be forever on the run. Everything he's fought for, thrown away in a moment.

He can't do it. He's not that man.

'What if we're infected?' he says quietly.

Lucy doesn't respond immediately. Instead, she looks over towards the vault. Rob follows her gaze. The door's open, and Danny and Bjorn have stepped out of it carrying something in a blood-soaked sheet. He knows exactly what it is: Marcus's body.

They carry Marcus over to the mess hall, Bjorn struggling

slightly with the weight of the corpse, and that's when Rob remembers why he came back here. To say goodbye to his brother, to give him a proper farewell. Now even that seems impossible.

'Whatever this thing is, we have to stop it,' he says. 'If this is the reason Marcus is dead, then we have to make sure he's the only one it happens to.'

Lucy nods, her expression grim. 'I agree,' she says, still watching the body. 'Maybe that's the best thing you could do for him. Make sure his death wasn't for nothing.'

23

EXTRACT: Notes from Kristian's slip box

20160912/A: `I never approve, or disapprove, of anything now. It is an absurd attitude to take towards life. We are not sent in to the world to air our moral prejudices.' A dangerous attitude, in my view. The purist approach risks leading us astray. We must be pragmatic: we have waited too long for a Saviour to emerge, and have found only confusion. We know what is good and bad, each of us, know the world we must build. Now is the time to pursue it. Actively. Vigorously.

20160912/B: `I pushed on. The colour vanished from the world, the treetops rose against the luminous blue sky in inky silhouette, and all below that outline melted into one formless blackness.' Too often this is how it feels in this place lately. Like all has become formless. Like none of it adds up to anything. We must keep

MARGINAL

pushing on, through the night into the day. But the path is faint and difficult.

20160914/A: *'I turned suddenly and stared into the uncertain trees behind me. One black shadow seemed to leap into another. I listened, rigid, and heard nothing but the creep of my blood in my ears.'* Aren't we all jumping at shadows these days? When did we last face a real threat? Nora's death, or the investigation? Bjorn's treatment in the media? All of them were years ago. The world has changed, cares little about us, and yet we're still so afraid.

20160915/C: *'"Evil is he who breaks the law," chanted the Sayer of the Law.'* One day you might see this card, Bjorn, stumble across it in your reading, and you'll know from the handwriting that it was me. So be it. If that's how it must be, then let's call it the leading of the Spirit. Because I see you, old man. Your creeping authoritarianism, the control you've amassed. There's a better way than this. One day we'll figure it out by ourselves, despite all your efforts. That'll be a beautiful day.

20150915/C/1: *'While the possible troubles of Maggie's future were occupying her father's mind, she herself was tasting only the bitterness of the present.'* Oh, how true. I can't remember the last time I felt joy. All of this has turned to ash. We had such high hopes once. This is an invitation to remember them, a reminder of the gap between what we hope for and what we currently have. And a challenge, too: to work towards that future, rather than merely hoping for it.

24

Everyone comes to watch when they carry what's left of Marcus out of the vault. Rob's not sure who spread the word, but it doesn't surprise him. Communes do strange things to people, bring out a kind of otherworldly intuition. You learn things by osmosis, can't ever trace the point where they were revealed to you.

At first they watch out of doorways, through windows as Danny and Bjorn haul those bloodied sheets out the door and lay them on a tarpaulin like pieces of broken masonry. They watch silently, with expressions of disbelief, burying their horror beneath masks of stoic resolve.

Elliot's stacking chopped wood by the bunkhouses. He sets down his armload and sidles over to Rob, who's leaning by the mess hall's entrance. 'I guess this is the last thing you want to talk about,' he murmurs, 'but I've got to know. What did you see in there?' He nods over towards the vault. 'You saw his body. Saw where he died. That means you've seen more than the rest of us.' Up close he looks sorrowful, rheumy, like an old basset hound. 'Maybe you think I'm prying. I'm sorry for that.'

Amy's watching them both from the vegetable patches. She clocks Elliot right away and makes only a token effort at looking like she's hard at work, stacking the day's harvest before she skulks over too, wiping her hands on her jeans. 'You think Bjorn killed him?'

Elliot stares at her, as though trying to make her out. 'You serious?'

Amy shrugs. 'Maybe.' It's got the cadence of a joke, but there's no humour in it.

'Huh,' says Elliot, rubbing his chin. 'How'd you feel if I told Bjorn about this conversation?'

'See, I don't think he did it. Not himself,' says Amy, as though Elliot hadn't heard her at all. 'Maybe he got one of the others to do it, but he would never get his hands dirty.'

'It's a hell of a mess,' Elliot says. 'Whatever happened.'

'You want to tell me what kind of animal did that?' says Ken, stepping out of the door of the mess hall. 'Inside the vault?'

'Can't have been an animal,' says Amy. 'If it was, it'd still be in there.' She shoots Rob a look. 'You see an escaped panther in there when Cat gave you the tour?'

Rob hesitates. Sees again those twisted bodies beneath the vault. Part of him wants to tell them what he saw down there, but he can't make himself speak the words. As though saying it aloud might make it real.

He shakes his head, forcing back the memory. 'No,' he says, his voice sounding hollow in his ears. 'No, nothing like that.'

Amy's eyes narrow, and he's sure she's seen through him. But she doesn't press him.

'I don't like this,' Elliot says. 'All this secrecy.'

Rob barely hears him. He's thinking of the dreadful moment where they're going to show him what's beneath that sheet, and wondering if it can be worse than what he's imagined.

It never ceases to surprise him, the malleability of the human mind. It can absorb almost anything, filling in gaps, erasing uncomfortable details. It's even worse in a situation like this, glimpsed at a distance, when there's such scant information available. Bjorn has all the power here, can tell people whatever the hell he likes.

There are others coming now, drawn to their little gathering by the edge of the mess hall. Rob should probably be glad about this, this groundswell of opposition against Bjorn, but it's all turning to ash in his hands. There's no joy in this.

Because Bjorn doesn't look powerful. Not anymore. He looks weary. Sorrowful. Defeated. And as Rob watches him, hauling his brother's remains out of the vault, it occurs to him – far too late – that Marcus deserves better than this. No matter that his brother was flawed in every way that mattered, that he failed Rob just when Rob needed him most.

He pushes himself up from the wall and crosses the site, feeling every eye on him. Bjorn stops, pausing at the top of the stairs to survey him warily. He's conscious of movement behind him, the sound of footsteps, and when he turns he's no longer alone. With him now are Elliot, Kristian, Amy, Ken, with more coming.

'Let me help,' he says, and Bjorn stares at him for a long time before he nods.

25

WHEN LUCY asks people about it all, in the aftermath, they speak to her in fragments, bewildered statements that hang in the air.

'Oh Marcus. What did they do to you?'

'They lied to us. They've been lying to us all week.'

'They killed him. They... they... those bastards. They killed him.'

It feels absurd, trying to stay professional at a time like this. Surely people must see through her the moment she approaches with her recorder in hand, must be able to see what she's imagining. Rob's skin splitting on the motorway; the car spinning off the road, flipping. Paramedics trying to stick a mask over his mutated face. Mice, bursting out of their skins in the sewers beneath London.

But the work helps her. Gives her a focus, a purpose, and something to occupy her hands. There's a value in recording this, she tells herself, even if she might not be around to talk anyone through it. She's at ground zero for this thing, after all. Her recordings can capture what it was like up here before things went to hell. Who knows what clues a researcher might spot in her audio?

Assuming it's not too late by then, comes the whisper in her skull. She brushes it off.

Of course, her recordings might be more useful if everyone wasn't so suspicious of her. Kristian's the first one to speak to her properly when she approaches him with the mic. He's in the mess hall, slumped back in one of the battered leather armchairs.

'Look,' he says, 'I didn't much like Marcus, but he was one of the chosen ones. And he sure as hell wasn't going to let you forget it. So I had to listen to him. All of us did. Like it or not. And I'll tell you this: whatever killed Marcus, it had to be strong. He wouldn't have gone down without a fight.' He shakes his head. 'He and I got in a fight once. Stupid stuff. I said something I shouldn't, and he smacked me in the mouth. It hurt, man. It really hurt.' He glances over towards the medical hut. 'Part of me wants to see, you know?' he says, with a smile that's not all there. 'Wants to know what got him.'

She can't help herself asking. 'You didn't much like him, did you?'

Kristian's smile widens, but it still doesn't reach his eyes. 'Nah,' he says after a long moment. 'Nah, I never liked him much.'

And it seems like he's not the only one. Elliot tells about how close Kristian and Marcus had been. 'Closer than Bjorn liked, really,' he says. He said it gave them too much power, that alliance.

'It wasn't that Bjorn was paranoid,' Elliot says. 'Not at all. He could cope with views that differed from his own. If he couldn't do that, then he'd have been a fool to start this place. But he wasn't ever a fan of factions. He believed in unity.'

'There doesn't seem much unity around here today,' she says, and Elliot looks thoughtful.

'No,' he says. 'No, you're right there.'

At dinner, Hazel whispers that Lucy ought to meet her outside. They talk in furtive whispers by the side of the mess hall, watching every shadow.

'He was a cynic,' Hazel says, her hands clasped around a steaming mug of tea. 'And you know what they say about cynics. They're frustrated idealists.' She takes a sip, winces. 'He was a true believer once, you know. Sent his own brother to the Pit. Went out searching for him when he ran away.' She shivers in the late evening cold. 'I think a lot of us believed he might be the next leader of this place. If Bjorn ever passed away.'

There's a hesitation in Hazel's voice, something she's not saying. 'But not everyone?'

'Hmm?'

'You said a lot of people believed that. But not everyone.'

'No,' says Hazel, staring into her tea. 'No, I think Bjorn had his doubts. Started wondering what he'd created.' She gives a sad little chuckle. 'Things were hard after Nora died. That was a hard year for all of us. But especially hard for Marcus.'

'Why was that?'

'Well, she was his mother, wasn't she? How would you feel if you were the one who'd sent your mother to her death?'

Lucy blinks at her, trying to take in what she's just heard. She feels for the recorder at her hip, praying it's still got memory, praying it's switched on.

'I'm sorry,' she says, 'maybe I'm being stupid. But… Marcus killed her?'

'Oh no,' says Hazel. 'I wouldn't go that far. I think she made that choice for herself, when Rob ran away. But Marcus was the one who got her sent to the Pit. A whole week she was in there, and whenever they asked her if she wanted to come out she told them to…' she mouths it, '…*fuck off*.' She shakes her head. 'You'd have imagined he'd be pretty cut up about it, but he never showed it. Maybe that's why Bjorn spent so long with him. He was never quite the same afterwards, though.'

After three hours in the Pit they let Cat out again. When she emerges, something's changed. Lucy can see it right away. There's a tension in her shoulders and a tightness around her eyes. Her movements are stiff and jerky, her hands clenching and unclenching at her sides.

It's Kristian who lets Cat out. He got sick of asking Bjorn: Lucy sees the whole thing play out. When she sees Kristian heading towards the Pit, she gets up from her seat in the mess hall. Makes like she's enjoying the fresh air, taking an evening stroll. She positions herself by one of the bunkhouses where she can listen in on them unobserved.

If Kristian thought Cat would be grateful for it, might take his side, he's misjudged it. Cat's tone is withering.

'You've got quite the nerve,' she says, 'doing this unilaterally. I'm almost impressed.'

'He's out of control,' says Kristian. 'I know you can see it.'

'I imagine he's saying the very same thing about you.'

Kristian frowns, runs a hand through his hair. 'You're not seriously talking about going back to being his lieutenant? After he locked you up?'

She stares hard at him. 'He needs me next to him,' she says. 'He's always needed me.'

'It's not working, Cat,' says Kristian, holding his palms up in an expression of despair. 'None of this is working. He's losing it. And we have to stop him.'

Cat takes a deep breath. 'Listen, if you want to know whether I trust him, trust his judgement – no, I don't. I think he's struggling. He needs help. But do I trust the System?' She hesitates. 'That's harder, you know. I can't just disregard it. Not after all these years.'

She glances around to check whether she's being overheard, and clocks Lucy. Holds Lucy's eye for just a fraction of a second – not long enough for Kristian to register he's being watched.

'And look,' she says with a sigh, 'you need to consider the bigger picture. The last thing we need is a panic. We need to keep things as normal as possible until we figure out whatever the hell is going on. That means holding your tongue. For now, at least.'

MARGINAL

'But… look at what happened to Marcus. Whatever did that to him, I don't much want to meet it.' He shakes his head. 'You can't have seen what I saw and then tell me we're supposed to carry on as is.'

'I know,' says Cat wearily. 'I see that. I do. Except… except maybe there's something we're not seeing.'

'What's it going to take to get you to acknowledge he's dangerous?' says Kristian, his exasperation beginning to show.

'More than this,' says Cat firmly. 'In all these years, Kristian, has the Spirit ever let you down? Has it ever led you into disaster?' She pinches the bridge of her nose, a gesture Lucy recognises from Bjorn. 'We both know the answer to that is no.'

'Okay,' says Kristian. 'I'm not saying you're wrong. Just that I'm… I'm beginning to have my doubts.'

'Don't let Bjorn hear you say that.'

Kristian gives a nasty chuckle. 'Oh, and what'll he do if he does?'

'Careful,' says Cat. 'Just because you let me out of there doesn't make us friends. Not even slightly.'

'Nothing's ever simple, is it?' says Kristian, rolling his eyes.

'Maybe it is,' says Cat. 'Maybe you just need to believe.'

26

BJORN SHUFFLES up to him in the mess hall just before 10 p.m., his shoulders hunched. Rob can feel the awkwardness radiating off him, as though he's not sure whether Rob still hates him.

'I'm sorry to keep you waiting,' Bjorn says. 'It's not intentional. Ordinarily I'd ask Cat to do it, but, well—'

'You locked her up?'

Bjorn frowns. He looks almost hurt. 'You know it's not that simple.'

'I'm not interested, Bjorn,' Rob says. 'Not now. Is anyone here going to talk me through what happened to my brother, or do we need to call a professional?'

'Reynaud,' says Bjorn sourly. 'He used to be a nurse. Helps Cat out in the infirmary sometimes.' He sighs. 'Really, I'd expected better of her,' he says. He's so matter-of-fact about it, he sounds more like a man whose bus was delayed than one who just locked a woman up in a dark room.

'Actually, she's out already,' he says, knowing this will get a reaction. 'I saw her a moment ago. Maybe you could hold off on shunning her until she's had chance to look Marcus over?'

Bjorn's eyebrows shoot up. 'Who let her out?'

Rob doesn't meet his eye. He's got no quarrel with Kristian, not really.

He can see Bjorn's frustrated now – his shoulders are tense, his posture stiff – but the older man shakes it off. 'Fine,' he mutters. 'Not that it matters much anyway. I've asked Reynaud to talk you through his findings.' He leads Rob over to the infirmary door and knocks on it twice, sharply.

It opens to reveal a man in his mid-thirties, wearing a sturdy denim jacket over a plain white T-shirt. His clothes look like they've come from military surplus: thick khaki trousers, black combat boots spattered with mud. But his slender, oval face is boyish, lightly freckled and framed by a pair of cheap glasses.

'Reynaud,' says Bjorn, 'thanks for taking over from Cat at such short notice. I'd like you to run Rob through what you think happened to Marcus.'

'Of course,' says Reynaud, offering his hand, which Rob takes. 'Rob, we've not met. Welcome. I'm sorry it's not under better circumstances.'

Reynaud holds onto Rob's hand for a moment, looking him full in the face. There's something owlish in his gaze – inquisitive, thoughtful, fiercely intellectual. His hand is broad and surprisingly rough: there's dirt around his cuticles and in tiny spider-webs across his knuckles.

'So, you've seen the body, and you know about the… the

state of it.' Rob can hear the words catch in Reynaud's throat, no matter how hard he tries to hide it. 'I'm going to talk you through some initial findings, if that's okay with you.'

'Sure. If you think you're qualified,' Rob says, suddenly emboldened. Again he looks at Bjorn. 'I've never seen anything like this, and my guess is you haven't either. So if I come out of here knowing what the fuck happened to my brother, I'll be happy. But if not, Bjorn, we need someone who can tell us that. Someone professional.'

Bjorn closes his eyes. 'I'm not trying to hide anything from you,' he says. 'But what happened… it's hard to explain.' He inhales deeply, as though trying to tamp down his frustration.

And then Reynaud speaks up. His voice still quiet and composed, and yet somehow authoritative. 'He's trying to say that he's afraid you'll overreact. Bjorn needs to be sure you'll listen to what he has to say – all of it – before you respond. Do you understand?'

'And what the fuck does he think I'll overreact to?' says Rob. He can feel the fury building inside of him, everything coming back in a rush. This place of shadows, this world of secrets. Where nobody speaks truly: where they've been holding back for so long it's become a habit. It's a kind of living death.

'Please,' says Reynaud. 'Let me show you.'

'No,' says Rob, standing his ground. 'No, because then I'm on the back foot again. That gives you all the power. How about you tell me what I'm about to see.'

'I assure you,' says Reynaud, his composure unruffled, 'it's better that you see for yourself.'

'I said no. I'm not going in there unless you tell me what's going on here.'

Now Bjorn explodes. 'For God's sake, man. Nobody's trying to trick you. We're trying to spare you.' His eyes are blazing, and although he knows Bjorn's never been especially strong, he still feels a terror he recalls all too well. All resting on that unspoken threat: *What if he shuts us out from paradise?*

'Spare me what?'

Reynaud sighs. From him it sounds like a real expression of sadness: there's none of the exasperation in Bjorn's voice. Despite himself, Rob feels a sudden rush of warmth towards this man. He's too good for this place.

'If it's any consolation,' says Reynaud with a single, slight nod, 'we believe Marcus died quickly. He would have died almost instantly.' He folds his arms. 'I don't imagine that's much comfort,' he says, and although his voice is still quiet, it seems somehow stronger. Rob feels a brief stab of guilt: he's pushed even this gentle man to his limit. 'But you need to know this: whatever happened here, we're not to blame. Nobody here did this.' He pauses, as though to ensure he's got Rob's full attention. 'Nobody *could* have done this.'

'Exactly,' says Bjorn from the corner. 'Exactly…'

The medical room itself is a tiny room in a corner of the mess hall. It's just large enough to accommodate a low bed against the left wall and a low counter on the right, but what little space was available has been carefully allocated. Nothing is out of place: beneath a row of cupboards on the right-hand wall are hooks from which hang a stethoscope, blood pressure cuff and various surgical implements. A standing light is pressed against the back wall, angled towards the bed, while on the counter bottles of rubbing alcohol sit alongside boxes filled with latex gloves and dozens of sterile syringes, safe in their wrappings. On top of the cabinets Rob can just make out a stack of half-a-dozen medical textbooks.

Rob recognises Cat's stamp on this place immediately. The attention to detail, the relentless efficiency. She's proud of this place, he's sure of it, proud of what she's achieved.

Marcus's remains lie on the bed, a misshapen form hidden beneath a thin white sheet. The peaks and contours of his body create an unsettling landscape. Because of the room's size, Lucy's forced to stand just outside the door, narrating the scene: it's doubly disorientating seeing this with audio commentary.

God, the anticipation is awful. Worse, almost, than just wrenching the sheet off and revealing what lies beneath. He imagines Marcus – or, at least, Marcus as Rob remembers him – reduced to a grisly mess. Imagines his brother's last moments, the panic as he fought off whatever had attacked him, the second he realised he was going to lose the fight. The rending of flesh, the combined rush of adrenaline and pain. Numbing him, paralysing him. And then, hopefully, oblivion.

'You don't have to do this, Rob,' says Lucy quietly from outside the door. But she's wrong. Rob owes it to his brother after all these years. He recalls Marcus's face on the night he'd fled the commune, the total commitment in it, the blind faith.

MARGINAL

Marcus's decisions led him here. Somehow. And Rob needs to understand why, how, all this could have happened. If not, he'll spend the rest of his life wondering.

'I do,' he says without turning. 'But thank you. Really.'

Lucy takes a step back so Reynaud can enter. He moves past Rob, pressing against the doorframe to squeeze through into the tiny room. He moves over towards the back wall, clicking on the standing lamp – light suddenly carving those contours into yet starker contrast – and then rolls back the sheet.

It's worse than Rob could have imagined. Marcus's lower half is relatively intact, but his torso is a bloody mess. It's like something tore through him with such force that it nearly obliterated his upper body. His shattered ribs jut out at unnatural angles, his spine a stark white column rising from the carnage. From the doorway, Lucy lets out a sharp gasp, her free hand going to her mouth.

Worst of all is the smell – a sickly sweet stench that's unpleasantly like the scent of a kitchen food bin. It's horribly domestic, the rotten-fruit air of it. He'd never realised how familiar he was with the smell of decay.

Rob can't shake the sense of being watched from all sides. It's not just Lucy, narrating the scene: Reynaud keeps breaking off from his examination to glance over at Rob too, apparently checking how he's coping. A part of him hates Reynaud, then, just for being there. For making Rob feel self-conscious, robbing him of the chance to mourn authentically.

Not that you know how to mourn authentically, something inside Rob whispers. *Not that you know how to feel at all.*

And it was true, wasn't it, that Marcus was virtually a stranger to him now. He had to work to recall what his brother had been like, to blot out the image of his corpse.

They'd played together as kids, naturally. Marcus was good at conjuring imaginary worlds. They'd played as explorers, fighting their way upriver to rescue a captured leader; they'd played as warriors, lost in the jungle, assailed on all sides. He'd had a knack for creating a world with a few well-chosen details.

But then Marcus had always been a storyteller. He could hold a room captive. People gravitated to him, drawn in by his words. He knew how to transport them, to liberate them, however briefly, from the tedium of food prep and farming and building maintenance. That was why he'd fitted in here. He'd had a place.

Except—

Except all of it was tainted. Their whole childhood took place among the Scriveners. It was impossible not to wonder how different things might have turned out if they'd had a normal life. Impossible not to recognise the seeds of their conflict, even when they'd been boys. They'd never stood a chance.

Reynaud's running his fingers along the skin of Marcus's torso now, pressing into the discoloured flesh. He seems particularly interested in Marcus's abdomen: he bends down to take a closer look, his head just inches away from that mass of bloodied flesh, and Rob can see him frown.

'Impossible,' he murmurs, shaking his head. He seems entirely engrossed in his work, as though he's all but forgotten that Rob's there with him. 'It can't be.' He reaches over to the counter, takes up a set of tongs, and then returns to the table, peering deep into Marcus's guts. Rob swallows back a rush of nausea.

'What's wrong?' asks Lucy, peering in through the door. Rob tries to distract himself, to think of the world beyond Craigdhu – anything, really, but this bloody mess.

'Just a sec,' Reynaud says without turning. 'It looks like… no, but that's absurd.' He shakes his head, obviously rattled. 'I'd have to speak to others to confirm it. To a specialist of some kind. Because the thing is, I'd almost swear that he was ripped apart from… from the inside. As if something was trying to claw its way out of him.'

Nope. He can't stay in here a moment longer. He'd thought he was prepared for this, but he's not. Not for this level of examination. He's seen enough now, can't sit for another hour watching Reynaud's back as Reynaud prods what's left of Rob's brother, turning Marcus into an object of scientific interest.

And then Rob sees movement. On the back of Reynaud's neck. Something is moving beneath Reynaud's skin. It looks like his flesh is roiling, as though there's a cluster of maggots just below the surface. At first Rob thinks he's imagined it, but then it comes again. Whatever it is moves in spasms, in waves, as though co-ordinated. Reynaud doesn't even seem to have noticed and continues with his examination, unfazed.

The revulsion comes on first, and then the terror. Whatever had killed those mice, it was in Reynaud too. And if it could get into Reynaud, that meant it could spread.

'Lucy,' he murmurs. 'Lucy, do you see that?'

But she doesn't respond; she's talking to Reynaud. Whatever is going on here, he has to stop it. He could lock Reynaud in here, get Lucy and then hatch a plan. Whatever. But he can't stay in here with Reynaud another moment. That much is clear.

Keeping his movements small, so as not to draw Reynaud's attention, Rob reaches over to the counter and gently unhooks a scalpel from the wall. Good: it's sharp, sharp enough that Reynaud might think twice about rushing him. Rob takes a step backwards, intending to make a quiet exit, to step out unnoticed and block the door before Reynaud realises.

Or at least that's the plan.

'What are you doing?' says Reynaud quietly, looking up towards Rob with his head cocked. Rob studies him: there's no trace of that strange, roiling mass in Reynaud's face now, nothing but a puzzled and slightly pained expression as he takes in the scalpel at Rob's side. But Rob knows what he saw. There's something inside Reynaud.

'Stay where you are,' Rob hears himself say, lifting the scalpel. 'Don't come any closer.'

'Rob, what the fuck?' says Lucy, taking a step into the room. She's trying to catch his eye, he can see that, but he keeps his eyes on Reynaud.

Now Reynaud's expression shifts from pained to angry – there's a new coldness in his eyes, a hardness to his jaw. 'I asked you what you're doing,' he says, standing upright. 'I've given you no reason to distrust me. All I'm trying to do is help you understand what happened to your brother.'

'And what did happen to him?' says Rob, gripping the scalpel tighter. Reynaud's given no sense he might make a break for it, but he remains disconcertingly composed.

Reynaud takes a long, exasperated breath. 'Like I say, it's… extraordinary.' His eyes flick to the corpse, his lips moving silently as though in wonder. 'It wasn't an animal that did this to him. It looks like some kind of… of mutation.' He holds Rob's gaze, but Rob doesn't respond. There's a faint V on Reynaud's forehead now. 'But I suspect you knew that already,' he says. Something like wariness has crept in to his voice.

'You're right, Reynaud,' says Rob, trying with all his power to keep his voice steady. 'You've been nothing but decent to me. So don't take this personally.' He takes a step back. 'We'll get you help. I promise. But whatever was in Marcus, it's in you too.'

Reynaud's shaking his head, his face set in a grimace. 'Bjorn warned me about you,' he says. 'Told me what you thought of us. Told me you might try something.' He takes a step closer to Rob, his hand outstretched. 'I can't let you leave here with that,' he says, nodding towards the scalpel. 'Hand it over and you can do what you want with me.'

'No,' says Rob, lifting it higher. 'Stay where you are.'

'You don't get to decide, Rob,' says Reynaud, still advancing across the tiny room. He's just inches away from Rob now, and Rob's almost at the door. His chance is slipping away.

'I'm sorry,' he says, stepping backwards and slamming the door.

He hears Lucy cry out in surprise and fear. 'Rob!'

But it's too late. Reynaud's slipped his arm through the gap, grabbing at Rob, and two sounds come almost simultaneously – the thud of metal on bone, and a howl of pain.

There's a moment's respite, and Rob allows himself to think that he's held off the threat before the door explodes outwards. It's as if the pain has energised Reynaud – he's hurling himself against the door again and again now, trying to dislodge Rob. His strength is incredible, and Rob's boots can barely find purchase on the floor. He grabs at chairs, at tables, at bookcases, anything to act as a barrier, but they're all beyond his reach. Worst of all, he can't even call for help: who would believe him?

Another explosion of force from Reynaud, and then quiet. Rob can hear the man's heavy breathing on the other side of the door; he can hear Lucy pleading behind him. 'Listen,' he says to Reynaud, holding the scalpel in his trembling hand. 'We can talk about this.'

'Fuck you,' Reynaud snarls. The door bursts open, and Reynaud stumbles out, his face a mask of fury. His eyes are wild and unfocussed. He charges forwards, reaching for Rob, and Rob can feel panic setting in, the same terror he'd felt when his bigger brother bested him in a fight, of circumstances getting beyond his control, and a punishment that wouldn't stop until he relented.

But he's different now. Older. Stronger.

He sees Reynaud bearing down on him and, instinctively, he thrusts the scalpel out in front of him. 'Stay back!' he yells, but Reynaud pays no attention. His momentum carries him forwards, directly onto the scalpel's blade. It sinks deep into his gut, and his mouth falls open in a silent scream. He staggers back, eyes widening, hands clutching at the wound.

27

This is bad. This is really bad. And it's all on her. She was the one who talked Rob into bringing her along, letting her record, knowing that would mean conflict sooner or later. That was the nature of the business, after all, no matter what she'd told Bjorn.

But this... this is way beyond what she expected. Sure, she knew Rob was stressed. Could understand if his imagination was playing tricks on him – especially after what they found in the vault. All the same: she hadn't planned for him stabbing a man in the gut.

'Rob,' she murmurs, her voice barely a whisper. 'What the fuck did you do?'

He whirls round to face her, his eyes wild. 'He's infected, Lucy. I saw it. There's something under his skin, something moving.'

God, this is not good.

'We have to get help,' she says, trying not to lose her shit. 'Cat. We need to find Cat.'

But before Rob can respond, there's a sharp crack as something collides with the inside of the door, followed by the sound of hands scrabbling against it. Lucy jumps back. Oh God. Oh God, he's trying to get out.

'Let me out!' Reynaud's voice is barely human, chocked with blood and rage. 'Let me out, you fuckers!'

For a moment she just stands there, her mouth agape, her mind blank. Rob shoots her a panicked look, as though waiting for her to come up with a plan, and then he seems to realise none is coming. He springs into action, throws his weight up against the door. 'Lucy! Help me!'

Still she stares at him, frozen. This is insane, she thinks. Maybe they could still talk this out. Apologise. Pay Reynaud off, hire a mediator if needed. Drive home and forget this ever happened.

From behind her come running footsteps. She turns to see Bjorn. There's something pure and innocent about his terror, his eyes huge and his mouth wide open, like he's a little boy caught stealing.

'Bjorn,' Rob says, turning to him. 'Bjorn… I… I fucked up.'

Bjorn just stares, and Lucy can't tell if it's in fury or bewilderment or terror.

And then the door bursts open, and there stands Reynaud, a great bloody stain on his shirt. He stares out into the mess hall with unfocussed eyes. He's trembling, his skin stark and pale, and he looks like he might be about to vomit.

'Bjorn,' he murmurs. 'Thank God.'

He staggers out from the medical room, trying his best to reach Bjorn. Tremors run up and down his body, apparently involuntary. He looks like a stop-motion film made by an amateur, all herky-jerky motions.

Bjorn backs off. Something's happening to Reynaud now, something is changing. The skin of his chest bulges, as though something within is trying to escape – it becomes a great rippling mass, a series of rolling waves in endless spasm – and Reynaud's eyes are wide, staring down at his body as though it were something alien. 'OhGodohGodohGod,' he's muttering, less a prayer and more an attempt to retain his sanity, 'ohGodohGodohGod.' And then come a series of wet thuds, low as depth charges, unmistakably organic, and the pitch of Reynaud's cries changes, rising to a higher pitch, a kind of strangulated scream, 'ohGodohGODGODMYGOD,' and then his ribs crack open, something maroon and glistening bulging out from them, streaked with veins, and as Lucy watches it seems to bloom – splitting into four, eight, sixteen segments like some monstrous kaleidoscope – and Reynaud's gasping, choking, up on his feet now, staggering backwards against the wall. His upper body is a mass of exposed tissue, and he looks like he doesn't know what to do with the weight – he stumbles back and forwards, swaying, dizzy as an old drunk at closing time. The spasms are still coming, coursing across Reynaud's body, his neck and right shoulder beginning to bulge, the skin there splitting as purple muscle erupts from beneath it, and Reynaud bats at it with one hand, scrabbling away like it burns, but his scalp is now joined to his shoulder by a mass of what looks like pure muscle, further weighing him down.

Rob gags. 'We have to get out of here,' she says to him, but he's rooted in shock, staring, horrified. 'Don't you hear me?' Lucy says, running to him, shaking him, 'we have to go. Right now.'

'No,' says Rob, his voice half a sob, but he's not speaking to her. At the sensation of movement in the corner of her eye, Lucy turns to see a third arm sprout from Reynaud's back, and then a fourth, a fifth, a sixth, spraying out in an unexpectedly elegant fan.

Now he's staggering across the floor towards Bjorn, whose eyes are huge, stunned. Every one of Reynaud's arms is reaching out, groping for him, but the weight of them is too great: now he's overbalancing, toppling over on his face, and yet somehow still dragging himself across the mess hall with fingers bloody and broken.

There's a dreadful, guttural sound coming from Reynaud as he heaves himself over the floorboards – a gasping, gagging noise like vomit in a clogged airway. His pace is slowing, his body spasming to no effect: there's no more organs emerging, not now.

It's unmistakable: she can recognise death even in a creature so deformed. He's dying, his body unable to support itself, crushed perhaps by his own weight. The sound is so pitiful, she can scarcely bear it. He didn't deserve to die this way.

But the thought of touching that thing, slippery with blood and mucus, raw as a newborn foal... that's inconceivable. She's not sure she can even bring herself to get near it, let alone flip it over.

Instead, she reaches for her phone, and flicks to the camera, and records its dying breaths. Somehow it seems more bearable through an LCD screen.

28

THE MESS hall suddenly feels far, far too small. Rob's up against the back wall, next to the door and preparing to bolt out into the night the moment he can get Lucy's attention.

By the other exit, Cat's pacing back and forth, muttering under her breath; Elliot's on the bottom step of the stairwell, head in his hands, rocking slightly. Neither is looking at Reynaud's body: hoping, perhaps, that if they don't look then the world will still make sense. Beneath the metal stairwell, a small group has formed, huddled together as though they expect to find safety in numbers. Hazel, ever the mediator, is trying her best to console Amy, but she's got her work cut out; Jenny appears to be hyperventilating, and Henrik too.

Kristian stands alone by the windows that line the east wall, staring out at the horizon with his brow furrowed. For a moment Rob thinks Kristian is deep in thought, facing this situation with stoic calm, but then he realises that it's more likely to be rage. In the centre of the room, by the thing that used to be Reynaud, Pyotr is frozen. He's the only one near the body: he looks rigid with shock, too stunned to move away.

Where the hell is Lucy? He can't see her anywhere. He can see Bjorn, making his way towards Pyotr through the scattered tables and chairs more calmly than Rob can believe possible; he hears him calling for people to listen up, although it's muffled by the ringing in his ears. She's dead – she must be – and it's all his fault. He should have been stronger, should have told her to stay away. He knows these people, knows how casually they treat human life.

At a flash of movement on the stairs he glances up and sees Lucy, thank God, peering down. She's sought out a vantage point that will give her the best view of the hall and its occupants. Ever the journalist. He'd rather she was out of here, of course: would rather they were both far from here, down in the village with a steak and a beer maybe. But he's starting to realise that's not an option, not after what happened tonight.

Not after what you made happen, something inside him mutters, and his stomach lurches at the thought of what happened to Reynaud. He tries to shake off the image of Marcus, alone in the vault, his body tearing itself apart. Can't quite manage it. When Bjorn starts addressing the group, he's almost glad of the distraction.

Bjorn's first challenge is to make himself heard over the cacophony of voices. He's standing in front of one of the room's two doorways, but getting close to him means putting oneself within reach of Reynaud's body, and Rob understands people's lack of enthusiasm. Bjorn glances over at Cat, who's by the other doorway, and she signals for him to move back a little.

He nods, takes a step or two back to stand under the frame. The group presses forwards, apparently closer to Bjorn than is comfortable. He needs to start talking, and fast, or he's going to lose them.

Not that he's ever had much difficulty commanding a crowd. Bjorn grabs a metal tray and slams it against the tabletop, and the room falls silent. He raises his voice to a commanding tone that Rob remembers from his most fervent speeches. 'I want your eyes on me,' he says, looking over each of them in turn. 'We need to stay united, you understand? Or else we're goners. That's never been truer than it has right now.' There's a strange quiver in Bjorn's voice, as though his authority is tempered by desperation. It's not helping his case.

'We are a family,' he says gravely. 'I've always thought that. There's a bond between us that's deeper than blood. And after something like... like what happened to Reynaud...' His voice breaks, and he puts a hand to his chest. 'After something so unprecedented,' he continues, sniffing back tears, 'we need one another. We need to stick together, to lift each other up and find... understanding.'

Bjorn pauses, swallows hard. Even Rob can't look away from him. There's a power in vulnerability, or at least in the performance of it. He glances up at Lucy, sees she's recording the whole thing. He'll be interested to listen back to it, when the moment has passed.

'I've never seen anything like this,' Bjorn says. 'None of you have, I suspect. I can't pretend to have any answers.' He looks them over, searching for connection. 'What I do know is that we are a community, and so whatever we do next, we need to do it together. Not to act selfishly, nor impulsively, but in a considered fashion. Like we've always done.' His eyes light on Kristian, then on Rob, and linger for a moment. 'Far be it from me to say this is a test. I wouldn't dream of being so crude. But the System is meant for times like this. It is our foundation, our way back to the Spirit among the chaos and clamour of this life.'

As he's been speaking Bjorn's voice has become quieter, so gradually that Rob barely noticed it happen. Now he sounds like a beacon of calm. 'I'm asking you to have faith,' he breathes, in a voice that's barely more than a whisper. 'Can you do that?'

The silence stretches out into eternity.

And then Kristian speaks up. 'You're not asking us to have faith in the System,' he says. 'You're asking us to have faith in you.' He takes a step forwards. Everyone's eyes are on him. 'Don't call us selfish, and don't call us impulsive. Not for wanting answers.'

Murmurs of agreement ripple through the room. Kristian continues, his voice stronger. 'I vote we get the hell out of here. Now. Before what happened to Reynaud happens to anyone else.' He turns to face the others, imploring them. 'He's trying to keep you here because he knows that, if you leave now, the Scriveners are over. But I'm telling you, you matter. Each of you matters. Not just as part of this group. You deserve the freedom to choose for yourselves.'

Bjorn tries to interject, but it's too late. Something has taken hold of the group, and it's spreading. Jenny's sobbing now, clinging to Josef like her life depends on it. Amy shakes her head, muttering 'no, no, no' over and over again, swaying on her feet, like she might collapse at any moment. Hazel's glancing between Bjorn and Kristian, her eyes wide and uncertain.

'We need to go,' Kristian says again, in a tone that invites no argument. 'Grab whatever supplies you can carry and meet outside in five minutes. We're leaving.'

He heads for the door without looking back. It doesn't take long for the others to follow, a frantic tide of bodies surging for the exit. Rob spots Lucy making her way down the stairs, camera still in hand, and fights his way through the chaos to reach her.

But she's heading for the door, apparently trying to stop the exodus. 'Wait!' he can hear her shouting, her voice straining above the din. 'We can't just leave!'

It falls on deaf ears. A couple of people glance in her direction, but the crowd has its own momentum now, driven by panic and uncertainty. Lucy grabs the arm of the person nearest her – Danny – and clings on for dear life. 'Listen to me,' she says, not trying to hide her desperation. 'We don't even know how this thing spreads. We can't risk this.'

Danny shakes his head, pulling away from her. 'I'm sorry,' he says, without meeting her eyes. 'I can't stay here. I can't do it.' He makes for the door, Jenny clinging to his side.

Lucy's looking around wildly, searching for anyone who will listen to reason. She spots Rob near the back of the crowd and calls out to him. 'Rob! We have to stop them!'

Finally she reaches the door, but it's too late, and Rob thinks she knows it too. There's only a few stragglers left in the room to hear her plea, although she sticks her arms out and blocks the door anyway. 'Please,' she says. 'I'm begging you. You can't do this.'

Kristian shoves past her into the night. 'Get out of the way,' he growls.

And then it's just Lucy, Rob and Bjorn in the mess hall. Rob can hardly believe it: not even Cat stayed by Bjorn's side. Lucy's slumped against the wall, her face pale, her whole body shaking. Bjorn stands in the centre of the room, his slip box hanging at his side, his expression unreadable.

Rob makes his way over to her. 'Hey,' he says. 'We can still fix this. It's not too late.'

Lucy shakes her head, her gaze fixed on the open door. 'This is bad,' she says. 'Really bad. There's no telling how far they could take this thing.'

Rob glances around the nearly empty mess hall, and his eyes fall on Bjorn. He hasn't moved from the spot where he gave his pitch. He's eerily calm, and there's something calculating in his gaze. A familiar unease settles in Rob's gut.

He leans in close to Lucy so he's not overheard. 'He's up to something,' he murmurs. 'I've seen him act like this before. Whatever he's got planned, it won't be good.'

Lucy tears her gaze away from the door and looks over at Bjorn, studying him carefully. 'You think he's been expecting something like this?' Lucy begins. 'He's prepared for it?'

'I don't know,' Rob says. 'But you'd think he'd be more worried. He's spent all these years building the Scriveners. If they somehow spread this thing, then they'll be infamous.'

Lucy chews on her bottom lip. 'Unless he knows something we don't.'

They watch Bjorn for a second or two, until he finally stirs from his reverie. He looks around, like he's just now realising the three of them are the only ones left. When his gaze meets Rob's there's a flicker of something in his eyes – resignation, or maybe acceptance.

'We should go after them,' Bjorn says, a little vaguely. 'Before they get too far.'

But there's something hollow about his words when he says it, as though he's reading from a script he no longer believes in.

29

Outside, the commune is on the verge of disintegrating: Kristian and Pyotr are running for a battered grey Volvo estate. Gillian, a petite woman in her early twenties, is kicking the tyres on a Range Rover. God knows how many of them are planning on leaving, but even one would be a disaster.

And Bjorn? Bjorn's leaning against the mess hall, rifling through his slip box. Lucy's so angry that she stumbles over her words: *apoplectic*, she thinks idly to herself. Furious at this man's cowardice, his stupidity and empty rhetoric.

'What the fuck are you doing?' Lucy says, her professionalism a distant memory.

He doesn't even glance up at her. 'You know what I'm doing,' he says sharply. 'I'm getting tired of having to explain it to you.'

'You're the leader of this place,' she says. 'You need to lead these people.'

'I *am* leading!' he growls. 'And that means trying to see the bigger picture. Cat's got this in hand. I need to think, not firefight.'

Lucy's trembling with anger, determined not to let him ignore her. 'Your people are about to carry an unknown contagion off this site without knowing a fucking thing about it,' she yells back. 'You need to make a decision, for God's sake.'

Bjorn lets out a sound that's somewhere between a groan and a sigh. 'What makes you think they'll listen to me now anyway?'

'They came all the way to the Scottish Highlands to find you,' she says. 'And even if you've somehow lost their trust, I doubt they'll want to run you over.'

For the first time, Bjorn looks taken aback. 'What?' he says, cocking his head.

Lucy shoots him a withering look, but before she can answer, Cat cuts in from behind her. 'She's saying that if they won't listen to you, then you ought to block the fucking road.' When Lucy turns, Cat gives her a single, curt nod. 'And what's more, she's right.'

Cat runs towards the Range Rover, and for several seconds Bjorn stares after her. Lucy can't place his expression – anger, perhaps, or just bewilderment. At the sight of Cat coming, there's a flurry of activity by the cars: bags being hurled onto seats, doors being slammed.

'Tell me you're not going to let her handle this alone,' Lucy says to Bjorn before she starts running too.

She's conscious of others following her, a blur of movement at her back, but she doesn't turn. Cat has her hands on the Range Rover's bonnet, and she's yelling something that Lucy can't make out over the roar of the engine. To one side, the Volvo is making a break for it, its tyres throwing up mud as it tried to find purchase.

Lucy breaks off from her path and heads towards it, reaching it just as it begins to move. She follows Cat's example, slamming her hands on the grey bonnet as though she might be able to hold back the vehicle with her bare hands.

For a couple of terrible seconds she can feel the car continue to press towards her, and has an image of being slowly crushed beneath its wheels. Two tonnes of metal rolling over her chest, cracking her ribs. The pressure on her as it reaches her skull, alleviated only by the crunch of bone. And then, thank God, it stops.

Through the windscreen she can see Kristian and Pyotr, both of them yelling something. Moments later, another pair of hands slam down on the bonnet next to her. Amy.

'You done this before?' Amy growls, and Lucy shakes her head. 'Well, don't panic. They're more scared than we are, believe it or not.'

In the corner of her eye, she can see others blocking the Range Rover's path – even Bjorn is pressed up against its bumper – and now Cat's striding round to its door, throwing it open.

'Out!' she yells, grabbing at Gillian's collar and dragging her towards the door. From the passenger seat, a set of unseen hands try to pull her back – Elliot's, Lucy thinks – but there's a ferocity to Cat, an authority that makes her hard to resist. 'Nobody's leaving this camp today, you hear?'

Again the Volvo revs its engine, and Lucy turns to stare into Kristian's eyes. He's banging on the steering wheel, shouting something, but Amy's right: he looks terrified, his eyes red, apparently on the verge of bawling. *Hard to blame him*, she thinks, and then pushes that thought far from her waking mind: now is not the time.

'Don't move a muscle,' Amy says from beside her.

Pyotr rolls down his window, leans out. 'You've no right to do this!' he yells. 'Get out of the fucking road!' Now even Bjorn turns and glares at him, and, to Lucy's surprise, Pyotr just glares back. 'You got something to say, old man?' he calls out of the window. 'You going to grow a pair all of a sudden now there's a journalist here?'

'Enough!' Bjorn calls back, although his voice is thin and hardly carries on the wind. 'We can't let you leave. Not until we know more about this… this… thing.'

'That's not your decision to make!' yells Kristian. His hands are off the steering wheel now, pressed to his forehead, and he looks pained.

'You know he's right,' Lucy calls. 'God only knows what damage you could do if you took this thing into a city. You must be able to see that.'

Kristian's eyes are wild, his teeth bared. Lucy knows what he's going to do before he does it. She can almost see him slamming his foot down on the pedal, accelerating towards her – and so, somehow, when he yells *goddammit* and tries to steer around her she's already primed to dive out of the way. The Volvo jerks off across the camp ground, bouncing over the rutted terrain at no more than 15 mph, and she gives chase.

She grabs at the Volvo's door handle in a desperate, last-ditch manoeuvre, and is shocked when it comes open. And then, before she knows it, Cat's streaking across the field and diving towards Kristian, doing all she can to pull him from the car.

Cat must have taken Kristian by surprise, as he tumbles out with minimal resistance, landing in a sprawled heap in the dirt. For a moment or two the Volvo veers from side to side, and Lucy can see Pyotr grabbing at the wheel to try and steady it before it finally comes a stop. When she looks back, Cat is straddling Kristian, her full weight on his chest, her hands on his shoulders pressing him down.

Pyotr's out of the Volvo now, striding towards Cat with a determined fury, but the others are just staring. Lucy glances over at the Range Rover and sees Bjorn and Amy standing by its open doors, ensuring that Gillian and Elliot remain inside. Lucy can't blame them: they have to shut this rebellion down somehow.

And then Bjorn speaks up from behind her, in a voice more commanding than she could ever have imagined he possessed. All his charm and affability have gone, replaced by sheer rage. 'I said enough,' he bellows, and even Pyotr stops dead, breathing heavily.

He looks round the group, this group of bloody and ramshackle people who'd come to the edge of the world to follow him. 'Listen to me,' he says fiercely. 'I'm not asking you what you think we should do. The Spirit has spoken. You know what that means. So we know this will bring us to a better world. That's a fact, not a feeling. We *know* it.' He swallows hard, his jaw set. 'I don't know how, not yet.' There's a catch in his voice now, a little tremor. 'But I… I have faith. I'm asking you to do likewise.'

Another voice comes from the crowd. It was Elliot, the crusty old hippy, his eyes weary and desperate. 'And what if we say no?'

'Then we'll stop you,' says Bjorn. 'By force, if that's what it takes.'

30

Lucy isn't sure how they even managed to get Reynaud's body into the infirmary. It had taken half a dozen people to lever it onto a tarpaulin with a shovel, all of them wearing thick gloves to try and avoid touching the thing. Rob has made himself scarce after what happened with Reynaud, and she can't blame him: he's going to need a hell of a lot more sessions with his therapist once all this is over.

Now they've got the body inside, the whole space seems to be filled with distorted flesh: they've had to pull another table in from the mess hall just to stop him from falling to the floor. Medical implements press into what was once Reynaud – stethoscopes, forceps, scissors – and several of Cat's neatly labelled bottles have fallen to the ground from when they'd first manoeuvred the body in here.

Sure enough, the moment they've got Reynaud on the table, Cat drops to her knees and begins scooping up the discarded bottles and boxes of gloves. Lucy sees Bjorn's irritation, and it's not lost on Cat either: she doesn't wait to finish before she starts talking.

'You need to talk me through what Reynaud was doing when this happened to him,' she says. 'As much as you can remember.'

Bjorn's arms are folded, his back pressed up against the door as though wanting to put as much space as possible between himself and the body. 'You're assuming that the same thing killed them both?'

'You're not?' cuts in Lucy.

'They died in totally different ways,' says Bjorn with a curt little shake of his head. 'Marcus was…' He fumbles for a polite form of words.

'Ripped in half?' says Cat.

'Yes,' says Bjorn wearily. 'While Reynaud, well…' He gestures towards the mass of flesh spread across the table. 'I'm struggling to see how the two are alike.'

'Shut up and get these on,' says Cat, pulling out two plastic-wrapped facemasks and throwing one to Lucy. 'If it's airborne, then we're most likely fucked already. But why not live in hope for once.' She hands a mask to Bjorn and then reaches back into the box for her own, rips the packet open and hooks it over her ears without hesitation. 'God, this is way beyond my training.' She glances over at Lucy, who's pulling on her own mask. 'You'd better be recording this.'

Lucy reaches into her bag for her camera. She sees Bjorn start to protest, and then he glances over at Cat and thinks better of it. Wise man. Lucy clicks the camera on, checks the viewfinder, adjusts her position to capture as much of Reynaud's body as she can. On the far side of the frame, Bjorn shuffles out of view, trying to make himself as small as possible.

'So you're working on the assumption that Marcus and Reynaud's deaths were connected,' says Bjorn quietly.

'Mm-hmm,' says Cat. The camera catches her selecting tools from the wall, lifting up a scalpel and a pair of scissors in preparation for her investigation of the body. Through the viewfinder she looks almost credible: she's got all the accoutrements required to be a medical professional, right down to the white coat. Lucy wonders what story their footage would tell, and whether they'll still be around to explain it.

'And whatever that thing was in the vault,' she cuts in. 'The mouse, or at least what used to be a mouse.'

Cat closes her eyes. Even a mask can't hide her look of dismay. 'Shit,' she says. 'That complicates things further.' She heaves a sigh. 'One problem at a time.'

'Forget Marcus for a moment,' says Lucy, doing her best to turn to Bjorn without losing her shot. She wishes she'd brought a tripod. 'Whatever killed Reynaud is the same thing that killed the mouse. No question.' She can see Bjorn's about to protest, but after a moment's thought he decides otherwise. 'Which means the question you have to ask yourself is this: what made each of them turn? What caused this transformation?'

'Exactly,' says Cat, with an approving nod. 'You're good at this.' She leans over the body, scalpel poised. 'Let's get this over with,' she says, bracing herself. She glances back towards Bjorn and Lucy. 'If I start to turn into one of those things,' she says drily, 'I give you permission to jam a scalpel into my neck.' She reaches out for a spare and hands it to Lucy. 'Here,' she says. 'Don't take it personally, Bjorn.'

Bjorn's expression shows he does, in fact, take this very personally, although Cat gives no indication she cares. She studies the body, lifting and grasping its folds of flesh with her scalpel and tweezers. Lucy watches everything through the viewfinder, zooming in to try and capture the full insanity of what she's seeing.

'I've never seen anything like this,' she hears Cat say. 'It's as though his body has replicated itself. In a wholly selective fashion.'

'What do you mean?' says Lucy, and when Cat frowns, she explains: 'For the tape. It's better if it comes in your own words.'

Cat takes a breath, apparently taken aback. 'I mean certain organs, certain muscle groups, seem to have multiplied,' she says eventually. 'See here? His anterior deltoids?' she points with her scalpel. 'There's a cluster of them, as though they've branched off one another, and it's the same with his heart, I'm sure of it.' She lays her gloved palm on where Reynaud's heart would, presumably, once have been. 'You see this great knot of muscle here?' she says, addressing the camera. 'Obviously those are his pectorals, but if we cut through…'

She cuts the skin, revealing a knobbed cluster of things that are unmistakably human hearts. There must be a dozen of them, pressing up against his ribs until they'd cracked outwards.

Even through the viewfinder the sight is vile. Lucy blanches, and as she looks away she notices Bjorn can't watch either. 'My God.'

'A horrible death,' says Cat, stonily. She turns to Bjorn. 'When was he last in the vault?'

'I don't know. I'd have to check the rota.'

'We need to find that out. For all we know this thing only made the jump between species recently. That's invaluable information.' A thought strikes her, and she frowns. 'Assuming that's where this all started, we can't let anyone else in there.' She's speaking to Bjorn, making sure he registers what she's saying. 'Maybe not ever.'

Bjorn's jaw is set, his face red. He looks flustered, unable even to process the idea of losing the System. 'I'll check,' he says, 'of course — leave it with me.'

But Cat's not leaving this. She's laid her scalpel down, as though wanting to ensure Bjorn has her full attention. 'If there's something in there, Bjorn,' she says with force, 'if there's even a chance… we can't take the risk.'

31

EXTRACT: Notes taken from the communal slip box for 21 September, 2016

> 'Evidently, after his fit of promptitude, Mr Tulliver was relapsing into the sense that this is a puzzling world.' A recognition of how little anything makes sense these days. Once we had clarity... now all that is dissolving. Have we lost our distinctiveness? Are we just like everyone else?

> 'Of good society, Teufelsdröckh appears to have seen little, or has mostly forgotten what he saw. He speaks out with a strange plainness; calls many things by their mere dictionary names.' We need, I believe, to be reaching out. Engaging more widely. We have become too lost in our notes, too afraid of outsiders. This path leads only to death.

TOM CARLISLE

'There again he is so sly and still, so imperturbably saturnine; shows such indifference, malign coolness towards all that men strive after.' A warning to our leaders. You are not so far above us; you are not so different from us. Do not forget your humanity.

'But do not let us quarrel any more, | No, my Lucrezia; bear with me for once: | Sit down and all shall happen as you wish.' We must put aside our debates. There has been too much quarrelling: the time is right for unity.

'Full often, taking from the world of sleep
This Arab phantom which my friend beheld,
This semi-Quixote, I to him have given
A substance, fancied him a living man.'
Perhaps we have spent too long living in dreams. How little we have truly accomplished: a vast library, and nothing more. This is no true achievement, only the semblance of one.

'Blossoms upon one tree, | Characters of the great apocalypse, | The types and symbols of eternity | Of first, and last, and midst, and without end...' We must learn to read the signs. This world in all its sorrow is coming to an end, and something new is straining to emerge. Will we recognise its coming, this rough beast slouching towards Bethlehem?

MARGINAL

'We will now discuss in a little more detail the struggle for existence. Nothing is easier than to admit in words the truth of the universal struggle for life...' *Our struggle is perpetual, but we mustn't give up on the task set before us. We are blessed to recognise our work. The fight may not be won in our lifetime, but we must not cede ground.*

'Hence, as more individuals are produced than can possibly survive, there must in every case be a struggle for existence.' *A warning and an exhortation. The struggle is great, may even now be at its most pronounced. We must take all necessary precautions to ensure we have the victory; must be prepared to do whatever it takes.*

'There is so much inviting us! — what are we to take? What will nourish us in growth towards perfection?' *We are, I believe, entering a new phase of growth. Becoming more and more like the people we were called to be. We must pursue whatever will help us in that goal, and cut off all that is dead. There is no other way.*

'It is not by wearing down into uniformity all that is individual in themselves, but by cultivating it and calling it forth, within the limits imposed by the rights and interests of others, that human beings become a noble and beautiful object of contemplation.' Let us not block the life that is emerging in this place. Only by recognising the patterns and leading of the Spirit can we possibly be changed; only by obeying can we possibly become beautiful.

32

THEY GATHER in the mess hall just after eleven. Most of them are slumped over tables, their heads in their hands. Hazel and Beatrice are hunched in close, their body language twitchy and paranoid, trying to keep their muttered conversations from being overheard.

Rob sits up when Bjorn enters the room. Everyone does. They need somebody to guide them, always have. Rob feels a little prickle of scorn. They're so easily led.

Bjorn looks harried, flustered. He makes a faltering attempt to get everyone's attention by rapping his knuckles on a table – a token gesture, really, a way to get them to look at him.

'So,' he says, wringing his hands. 'What happened tonight. Not our finest hour, I fear.' He sighs, runs his hands through his long, greying hair. 'You saw what happened to Reynaud. And those that didn't will have heard about it.' He drops his head, his eyes closed. 'It was… horrible. And unprecedented.' Then he looks up, his eyes lighting on each of them in turn, silent for what feels like an eternity. When he speaks again his voice is more forceful, as though he knows he's on steadier ground. 'But tonight, I'm going to ask something of you, each one of you, that you might find hard,' he says. 'I'm asking you to trust the System.'

From his satchel he removes the slip box. 'You know how this works,' he says. 'Today is no different from any other.' He looks them over again, something a little professorial about his mannerisms even now. 'I have seen your confusion. I have seen your hope. And I have seen your insight.' He puts a hand to his heart. 'Let us gather together in a spirit of unity, and listen for inspiration. Let us visualise a better world, and know the steps we must take to realise it. Above all, let us be changed.

'It is time to listen,' he says. 'To ask what the Spirit is telling you.' He reaches into the box, and withdraws a stack of cards. Bows his head. 'We are attentive to your leading.'

He looks down at the card in his hand. Nods. Reads the notes aloud to the room. Rob remembers this all too well. Trying to decipher what the cards were saying about the mood here: using them to discern how safe he was.

He's struck by how many dissenting voices there are. There's no unity here today: it's the closest thing he's ever heard to open rebellion. And yet Bjorn doesn't seem to see it: his face remains neutral, unruffled.

Once more Bjorn surveys the gathered crowd. 'You've heard the words of the Spirit. What do you make of them?'

Kristian raises his hand. 'I have something to say,' he says. 'If I may.'

'Go ahead,' says Bjorn. 'We're listening.'

'What I hear is concern. Anxiety. About the direction of this movement, and its leadership.' He looks around the room. 'I'd bet others heard the same.'

Bjorn gives a sage nod. 'Very well.'

Kristian stares at him. 'Is that all?' he says. 'You do understand what I'm saying here? That you're at fault.'

'I hear what you're saying,' says Bjorn. 'And I note your concern.'

The silence is deafening.

'So…' continues Kristian. 'What do you propose to do about it?'

'Nothing,' says Bjorn, his gaze unwavering.

'Nothing?'

'That's right.'

'This is a crisis, Bjorn,' says Pyotr, rising to his feet. 'You're acting like what happened to Reynaud couldn't happen to us.'

'I agree,' says Bjorn. 'I acknowledge the crisis. And yet I choose to trust.'

Pyotr's trying hard not to lose his rag. 'And what about us? Everything we heard, all those words of caution… don't they count for anything?'

'No,' says Bjorn. 'It's just that the Spirit's leading can be cryptic. It requires some discernment. There is no clear word on this, not in this room. That's why a community like this needs a leader.'

'So you're the one who decides,' says Kristian. 'That's what you're saying.'

'We're not a democracy, Kristian. We've never been a democracy.'

'No, but in case you hadn't noticed, none of us have had eight fucking arms bursting out of our backs before, either,' says Kristian, glowering. He's starting to gather momentum, pulling others into his argument like a black hole. Rob can see Elliot, Amy, Ken starting to nod. 'I think you'd agree that things have changed.'

Bjorn stares at him for several seconds with a new intensity. It's a stare that looks very much like hatred.

'Some things never change,' he says finally.

'This isn't a dictatorship, Bjorn,' says Kristian.

Bjorn's eyes flash. 'That's exactly what it is,' he says. 'A dictatorship of the Spirit.'

Rob sees Cat close her eyes and sink down into her chair. Sees Kristian's mouth hanging open, trying to take in what he's just heard. Sees Elliot chewing on his knuckle.

'We don't have a clue what this thing is,' Bjorn says. 'We don't know how it spreads, nor how to protect ourselves from it. All we have is what the Spirit has revealed.' He pinches the bridge of his nose. 'I'm not going to pretend this is an easy message, nor that I understand it myself. Perhaps this is a test. But I won't abandon everything this movement is built on, not when we need it most.'

'And what about the rest of us?' calls Amy. 'What if we disagree?'

'Oh, Amy,' says Bjorn, a smile breaking across his face. 'What kind of leader would I be if I let you turn away from the words of life? What kind of man would I be?'

MARGINAL

Rob turns, then, and catches Cat's eye. Her expression is grave, and despite himself he feels a prickle of excitement run down his spine.

Finally, he thinks. *Finally she gets it.*

33

H<small>E WATCHES</small> Cat head into the kitchen after the meeting, and gives it a few minutes to check no one's joined her before he follows her in. Something changed in her during her three hours in the vault, that much is clear. If he and Lucy are to have any chance of getting out of this alive, they need her as an ally.

He's not prepared for what he finds. Cat's hunched over the central counter, a metal skewer in her left hand and her right arm laid out flat. She glances up as Rob enters the room, and, as though Rob's appearance gives her the push she needs, she presses the skewer against the skin of her wrist. He hears flesh sizzling.

'FUCK!' Cat's voice isn't quite a yell – she's holding something back, perhaps hoping not to draw too much attention to what she's doing in here. But she can't entirely contain it.

'What the fuck are you doing?' Rob half-screams, but Cat doesn't answer. Instead, she crosses the room, flicks on the cold tap, and shoves her arm underneath the streaming water.

She heaves a shuddering sigh. When she finally turns back to look at Rob, her arm still held beneath the tap, she wears a manic grin.

'Well, thank God for that,' she says, and Rob can hear the relief in her voice. 'I guess we can be sure that I'm not infected.'

He can't hold his anger back. 'You don't know a thing,' he says. 'This isn't evidence, it's... self-mutilation. What if you'd transformed?'

'Then I'd be dead.' Cat stares at him, her eyes so hard and resolute that Rob has to look away. 'And no harm done.'

'You don't know that,' yells Rob without really meaning to, and Cat hisses at him to *ssh*. 'Even Bjorn said it,' he continues, his voice a furious whisper, 'we don't know how this thing spreads.'

'You're right. But I have a theory.'

'Oh, you do?'

God, he's pissed off. He can't keep the bitterness out of his voice.

Cat cocks her head. 'I do.' She's smirking. Fucking smirking. Trying to hide it, sure, but not trying especially hard. 'Do you want to hear it? Or are you too busy sulking?'

It takes Rob longer than he'd like to regain his equilibrium, and when he does speak it's through gritted teeth. 'Go on, then. Spit it out.'

'Right,' says Cat, eyebrows raised. 'So listen. You saw something to make you turn on Reynaud, didn't you?'

He thinks back to the strange ripple under Reynaud's skin, the shimmer of movement at his neck. Even now he couldn't swear it wasn't his imagination.

'So that means that if this thing is inside any of us,' Cat goes on, 'there must be some sign of it. You follow?'

'And, what, you thought you saw something in your arm?'

'No,' says Cat, her tone impressively level considering the triangular scorch mark on her skin. 'But if there was anything in me, I'd bet all I own that it would react to me doing that.' She sniffs. With her unburned arm, she reaches down into the sink and retrieves the skewer. 'How about it?'

Rob recoils. Maybe it's the smell of searing flesh, or Cat's matter-of-fact approach to branding herself, but this whole situation makes him want to jump out of his own skin.

No. He has to be rational. He has enough tools to handle this situation, enough ways to stop himself from shutting down.

This isn't new. Or, at least, not all of it is. Yes, there's high emotions. There's personal risk. The outcomes are uncertain, the next steps unclear. But, his therapist would say, he's dealt with these things before. All that's changed is the context.

He takes a breath, grounds himself. He tries not to think of Reynaud. He can see Cat watching him with a twisted little smile, and fights back the urge to call her a stupid bitch. They have to stick together here.

'You don't get to decide this for me,' he says. That's good. Frank, assertive, not too confrontational. At least they both know where they stand.

'Sure.' Cat lets the silence linger, but there's something combative in it. For a few moments the only sound is running water.

'You can't force me into this,' he says finally. 'Not now.'

MARGINAL

'Okay,' says Cat, in the same level, calm tone that seems so profoundly wrong coming from her mouth.

Again, silence blooms between them. Some part of Rob envies Cat her certainty. She knows, for now at least, that she's safe. That's a gift.

All the same, he can't get the image of Reynaud out of his head. His bloated, deformed body; organs multiplying, pressing up against his skin. The thought makes his skin prickle.

No. He can't think this way. If this thing was inside him, it would show itself. There'd be signs. And then he'll take matters into his own hands. Something non-violent, that takes it by surprise. Pills, hanging, drowning. Plenty of options.

Cat's staring at her arm again, pressing gingerly against the skin around her wound. It's already edged with a violent pink corona.

'But then if I don't do it,' Rob says into the silence, 'then I guess you'll always wonder. What it was that made me hold back. What exactly I've seen under my skin.'

'I—' Cat glances up, and her words catch in her throat. Now it's Rob's turn to let the statement hang in the air. One second. Two. Three. Four.

'You see?' he says. 'Knowing changes things. It forces your hand.'

Cat closes her eyes. 'Okay,' she sighs. 'That's true. But that doesn't mean it wasn't the right decision.' Now she meets Rob's eye, and nods over to the cooker. 'Are you sure you won't do it?'

'I guess I don't have much of a choice,' Rob says heavily. 'But I want you to promise me something.'

'Sure.'

He crosses the kitchen and removes the longest chef's knife he can find from the magnetic rail. 'If I start to transform, I want you to stab me in the neck.'

Cat blinks once, hard. 'You're serious. You want *me* to do this?'

'Dead serious.' He moves over to the sink and sets the knife on the edge. 'You'll do it, right?' Cat remains silent, staring at the knife. 'I need you to promise.'

'I— I want to,' she says shakily.

'That's not good enough,' Rob says fiercely, laying her hand on the knife again. 'I won't become one of those things. If you see that happening to me – if you get even a hint that something's up – do it.'

'Christ.' Cat swallows. 'Okay.' She still hasn't touched the knife. She chews at her lip. 'No. What if I fail? What if something goes wrong?'

'It's simple. I'll be screaming. It'll be a mercy.'

Cat's head is bowed. She nods a couple of times, gently, and Rob can see her talking herself into this. Good, he thinks. Proof she's still sane after all.

Finally, Cat reaches for the knife with her uninjured hand. Feels the weight of it, tries a tentative stabbing motion. Swaps hands, and winces as she tries to grip the handle. 'Okay,' she says again. 'But can I just ask one thing?'

'Of course.'

'Do you feel, y'know, normal?'

'I feel great,' he says, crossing the kitchen to the gas burner. 'Now let's do this.'

34

Lucy clocks the wound on Rob's arm the moment she enters the kitchen. He's not even tried to be subtle about it: big white swatch of bandage on his arm, making a matching pair with Cat. She supposes she ought to be glad: any new ally is good news. Hell, think of the narrative: she'd never imagined a redemption arc for Rob. But they're a long way from that now, and really all she wants to do is scream.

She knows what they've done. It didn't take a genius to work it out. It's some kind of test, some way of working out if they're infected. Thank God it didn't backfire. They've lost enough people already.

'Well this looks awfully cosy,' she says. 'Shame I wasn't invited.'

Rob is, for a moment, like a little kid caught stealing. 'It was an impulse decision,' he says. 'A stupid one.' He mouths *sorry*, and Cat glowers over his shoulder.

'I don't know what you think this proves,' Lucy says, 'except that it doesn't respond to heat.'

'It's a hypothesis, that's all,' says Cat, raising her eyebrows. 'But a working one. One I'd like to test a little further.'

'Don't let me stop you,' says Lucy. 'But personally, I'm not sure this goes far enough. I've been wondering about what you said to Bjorn about transmission. Whether there might be a way to protect ourselves. Do you have anything that could help us do that?'

'What do you have in mind?' says Cat, her eyes narrowed.

Lucy rubs her temple. 'I guess I want to know how this thing spreads,' she says. 'How it got into Reynaud, or into Marcus, in the first place.'

'It's a good question,' says Cat, leaning back against the counter. 'Every one of us got a lungful of air from the vault and yet we don't seem to be infected.' She catches Lucy's eye. 'As far as we know.'

'So we can rule out airborne transmission?' says Rob.

'Not exactly.' She rubs her chin. 'I'd say it's unlikely, though. Bloodborne I think is out: no exchange of fluids. Sexual: same. I guess it could be spread through touch? Droplets?'

Rob puts a hand to his head. 'We'll never pin that down,' he says. 'It could take weeks.'

'Agreed,' says Cat. 'Maybe we're overcomplicating it by looking at transmission...' Her fingers beat a tattoo on the edge of the counter. 'Bacterial, fungal, viral. Those are the most likely candidates. And if it's one of them...'

'We can stop those, right?' says Lucy. 'There are antibiotics. Antifungals.'

'It's not enough,' says Rob in a tone of despair. 'We need to cover every base or this whole exercise is worthless.'

'No,' says Cat firmly. 'No, it's not. Just think about it a second.

MARGINAL

If we could rule out bacterial or fungal infections, and this thing persists, that tells us something. It tells us that it's viral. And perhaps that gives us the information we need to stop it.' She paused, and then said more quietly. 'Or it gives somebody the information they need to stop it, anyway.'

Rob lets out a long sigh. Whatever lightness he'd had after his self-mutilation has long vanished, and his expression is tired and grave now. 'It's not enough,' he says. 'What if the antibiotics – the antifungals – what if they're not strong enough to beat this? What if they do nothing at all?'

'That's a chance we have to take,' says Lucy. 'We'll deal with that when it happens. But we've got to do something. I'm not sitting on my hands waiting for this thing to get me.'

She regrets saying it the moment she opens her mouth, but she can feel despair blooming inside her, and it scares her. To her relief, Cat nods slowly. 'I can get behind that,' she says. 'But there's an issue.'

'You don't have the drugs.' Lucy should have known: the medical room was tiny, with limited storage space.

'Exactly. So we'd have to get them somehow.'

'How easily can you do that?'

'I've got a contact,' says Cat. 'I reckon he can get us what we need. All I need is to get him a message.'

'It's that easy?' mutters Rob. 'You just send him a text and he shows up with drugs?'

'No,' says Cat, rolling her eyes and for a moment sounding as if she were Rob's older sister. 'There's no reception up here, is there? We use email. Obviously.'

'Bjorn's okay with this?' asks Lucy, and Cat raises an eyebrow.

'It's not like I'm asking him to get me cocaine,' she says. 'It's mostly antihistamines, hydrocortisone cream. Bjorn knows we need medical supplies, and Francis is... well, he's reliable enough. Keeps himself to himself.' She rubs her chin. 'But we need to be careful, you understand. We can't give him even the slightest indication of what happened to Marcus and Reynaud, or he'll panic and call the authorities.'

Lucy frowns. 'Are you sure this is the right call, Cat?'

'What do you mean?'

'I mean...' Lucy sighs. 'I mean, are we really talking about just getting some drugs and carrying on like everything's normal? Wouldn't it be better if someone were to, you know... take things out of our hands? If you were to drop your contact a hint that we're in trouble?'

Cat glares at her. 'No,' she says firmly. 'If we bring outsiders in now, we're goners. They'll stick us in a lab for the next six months, if we're lucky. We'll lose any chance of figuring this out on our terms.'

Lucy chews her lip. She can see what Cat's saying: there might still be a way of getting out of this alive, and she's got no desire to be vivisected. Still, she can't shake the sense that they're way out of their depth. She wants someone else to be in charge for an hour or two.

'Okay, then,' she says heavily, 'what's the plan?'

'Let me reach out to Francis, set up the meeting like usual. But I'll stress the need for discretion. No unnecessary risks.'

'I'm coming with you,' Lucy says. 'In case something happens.'

She doesn't need to clarify: she's certain that she and Cat are thinking the same, horrible thoughts.

Cat hesitates. 'Alright,' she says after a moment, with a curt nod. 'But you follow my lead. We get in, we get the drugs, we get out. No drawing attention.'

'Understood,' says Lucy. 'When do we leave?'

'Tonight. The sooner we have some protection, the better.'

Cat's smile is half-hearted now, the mood changed. 'Leave it with me,' she says. 'He's usually pretty quick.' And then she takes off out of the door in search of a computer.

Still, at least they're making progress now. Taking action, moving forwards. She can't stand sitting around, waiting. Too much time to think. Too much time to dwell on that thing that used to be Reynaud, and its vast, deformed shape – inexplicable and grotesque and yet recognisably human.

Really she ought to be interviewing people about it, ought to be exploring, asking the pertinent questions, but she can't bring herself to do it. Can hardly bear to look at the thing. They'd moved it to the medical room, managed somehow to get it through the door, and now everyone's giving it a wide berth. It's probably for the best, although God knows what they'll do if it starts to rot.

Maybe she'll have to help dig his grave. The thought makes her want to laugh, but it's not the good kind of laughter: it's the kind that hurts all over.

She'll have a hell of a story to tell when this is finished, though. Assuming the government let her. Assuming she lives to tell the tale.

She meets Cat at the edge of the woods just before two. It's pitch black out here, the stars hidden beneath thick cloud. Again it strikes her how far they are from civilisation: the faint glow of the quarry's lights, and the few scattered pinpricks in the village, are dwarfed by the darkness.

They walk about 500m down the road, just far enough to be out of sight of the camp, and stop at a bend. Cat leans back against a tree, removes a small head torch and straps it on. Beneath it, her face is grave.

'Did you have any issues with your contact?' she says into the darkness.

Cat hesitates before answering. 'He's not happy about it.'

'But he can help?'

'He has questions.' She sticks out her lip. 'I can't say I blame him.'

'What did you tell him?'

Cat must have heard the concern in Lucy's voice, as her reply is defensive. 'I'm a nurse. I know any number of reasons why we could need antifungals.'

The silence crackles between them, the darkness like a physical presence. 'Can he get enough drugs? Your contact?' Lucy says after a minute or so, picking up the thread of their abortive conversation as best she can.

Cat sighs. Lucy can't tell if it's due to the subject matter, or simply from being expected to talk at all. 'Well, that's where we have a problem.'

Of course there's a problem.

'How much can you get?'

'Enough to treat three, maybe four people, for a week.'

She forces herself to stay positive. 'That's not nothing.'

'Hmm.' Cat seems hesitant, her fingers on her thigh, her brow lightly furrowed. This time, Lucy braves the silence, lets her think. She's seen this before. Cat is working up to something: these are the initial, faltering steps towards trust. After thirty seconds or so, her hunch pays off. 'That… that *thing*,' says Cat with a shudder, her eyes still on the road. 'It— what it did to Marcus…'

'You're wondering if that dose is enough.'

'Yes.'

'I wish I had the answer to that.'

Cat considers this for a moment.

'Yes,' she says with a sigh. 'Me too.'

After they've been there less than five minutes, she sees a pair of tiny headlights climbing the hill, flickering in and out of view as the vehicle navigates the winding road. She can hear the engine struggling on the hill, and feels oddly relieved: it's hard to be afraid of someone who drives such a crappy little car.

The driver parks up on the side of the road and kills the engine. When he opens the door she can make out a tall, skinny man in a red flannel shirt. He walks round, surveying them both with an oily smile.

'Cat,' he says. 'Always a pleasure to see you.'

'Francis,' she says, a little tersely. One hand hangs at her side, her fingers drumming on her thigh. 'This is Lucy.'

'Charmed, I'm sure,' he says, his voice dripping with irony, and offers Lucy his hand. Lucy takes it, startled to find it dry and callused, his handshake stronger than she expected.

Cat doesn't bother with a handshake: her hands are still on her hips, and she doesn't look any more keen to chat with Francis than she was with Lucy. 'Do you have the pills?'

'Okay, okay,' he says, mock-offended. 'I'm just trying to be polite here, no need to get your knickers in a twist.' His smile widens. It's disconcertingly toothy. 'Product's in the boot. I assume you've got the money.'

Cat sighs, moves round to the back of the car. Francis lifts the boot, revealing dozens of white pharmaceutical packets. He removes a sheet of paper from the pocket of his shirt and peers at it in the light from his phone torch.

'Let's see, let's see,' he says, checking his list, and Lucy hears the amusement in his voice. 'In your email you said you'd been having some issues with… fungal infections. Your lot had an outbreak of thrush up there, Cat?' She tries to laugh, but it comes out tight and forced, and even Francis seems to notice. A note of malice creeps into his voice. 'Hardly surprising, at least if you believe what people say.'

'We're not that kind of community, Francis,' says Cat tartly. 'I'd have thought you'd know that by now.'

Francis looks Cat up and down with an expression of distaste. 'You're the only one I ever see,' he says, with a shrug. 'Not that I'm complaining.'

Cat's growing exasperated. Shifting from foot to foot, her voice irritable. 'Can we get this over with?' says Cat. 'I don't like being away from camp for long. Somebody will spot us.'

'Alright, alright,' he says. 'But I'd like something extra from you today.'

'I've got money,' says Cat curtly.

'Oh no,' says Francis. 'No, nothing so squalid as that. No, what I'd like is information.' He rubs his cheek. 'See, there's something awfully suspicious about all of this. Late-night meetings, and your new friend here. It stinks.'

'Careful, Francis.' Cat's tone would have sent Lucy running, but it has no effect at all on Francis. He turns to Lucy.

'How about you, then?' he says, raising his eyebrows. 'You going to tell me what this is all about?'

She's unsure what Cat already told him, and doesn't want to make things more complicated. 'Your guess is as good as mine,' she says. 'Better ask her.'

Francis is smiling again. Too many teeth. 'She's got you well trained, hasn't she?'

'Didn't anyone tell you it's rude to talk about people behind their backs?' says Cat.

'Don't recall talking about you behind your back,' he says, leaning forwards, his smile widening still further.

Cat ignores him, reaches into the boot. 'Is this them?'

'Mm-hmm.' Francis picks up one of the boxes, rattles it, and then opens the end. 'It's in liquid form, like we discussed,' he says. 'If you want pills, it'll be next week. I can give you it in a bottle, or I've got some auto-injector they sent me as a sample. It's up to you.'

'Can I take both?'

He raises an eyebrow. 'I mean, sure,' he says warily. 'If you can pay.' He pushes the boxes across to her, and studies Cat's face as she reaches for them. 'All this has you kind of rattled, huh?' He cocks his head, glances over at Lucy as though she might give him something more. 'Listen, I hate to pry. But if something's going on up there—'

Cat cuts him off. 'Can we just pay and go? I want to get back.'

'Alright,' he says, although the wariness hasn't left his eyes. 'Four hundred.' With a sigh, Cat reaches into her pocket and withdraws a wallet filled with £20 notes. She counts them out and hands them over to Francis with a distinct lack of grace.

'We done here?' she says.

He sticks out his lip. 'I guess. But I'd prefer to know what I'm getting into. In case anyone comes around asking questions, you know.'

'If it mattered so much to you, you could always have sent me packing,' says Cat.

'Sure,' says Francis. 'Sure.' He sucks on his teeth. 'Except, I mean, people might talk about your friend here. What she's doing here. And without knowing any better, I might have to join them in their speculation.' He glances over at Lucy. 'So go on, what is it?' he says to her. 'You her bodyguard?'

'I'm certain she can defend herself,' Lucy mutters, and Cat shoots her a look.

'Aye,' says Francis, glancing at Cat with a half-smile, 'you're probably right there…'

Cat's stare is withering. 'Are you going to let me take these drugs now?'

'Alright. Take a chill pill.' Francis is still looking at Lucy, rubbing his chin. 'I saw you and your friend passing through when you first came up here, you know,' he says thoughtfully. 'Not much to see out here, so we take whatever excitement we can get.'

Lucy feels a little prickle of irritation. 'I assume there's a point here.'

Francis gives a tiny shrug. 'Only that they don't get a lot of visitors up at their, uh, commune. Not anymore, anyway.' There's an unspoken question there. She doesn't like it.

'I've got my reasons,' she says, looking for a tone that invites no further discussion.

'No doubt you have,' he says with a droll smile. 'And that wouldn't be anything to do with why you need these, now, would it?' He rattles the boxes.

He's not stupid. He knows something's up, and that makes him dangerous. The last thing they need is people sniffing around the camp, not when they've no idea how people get infected. She makes a calculation, a judgement call, and doesn't let herself look at Cat for fear of losing her nerve.

'I'm going to tell you something in confidence,' Lucy says, swallowing hard. She can hear Cat pointedly clearing her throat and ignores her. 'My friend's brother... he passed away two days ago. There was an accident. That's why I'm here. For his body.'

Francis's eyes narrow.

'I needed to get out of there. Just for an hour or so. It's... heavy.'

'Were you going to mention this, Cat?' says Francis, turning to her.

'It's not your concern,' mutters Cat.

'No. No, I suppose not.' He looks at the boxes piled in the boot and gives a little sigh. 'Well, now you've got me,' he says. He picks up one of the largest boxes and hands it to her. 'I'm sorry for your loss.'

'Thank you,' she hears herself say, a little tartly. She sniffs. 'You can tell people what happened if you want. But don't dress it up as something it's not. They're not monsters.'

Francis is silent a moment, looking down at his shoes. When he speaks again he sounds slightly abashed. 'If you'd only heard the stories I had…'

'They're just that. Stories.' She taps the top of the box, hears the ampoules rattle inside. 'Thanks for these,' she says, then turns to Cat. 'Let's get out of here,' she mutters.

She can feel his eyes on them the whole way back up the hill. She holds the box of ampoules tightly beneath her arm, listening to them clink together with every step.

The clouds have parted slightly now. Next to her Cat is dimly visible in the moonlight, glancing over at the box from time to time as though she can't quite believe the drugs are real. Under different circumstances it would piss Lucy off.

'I've got them,' Lucy says eventually. 'I'm not going to do anything stupid, I promise.'

'Yeah, well hold on to them carefully,' says Cat tersely. 'If you drop them, we're fucked.'

They're both quiet a while, brooding. Already she can feel Cat retreating, feel that distance between them growing again. Cat wanted to bury herself, to live out her life in splendid isolation. That's a luxury they can't afford right now. 'This is horrible,' says Lucy finally, choosing her words carefully. 'The uncertainty.'

Again Cat's silent, for so long that Lucy wonders if she's misjudged the mood altogether. It wouldn't be the first time. But then, Cat speaks again.

'It is,' she says. 'Horrible. All of it. Fucking awful.'

Lucy takes a long breath. 'I've been thinking—' she begins.

'About who we give the meds to?' Cat nods. 'It's a good thought.'

'Uh, yeah. Exactly that.' Cat continues to surprise her. She's always watching, always thinking. Lucy isn't sure what she'd been expecting. One of the archetypes, most likely: a brutal priestess, a subservient lackey. Cat's neither. There's a savviness about her, a steeliness, that Lucy likes a lot.

'So you want to know who was closest to Marcus? Or to Reynaud?'

Again, that spooky ability to predict what Lucy's thinking before she says it.

'Listen, I know this will sound like prying…'

Cat's eyes narrow. 'You want to know if Marcus and Reynaud were fucking?'

'Well, yeah,' says Lucy, her laugh more from surprise than embarrassment. 'In short.'

Cat gives a tiny shake of the head. 'No. Not that I know about, anyway.' There's something almost like amusement in her face. 'It's not that kind of commune.'

'Were they friends?'

'Doesn't matter,' says Cat with a shrug. 'They'd have spent enough time together anyway. Working the gardens, or in the kitchen, or just down in the vault.'

Again they're silent in the darkness, thinking.

'If people find out we're offering protection,' says Lucy, 'or even just the chance of protection… I don't know what we'll do. There's not enough drugs here for two dozen people.'

Cat takes a deep breath. 'Listen, not everyone thinks like you,' she says, and for the first time in several minutes she sounds reserved. 'We're a pretty cautious bunch.'

Lucy chooses her words carefully. 'Not everyone,' she says. 'Not according to Rob.'

'You mean Pyotr? Kristian?' Cat's face hardens. It's a tiny, barely perceptible movement – everything she does seems to be restrained – but the difference it makes is palpable. 'The trouble those two have caused…'

'I think they'll go for this. If you ask them.'

Cat gives a hard little laugh. 'You just watch what happens if I ask them anything,' she says. 'Anyway, even if I won them over, they're not going to sway anyone. They're thick as thieves, but they keep themselves to themselves.'

'We just need somebody to agree to be a guinea pig. To show it's safe.' She can feel herself sounding Cat out, isn't sure how hard to push. 'If they're reckless, then perhaps—'

'I never called them reckless,' says Cat tersely, and Lucy's heart sinks. 'Troublesome, that's what I called them. They've no concept of community, never have.'

There's a fierceness in her voice now, something like venom.

35

They make straight for the mess hall, and the moment she steps through the door Lucy seeks out Kristian. She notes the reaction when she walks in of naked suspicion on the faces of people around the room: Pyotr, Elliot, Miranda.

Still, at least she has Rob here with her for company, although right now he's sitting alone at a table with his head bent over his journal, glowering.

'Kristian,' she says, approaching his table. 'Hey. Do you have a moment?'

She can see Bjorn watching, his fingers tapping restlessly against his thigh as he weighs up how to challenge her. He's not the only one. For the first time since she's arrived, even Kristian looks wary.

'What's up?' he says, frowning.

'I'd rather not talk here. Can we talk outside?'

He gives a low chuckle. 'You know anything you tell me isn't going to stay secret for long, right?' he says, nodding to one side and the other.

'Humour me.'

Kristian shakes his head. He's hating this, she can see that. Being singled out, being made to look like a collaborator. Well, good. She can work with that. It gives her some drama. Then Kristian glances to one side. 'Pyotr,' he calls. 'You got a second?'

Pyotr walks over, scowling and tense, trying to make himself appear bigger than his scrawny frame will allow. Kristian raises a bushy red eyebrow. Lucy can't tell who it's aimed at. 'Whatever you have to say to me,' he says, 'Pyotr can hear it too.'

Lucy tries to keep her voice calm.

'This isn't a trap, Kristian.'

'Then you won't mind my buddy coming,' he says with a shrug.

She rolls her eyes, exasperated. 'Fine,' she says. 'Let's do this outside. Now.'

At that Pyotr pulls an absurd face, and makes a pantomime of waggling his eyebrows as though wondering if he might get lucky. She ignores him, and the others. Crosses the room and heads for the door.

Kristian and Pyotr come out on to the porch, obviously feeling the evening cold even if they don't want to show it. Kristian has his arms folded, and Pyotr's lounging against the edge of the building. They've got the air of a couple of sixth formers – a little too cocky for their own good. Lucy looks them up and down, weighing them up.

'Right then,' she says. 'Which one of you wants to get jabbed?'

Pyotr and Kristian share a look. 'Jabbed?' says Kristian slowly. 'With what?'

'Antifungals,' Lucy says, removing an ampoule from the box. 'Stick 'em in your arm and they'll auto-inject.' She can see from their mystified looks that this isn't enough. 'Listen, Cat thinks this thing might be some kind of contagion. Fungal, most likely. Based on, well, you know.' She doesn't want to remind them of what happened to Marcus or Reynaud too vividly: that won't help anyone. 'And so maybe antifungals will kill it. Even better, maybe you'll get some lasting protection. But we need a guinea pig. Someone to test it on.'

Kristian cocks his head. 'Why not test it on yourself?'

'People here trust you. They've seen how you stood up to Bjorn. Doesn't take a genius to see that.' She looks Kristian dead in the eye. 'You're credible. More credible than I am, anyway. We need you.'

Pyotr can't help himself smiling, and Lucy feels a faint thrum of satisfaction. She's good at this job and she knows it, but it's always nice when your skills prove useful. Kristian still looks sceptical, his lips pursed beneath his beard.

'And they're safe?' he asks gruffly. 'You can vouch for that?'

Lucy meets his stare. 'You can get them on the NHS,' she says. 'They sell them in pharmacies. I'm not going to ask you to be a guinea pig for some untested medication.'

'That doesn't answer my question.' His stare is intense, boring into her. 'I don't like being hurried into decisions like this, not without all the facts.'

'Okay,' she says. 'I hear that. But if you want that certainty, you're going to be waiting a long time for it. What if you wait too long, and you end up like Reynaud?'

Kristian takes another long breath. 'What happened to Reynaud was… horrible. And I understand why you're scared it'll happen to you—'

'And you're not?'

'Okay,' he says, swallowing hard. 'Yes. Yes, I'm scared.' She sees Pyotr glance over at him then, with something like shock. Kristian doesn't meet his eye, although Lucy can see how much that admission cost him. 'But you're right. I don't want to end up like Reynaud.' He moves past her, stares off into the night.

'You know, I came here because I was tired of how the world did things,' says Kristian. 'I didn't know what I thought anymore, and I couldn't quiet the noise long enough to focus.' He's silent for longer now. His head bowed, his voice quieter, as though speaking to himself. 'What Bjorn was offering – it felt like bliss. It still does.' He glances up at Lucy. 'If you'd been in the vault before what happened to Marcus, you'd have seen it. You can lose yourself down there.'

But now, to one side, Pyotr's frowning. Kristian looks up from his reverie and notices him. 'You don't agree?' he says, with a note of challenge.

Pyotr grimaces, his whole body emanating discomfort. 'I don't know, man,' he says with a little sigh. 'I don't know.'

'But that's… that's everything this place is about.'

Pyotr's eyes are closed, as though he doesn't have the appetite for this fight.

'Go on,' says Kristian.

'No,' says Pyotr reluctantly. 'No, it's not. Or at least that's not how I saw it.'

'Then *what?*'

Pyotr's sigh is deeper than before. 'It's like you think... it's like you think this isolation is a good thing.' He holds out his hands in a gesture of hopeless surrender. 'The System – it's transformative, man. Like, it could change the world. I swear it could.' He rubs at his shoulder. 'I guess I thought the plan was to take it outwards. To, you know, actually tell people about it.'

Kristian still sounds furious. 'You know why we can't do that.'

'I know why Bjorn *says* we can't. But I'm not so sure anymore.'

'They never understood it. They always wanted him to compromise.'

Pyotr bows his head, and when he speaks again he sounds very tired. 'Those times in the vault, they've been some of the best times of my life, Kris. That's too good to keep in here.'

'You know this, Pyotr,' says Kristian tersely. 'Your being here is an act of service. The work you do here is for the good of everyone...'

Pyotr's on the verge of giving up. He looks exhausted, his nervous energy ebbing away, all the fight gone from those long limbs. 'You're right,' he says hollowly. 'Of course you're right.' He raises his eyebrows. 'Thanks, man.'

'Don't mention it.'

And then Pyotr turns to Lucy and puts out his hand. 'Give me one of those,' he says, nodding to the ampoule. Kristian rolls his eyes.

'You're a bloody fool,' Lucy hears him mutter, but Pyotr ignores him.

'It's like you said, Kris,' he says, flicking off the ampoule's cap. 'This isn't just about me. It's about what's best for everyone.'

'Pyotr, no!' Kristian's moving towards him now, but he's too late. Pyotr rolls up his sleeve and jams the ampoule against his upper arm and there's a click as the auto-injector mechanism fires. It takes less than a second.

There's a smile spreading across Pyotr's face, like oil on water. His eyes are widening, and he looks positively beatific. 'God, I've missed the centre ground.'

Kristian takes a step away from him, aghast. 'You've no idea what this thing is,' he says, 'or how it'll react to medicine.' His face is ashen. 'That was fucking reckless, you know.'

Pyotr raises an eyebrow. 'I'm still here, aren't I?' He turns back to Lucy, gives a giddy little chuckle. 'Hey, how long does this stuff take to work?'

Lucy feels her stomach sink. 'I don't know,' she says. It occurs to her that she doesn't really know anything about the medication in her hand. She'd handed all the responsibility for that over to Cat, trusting the older woman knew what she was talking about.

'You don't know?' says Kristian. 'Don't you think that would have been a useful thing to figure out *before* he stuck it in his arm? Along with, like, a sense of how you'll know whether it's worked?'

He's right, and they both know it. She can feel the silence stretch out, horribly, into eternity. Finally, the weight of Kristian's fierce glare becomes impossible to bear. 'Like I said,' she says. 'You can buy this stuff over the counter. I'd be shocked if anything happens.'

But now Pyotr's smile is faltering, his brow furrowed. He presses a hand to his stomach. 'God,' he mutters. 'That can't be good.' Then suddenly, he's doubled over, letting out a sharp gasp.

'Pyotr?'

'Pyotr?' says Kristian, moving around in front of him and grabbing him by the shoulders. Still he doesn't look up. 'Is everything okay?'

'God, Kris.' Pyotr's on the ground now, curling in on himself. 'God, it hurts. Like something's… tearing.' He lets out another choked sound.

'Pyotr. Look at me.' Kristian puts a hand under Pyotr's head, lifts his chin with surprising gentleness. 'Talk to me.'

Pyotr's voice is a haunted thing, hollow and frightened. 'Something's wrong,' he says. He's shaking his head now, more animatedly than seems normal. 'Something's really, really wrong.'

Lucy speaks to calm herself as much as him. 'Okay. Okay. Is it just your stomach?'

'No, man,' says Pyotr, with a horrible, pained swallow. 'It's this place. Can't you feel it? This whole place? It's *fucked*.'

Kristian takes a deep breath. 'Let's get you inside,' he says, 'get you a drink.' He kneels down and drapes Pyotr's arm awkwardly over his shoulder. 'Get his other arm,' he says viciously, turning to Lucy. 'Whatever this is, it's on you. You get that, right?'

Lucy kneels too, and takes Pyotr's other arm. He's limp, without energy, surprisingly heavy despite his skinny frame.

God, this is bad. She needs to get Cat, to get Pyotr somewhere they can examine him without a dozen observers. But Kristian's already pushing open the door and manoeuvring Pyotr through into the mess hall. Bjorn is on them in moments.

His expression is grave. 'Something's wrong,' he says. It isn't a question.

She's surprised by how grateful she is to have him there. His certainty, his assurance. As though he can see things for what they are.

'Yes,' she says. 'Pyotr… he's…' But she stumbles, the words eluding her, the nature of this thing too slippery and elusive.

Bjorn speaks in a hushed whisper. 'What did he say?'

'He said it felt like something was… tearing,' says Lucy, the words catching in her throat. 'In his guts.' She hears a tremor in her voice.

Kristian's face is ashen. 'She's right,' he says. 'And he just slumped over. Like he couldn't bear it anymore.'

Bjorn's frown deepens. 'Someone had better get Cat,' he mutters, peering into Pyotr's eyes in what seems to Lucy like a rather perfunctory fashion. But a moment later, his eyes widen and he jumps back. 'Jesus. Jesus, what is that?'

Lucy can feel something now: a rapid, pulsating vibration, like a pneumatic drill, radiating from within Pyotr. Clearly Kristian feels it too. He leaps backwards, forgetting he's supposed to be holding Pyotr upright, but it no longer matters. Pyotr's gained some new strength, is supporting himself, despite his whole body shaking violently.

Kristian just has time to mutter 'What the fuck?' before

Pyotr's arm distorts into a great bulbous mass. It happens in slow motion, and her first thought is of the Hulk. But this is something altogether more disorderly: tendons form in real time, jagged spurs of bone break the skin as more and more limbs emerge from what was once Pyotr's shoulder. She feels like she's watching time-lapse footage of evolution, millennia of adaptation compressed into mere seconds. Pyotr's arm has doubled in size. He now sports a kind of huge, trailing claw, and his transformation shows no sign of stopping.

Pyotr screams, a terrible animal howl, and his face contorts in agony. His new limbs have a mind of their own. They sweep round with incredible speed, hurling Kristian against the wall of the mess hall. Lucy runs over to help, but something slams into her, knocking her to the ground. Her palms smack against the bare floorboards, but years of self-defence training kick in, and she pushes herself back to her feet. Pyotr's still hunched by the door, his body exploding outwards in a mass of bone and sinew.

She realises it was Bjorn who knocked her down. 'Leave him!' he yells. 'Get to shelter!' Pyotr's body is expanding now, muscles and tendons blooming, splitting skin and sending blood spraying across the floor in a delicate fan. Bones crack as the force of the expansion wrenches Pyotr's skeleton out of shape, and she smells iron and salt and shit.

She can't catch her breath. The air around her seems to be boiling. She can hear the floor timbers straining beneath the additional weight of the creature and she's conscious of a constant, roaring scream that she assumes comes from what's left of Pyotr, still alive inside that thing, now a raw mass of purple and browns, bruised flesh and yellowed skin and the slick pink of minced flesh. She glances over at Kristian, lying in a dazed heap on the floor; she sees the creature hauling its body across the room; she sees Bjorn running for the kitchen's open door with Rob close behind.

And then she makes a choice of which she's not proud. She follows him.

36

So, Rob thinks, *this is how I'm going to die.* His cheek pressed up against the steel of an industrial fridge, waiting to be torn apart.

Outside he can hear the beast. The shrieking and the banging, the banging and the shrieking. It's strong, that much is clear. Every time its blows collide with the walls they shake. He wonders, idly, how long they'll take to collapse, and whether being crushed is preferable to being dismembered. These cabins are well-built, ex-military, but even they won't survive this kind of battering for long.

He can't believe the creature's still standing. Surely it must be in agony, but the pain doesn't seem to stop it. Something keeps it conscious, keeps it thrashing about. Perhaps that's deliberate. A way of spreading itself further still.

He feels a sudden rush of hatred towards Lucy, who's crouched up against the kitchen island. She's caused this. Not all of this, true. But until she came back with that medication, Pyotr was just a gangling irritation, and not something that could tear out a man's spine without thinking.

The air's ripe with the stench of sweat and fear. He can see panic in people's faces: they're twitchy, directionless, in need of a leader. Not that Bjorn is much help on that front. He's sitting on the floor, legs out in front of him. Hand pressed up to his forehead, grimacing. Probably thinking of his slip box. Behind him on the wall are a set of knives stuck to a metal bar, but he doesn't even seem to have noticed.

And then, from nowhere, a memory: Bjorn, in the gloom of the vault, sitting at the next desk along from a teenaged Rob, telling him he'd never wanted to be a leader. Maybe he thought he did, once, but the years had taught him otherwise. All he really wanted was to be left alone with his books.

Well, that was hardly an option now.

Another fearsome blow, further down the wall. The creature's searching for a way in, seeking out flaws in the structure. It won't be long now.

And then a crash as the creature pounds on the metal shutters. Once, twice, three times. The shutters buckle and groan. The first blow twists them out of position, the second splinters the metal, warping it into jagged spurs. Then there's a sickening crunch as the creature punctures the shutters, and suddenly it's trying to haul itself through the gap it's made. Its mutated form is far too wide, and as it tries to clamber through Rob can see its weight drive the jagged metal deep into a muscle. It lets out a bellow of pain, and somewhere inside Rob feels the flicker of hope.

If it felt that, that meant it could be injured. Somehow. Perhaps pain might be enough to drive it away, however briefly. From the look of it, the same thought has crossed a few people's minds. *Strange how trauma can bring you together*, he imagines his therapist saying when he tells her about this. If he gets out of here, he's getting a new therapist.

Cat catches Elliot's eye. Staying as low as she can manage, she shuffles across the floor towards him. Rob flinches, expecting another roar from Pyotr. But it doesn't come. Maybe Cat's quiet enough, or maybe its sheer mass has enveloped its ears, its eyes.

'You think you can distract it?' he hears Cat whisper to Elliot. 'Open the door and throw something out there for it to chase?'

Elliot swallows hard. 'I guess so,' he says. 'You think it'll work?'

'Uh-huh,' says Cat, although she's not completely convincing. 'Whatever that thing is, it's not Pyotr anymore. It's like an animal. It's acting on instinct.'

Bjorn's jaw is set. 'That's Pyotr,' he hisses. 'It started off as him, and he's still in there. Somewhere. I'm certain of it.'

'What?' Elliot's expression is naked bewilderment. Rob can hardly blame him. This isn't really the moment to pick this fight. He sees Cat wince.

'I'm hypothesising, Bjorn,' she murmurs, but Bjorn shakes his head.

'Whatever did this to him, it's something we've never seen before. We don't understand it. Not at all. And we can't underestimate it.'

'Fine,' snarls Cat. 'So we chuck the spoon and see what happens. It's an experiment.'

'That's not an animal, Cat. Not at heart. It's Pyotr.'

His words hang in the air, and it takes Rob a moment to realise why. The blows have stopped. He knows they're thinking the same thing he is: they have to be. Has the mention of Pyotr's name brought him back to himself, surfaced some remnant of the man that was buried among all that bloodied flesh?

But then comes a sound like a thunderclap, an agonised roar that far eclipses anything that came before. Rob manoeuvres himself into a position where he can observe the creature through the hole in the shutters. He sees, to his amazement, that it's still expanding. There's yet more tumorous growths, more spurs of bone driving up against the skin where Pyotr's neck might once have been.

Amy and Elliot and Margaret and Danny are huddling close to each other now in the corner of the kitchen. Trying to make themselves as small as possible, hoping somehow to avoid its gaze. Rob can't hide his contempt at these men and women who have destroyed families, persuaded children to leave their parents, to hand over their life savings in pursuit of some hopeless dream. They've spent their lives here telling themselves they were courageous, but their story doesn't hold up, not when it really matters.

Come to think of it, nor did his. But it's hardly the time for that now, either.

Cat is watching him, her expression thoughtful. She nods towards the others, as though suggesting Rob joins them, and then shuffles across the tiles towards them. If Bjorn feels affronted at her wresting control of the group from him, he shows no sign of it: his head's bowed, his face still set in a grimace, an expression clearly meant to show he's deep in thought.

'Listen,' says Cat in a hushed whisper. 'That thing out there isn't going to stop, and I think we all know that. So we've got to do something. And I know you want to try and hide from it, but it's going to find us eventually.' She surveys people's expressions, but nobody says a word back to her. Not yet. They're waiting for the plan. 'I think we can take it down.' That gets a reaction, and not a positive one: Amy can't hide her terror, lets out a little squeak, her whole body starting to shake involuntarily. Elliot lays a trembling hand on her shoulder. Danny's head is between his knees, and he's hyperventilating.

'They're terrified, Cat,' says Rob, 'and you can hardly blame them. You're asking them to fight that thing off with kitchen equipment.' He turns to Bjorn. 'Surely you must have other weapons up here. Somewhere.'

Bjorn's appalled. He's reddening, stumbling over his words. 'After all this time – there's never been a hint of violence – and still that's what you think of us?'

'You're damn right I do. I haven't forgotten what it was like, even if you have.'

But then Cat cuts in. 'Enough,' she says forcefully. 'I have a gun.'

Bjorn's head flicks towards her, aghast. 'You do?'

'I do,' she says, looking him dead in the eye. 'I bought a shotgun. After the bad times.' She sighs. 'But that's in my room. So what we have now is… kitchen implements.' She looks round at the group's more terrified-looking members, trying without success to rein in her exasperation. 'Look, we can get my gun if you want, but that means somebody's going to have to go out there. Distract it.' She runs a hand over her jaw. 'You can either volunteer to do that, or start finding something sharp. It's your choice.'

There's something horribly methodical about the creature's blows now. They come at semi-regular intervals: a crash, the sound of pounding footsteps, and then another. It's testing for weaknesses. Cat's right: sooner or later it'll get through to them. It might be unwieldy, but there's a brain buried under all that flesh.

Cat is still watching Rob, her eyes wary. When she speaks, it's addressed to him. 'I don't know if we can beat that thing. I don't know if it can even be killed. But I'm certain that if it can be done, we stand the best chance of doing it together.'

'So we need something that can draw its attention,' he hears Lucy say. 'Something noisy.' He turns to find her holding up a large metal serving spoon, and his expression tells her all she needs to know. 'It's low-tech,' she says, with a hint of defensiveness. 'Low-tech is good. It's reliable. Predictable.'

He wants to shout *No*: to tell her she can't do this, that it's madness, that he can't let her throw her life away like this. But he can't do that, because then they'll look to him for a solution, and what does he have to offer in return? *Let's stay in here until it breaks open that hatch and tears us apart.* The words of a coward.

Cat blinks hard, twice, a little stunned. 'Okay,' she says, looking through Lucy. 'Okay, that could work. But we need more than just noise. We need to give it a reason to chase you.'

She glances round at the various implements within arm's reach. 'Grab a knife, or a blowtorch… anything that can do it some damage. If you can hurt it, even just slightly, then you might be able to draw its focus long enough for us to get to the cabin.'

Lucy swallows. Rob can see her trying to squash down her panic. *Still, at least it'll be quick,* he catches himself thinking. *Maybe it's better than becoming one of them.* He wants to vomit. In a desperate attempt to feel like he's doing something – anything – to be reassuring, he reaches out and lays a hand on her shoulder. As he does, the creature makes another fumbling attempt to open the door. Handle rattling, doorframe shaking. Somehow it's still standing, although surely the hinges can't hold much longer.

'What about the rest of you?' Lucy asks, looking round the room. 'What will you be doing while I'm out there being bait?'

Cat's smile is grim. 'We'll be getting ready,' she says. 'Gathering whatever weapons we can. Waiting for the best moment to strike.' She turns to the others, surveying their terrified faces. 'What the hell are you waiting for?' she says. 'There's everything you could need in here. Knives, skillets, blowtorches, gas canisters. Hurry the fuck up and arm yourself.'

Elliot, Amy and the others haul themselves upright, their fear giving way to grim determination as they realise this is the only way they're getting out of here. Elliot reaches for a chef's knife, fingers flexing as he tests the weight of it in his hand. Amy's knuckles whiten as she grabs a cast iron skillet. Even Beatrice – sweet, gentle Beatrice – is now standing with a meat tenderiser in hand.

Only Bjorn is still scowling. 'You're treating it like it's stupid!' he hisses. 'It's not blind. You've no evidence of that. Why should it be distracted by noise?'

For a moment Cat pauses, glancing over at Bjorn and holding his eye for a moment. But then her brow furrows, and she breaks eye contact, turning on him. She's in his face in seconds, towering over him. 'Do you think *this* is helping?' she says. 'Do you? Do you think sitting here and *talking out* our approach is going to stop that thing tearing us to bits?' She throws up a hand in exasperation. 'I don't like this any more than you, Bjorn, but if we can't improvise then we're fucked.'

'But you're not thinking, Cat. You're not.'

'And what the fuck does it matter to you?'

'Because I don't want you to die!' This time Bjorn forgets to keep his voice down: his raised voice brings on another flurry of blows from outside the kitchen. When he speaks again he's quieter, unable to meet Cat's eye. 'That thing's furious,' he says. 'If you go out there now, you won't stand a chance. We need to back off, let it calm down.'

It seems like an eternity before Cat speaks up again.

'If we wait, we die.' She shrugs her shoulders. 'Simple as that.' She glances over to Lucy. 'You sure you're ready for this?'

'Not at all,' mutters Lucy.

'I'm begging you to stop,' says Bjorn. 'Think about this just a moment longer.'

Cat ignores him. 'Try and lead it outside,' she says to Lucy. 'It's more dangerous in a confined space. Out there, on the open ground, you can escape it. Allow us some time to get in position.'

'Right,' says Lucy, swallowing hard. 'Okay.' She holds the spoon up in her hand, looks at it as though realising for the first time how inadequate it is as a weapon. 'You think I ought to take anything else with me?'

Rob can't believe how useless he feels, how passive. He grabs the fire extinguisher from the wall and hands it to her. 'Try this,' he says, and when she looks at him quizzically, 'pretty distracting, right?'

'That might actually work,' says Cat, sticking out her lip and surveying Rob with something that doesn't look entirely like contempt. 'You think you can run with that thing?'

'I can try,' says Lucy.

God, this is awful. He knows he should offer to go with her, offer himself as a second sacrificial lamb, but he can't bring himself to say the words. All these years he'd focussed on staying alive. He can't just throw it away now. Not here. Not now. He can see in Lucy's face that she knows it all already. She doesn't even have it in her to look disappointed.

Danny and Amy are armed with the most vicious chef's knives they can find. Elliot's stuffing a rag into a bottle of vodka to make a rudimentary Molotov, and Margaret's grabbed a kitchen blowtorch. What they lack in range, they make up for in power.

Cat motions towards the door. 'I'll open it,' she murmurs. 'And then you fling that thing in one direction and run as fast as you can in the other.'

'Got it,' says Lucy, her hand tightening on the handle. And then she's up against the doorframe, Cat turning the lock, and there's a rush of cold air and the *thunk* of the metal spoon on the parquet floor and then Lucy's sprinting out into the mess hall.

There's a momentary pause, and then something — flesh, bone? — scraping against the ground as the creature turns towards the sound. Perhaps Rob imagines it, but it almost feels like the creature's reaction has a trace of disdain.

You thought I'd be fooled by this?

And then there's an explosion of noise and it's hurling itself after her, dragging its lumbering bulk across the room. It's a mass of twisted flesh, graceless and uneven, but animated by some power that gives it an unexpected speed.

It's faster than Lucy. Rob can see that right away. It's going to reach her before she reaches the door. He imagines it pinning her against the wall, squashing her like a bug. He imagines her wrenched from the ground by an arm with the strength of ten men, and thrown like a ragdoll across the room, shattering her skull and spine.

'Lucy!' he yells, and in one fluid movement she turns with the extinguisher and discharges it into what looks most like the creature's face. Covered in thick white foam, it takes a step back, staggers. It moves uncooperative limbs across itself, trying and failing to brush itself clean. It's gasping, wheezing. Overwhelmed by the sensation.

Then it starts flailing, tables are swept out of the way by its massive arm, limbs crash against the wall, shattering plasterboard and leaving deep grooves. Lucy dives out to one side as it comes for her, wrenching open the door, but the creature retains enough awareness to feel the fresh air and charge in its direction.

Splinter of doorframe, creaking of timbers. This place is well-built, but it's not invincible. How long before the ceiling falls on them? No, that doesn't bear thinking about. Not now.

From somewhere far away he hears a voice. Can't make out the words, just a muffled shouting. A hand on his shoulder, shaking him. Hard. He turns to see Cat, a huge knife in her hand.

'What the fuck are you waiting for?' she yells. 'Go and help her!'

37

COOL AIR on her face, damp earth beneath her feet. Freedom. Surely she can outpace it on the open ground. She's nimble, agile. Yes, that thing is huge. She felt that when it came for her. The weight of it, the force. If it had landed a blow she'd have been flattened. But it didn't happen. She's still standing. A little bit shaky, her heart pounding in her chest, but very much still alive. For now, at least.

She can make out the cabins ahead of her. Tries to remember what Rob told her when they arrived, which one was Bjorn's, which had been his. Tries to visualise the map Cat had sketched in mid-air in the kitchen.

She crosses her fingers and prays she's right. Ahead of her she sees lighted windows in the darkness, a fairy-tale silhouette. It can't be more than a hundred metres away. Is the thing behind her? Surely not. She'd hear it. Thudding footsteps, wheezing breaths. All the same she glances over her shoulder. It's still inside. Sounds of commotion from the mess hall. Yelling, screaming.

She can't think about that now. She has to stay on track.

And then, from nowhere, the muffled *thud* of an explosion, the force of the air at her back, and when she turns there is a hole in the wall of the mess hall, outlined in flames, and the creature is charging through it into the open air.

Shit.

She's sprints for the cabin, hoping against hope that she can find the gun before the creature reaches her. She can feel it behind her now, pounding towards her, shaking the earth, hears that snarling wheeze in each breath, something terribly human about it. The asthmatic inhale, gasps that might once have been words.

She's almost at the door when it lunges towards her with a guttural roar. She dives into the room and slams the door behind her. The thing collides with the outside wall and collapses. There's a scrabbling of limbs, the sound of something heavy hauling itself upright, and then it charges at the doorframe again. A creaking of timbers, glass shattering.

Again and again it raises up. Charges. Falls to the ground. Begins again.

There's something kind of tragic about the repetition of it. As though condemned to play out the same human actions over and over by some animal compulsion. And something beautiful, almost, in its tenacity. The determination, the single-minded pursuit of a goal.

She shakes herself alert. What's she doing? The others bought her time. Not much, but enough. It's crazy to waste it. She has to get the gun.

The room is small and highly organised. Cat's bed is tucked in the corner, mattress on a simple metal frame. Covers neatly folded, tight hospital corners. Of course. Set of cheap plastic storage boxes underneath. Lucy hurls herself across the room, lies on the floor, wrenches the boxes out. It feels like a transgression, to ruin Cat's carefully constructed order, but they can worry about that later. Behind the boxes, pressed up against the wall, sits a shotgun and a box of cartridges. Her fingers close around metal... and then the door disintegrates, a spray of wood across the floorboards, and the creature stumbles through into the tiny space. She flips herself over. Fumbles for the safety catch, flicks it off. The creature is halfway across the room now, its speed incredible, one arm upraised and preparing to slam down upon her, and she looses a blast without aiming. Hits it in the shoulder, the upper arm, knocking it briefly off balance, just enough to get to her feet. And then she's running past it, down the steps, out into the night.

She can see the others hurrying towards her, and they're shouting something – but their voices are lost in the distance, overcome by terror and adrenaline. Behind her, the sound of the thing's pounding footsteps, impossibly fast, growing closer and closer.

She spins around and it's there, right behind her, and she mutters a prayer to a god she's never much believed in and pulls the trigger once more. It's a good shot, better than she could ever have managed if she'd been trying. Right into the closest thing the creature has to a face. The blast echoes across the site, the ringing in her ears deafening.

The creature stops then, and lets out a series of pained grunts. It hunches over, its body twisting and contorting, and for a moment Lucy wonders if it's about to burst, or else overbalance altogether like Reynaud, defeated by its own biology.

Instead, with a tearing sound from its shoulder, the creature sprouts what looks like another arm. And then another, and still more, entwined with one another, all stuck together in a grotesque chain. A half-dozen and counting now. And its abdomen is shifting, splitting in two, apparently growing more legs, and it moves again, coming at her incredibly fast…

She backs up, but nowhere near quickly enough. The creature scuttles towards her on those impossibly bent legs, and she can see in its face something that looks unmistakably like recognition, and not just recognition but *malice*. It sees her, it knows her for its enemy, and now its fingers are digging through her flesh with incredible strength and it's scooping her up like she's weightless…

Then the world's spinning around her and she's flying through the air. There's a faint breeze, and a bonfire smell on the air that feels weirdly nostalgic, and for an instant she thinks of that as a kindness. She's always loved that smell, and so she's going to die happy. Who cares if it's an olfactory hallucination: it hardly matters now anyway.

That's when she collides with the ground. The impact is brutal, knocking the wind out of her lungs. She skids across gravel and collides with a rock, feels her right shoulder crack. The pain of that takes a moment to register, although she hears the *snap* right away.

Half of her face feels scraped raw: one eye can only squint. She lays there on her side, the world woozy and unreal, her main thought being, *This really stings*. It takes a second or so before that pain is blasted away by the deeper pain, the kind that tells her she's broken inside. An 'all systems red, critical hull malfunction' kind of situation.

She tries to look around to see where the others are, if help is coming, but moving her head even slightly causes her such pain that she can hardly breathe.

She can't think like that. She has to get up. But her hands won't co-operate, her whole body's in shock, and now she can see the creature again. It's silhouetted in the light from the mess hall, fighting off the others with ease. Its strange new grace, the sweep of its many arms atop its split torso.

It's learning, she thinks to herself. *It's learned from its mistakes*. Then it's coming towards her again, scuttling on its many limbs, speeding up as it approaches.

She forces herself to keep her eyes open, to face her own death with courage, but although the thing charges in her direction, and although she sees its eyes rest briefly upon her, this time it doesn't come for her. Instead, it veers away as though it's done with her, and scuttles past and into the darkness beyond the camp.

She lays her head on the dirt, closes her eyes, and waits for oblivion.

38

Later, when he tries to reconstruct its shape, its sprouting limbs and scuttling gait, it will seem so impossible his brain will refuse to hold the image. It'll slip away from him, leaving his mind a flat blank. None of it will make any sense to him: not how it existed, nor how it moved, nor how it hijacked the internal mechanisms of Pyotr's body.

But Lucy lying, shattered, on the ground? That he'll remember. That he'll remember until the day he dies.

When it's done with Lucy, when it has hurled her across the site like a ragdoll, it stands by the gate on those spindly legs, watching for their reaction. Wondering, perhaps, what they'll do next. None of them dare approach it: most of them can hardly bear to look at it. The skin stretched tautly over its distorted limbs, splitting in places to reveal glistening musculature. The warped grimace of a face they used to know, still discernible beneath it all.

Is it… God, is it trembling? Is it scared? Rob almost thinks it is. There's something human about it, even after all it's done to Pyotr's body. Surely the others must be able to see that.

'The fuck is it doing?' growls Kristian. 'What's it waiting for?'

'It's watching us,' says Amy. 'Trying to figure out what we'll do next.'

'Then we need to surprise it. Show it that it can't pin all of us down.' Kristian glances around, looking for allies. 'Who's with me?'

If Kristian is expecting an immediate show of support, he doesn't get one. A couple of half-hearted nods from Miranda and Adam, but Cat is the first to speak up. 'Look at it,' she says to Kristian. 'Just look.'

Kristian stares at her instead. 'I don't want to spend another second looking at what it's done to Pyotr,' he says. 'I've seen enough.'

'Look at it, for fuck's sake.' Cat's voice is authoritative, her face hard. 'If it wanted to come for the rest of us, it could have done it by now.'

'It's learning,' Kristian says, through gritted teeth. 'The longer we wait, the more it knows. We need to surprise it, split up, scatter. If we can surround it…'

'You can't seriously be considering fighting that thing,' Elliot says. 'After what it did to Lucy.'

Rob doesn't want to look at Lucy's shattered body any more than he does the creature, but he can at least do it without stifling his gag reflex. She's unconscious, sprawled out on a patch of ground where the camp gives way to the woods. Face down, her arm bent at an awkward angle, but still breathing... For now.

'We've got to get to her,' Rob says. 'We can't just leave her out there.'

'She's not our priority,' Kristian says curtly. 'We need to focus on killing that thing.'

'You really think we can take it down, Kristian?' says Cat. There's something caustic to her tone, a disdain that feels long-standing.

Kristian actually thinks for a second, although Cat's was clearly a rhetorical question. 'I do,' he says. 'You saw how it reacted to the fire extinguisher. A couple of us could distract it while somebody tries to get a blade into its head.'

'And if it grows another set of arms?' snaps Cat. 'It'll go through us in seconds, and then we lose our advantage. Assuming you can even bring yourself to touch it.'

'What are you proposing, then?' says Kristian, rounding on her. 'We can hardly just leave it there, watching us, can we?'

It's clear Kristian isn't expecting the thoughtful silence that follows this question.

'Oh, no. No. No, no, no.' He looks round each of them in turn. 'We are not doing that, you hear? That thing is wearing Pyotr like a skin.'

'Maybe Bjorn's right,' says Cat, a little tentatively. 'Maybe's he's still in there. Some part of him. Maybe we could reach him.'

'Fuck that,' says Kristian, with a strangulated half-yell. 'That's not him, you hear? It's not. I won't let you say that.'

'You won't *let* me?' says Cat, incredulous. 'Bjorn, are you hearing this?'

Bjorn has his fingers to his forehead, his expression pained. 'You are better than this,' he murmurs. 'You were supposed to be better than this.' He looks up, glowering, at both Cat and Kristian. 'Enough bickering. Somebody needs to show some courage here.' He looks first to Cat, who glowers back at him, then to Kristian, and then to the rest. Finally his gaze rests on Rob, lingering a little longer than it did on the rest, something interrogatory in Bjorn's eyes. 'Who among you will be bold enough to take that first step? To go to her?' He raises his eyebrows, looks from one side of the group to the other. Rob follows his gaze. A sea of faces: angry, tired, scared. 'What are you made of?'

He hears himself say it before he has to think again. 'I'll do it,' he says. 'I can't just leave her out there.' He can't tell how much of the gesture comes from wanting to show the rest of them up. It's more than he'd like.

Bjorn nods grimly. 'Good,' he says.

The creature is still standing on those spindly, distorted legs, swaying slightly. Pyotr's eye is fixed on Rob, watching as he moves. He doesn't like meeting that gaze. There's some kind of strange intelligence behind it he doesn't understand.

Instead, he fixes his eyes on Lucy, glancing over only sporadically at Pyotr — or the creature that used to be Pyotr. To one side he can hear Kristian muttering that this is a bloody stupid idea, and Amy trying to steady her breathing. He tries to ground himself, like he was taught. To feel the earth beneath, the air entering and leaving his lungs, the cool breeze. Underneath it all, the smell of blood, and sweat, and terror.

He takes a first step towards Lucy and braces for the reaction. Imagines the creature hurtling towards him like some kind of stop-frame nightmare. Herky-jerky movement, insectile motions.

Nothing happens. The creature doesn't move. He thinks he hears someone say something behind him, but he's not sure what. All he can hear is his own breathing, the blood pounding in his ears. He takes another step, his eyes still fixed on Lucy. Dares to glance up at the creature – but it still hasn't moved. It seems almost weary, tired from the exertion of the attack. He knows it's unwise to humanise it, especially after what it did to Lucy. And yet he can't help himself. Not so long ago it was a man. Some vestiges of that man must still remain.

Another step, and then another. Still nothing. He considers picking up his pace but stops himself mid-thought. Doesn't want to seem like a threat. It occurs to him that he's no idea how he'll get Lucy back to the others. It's only about ten metres, but it might as well be a mile. He'd call someone to help were it not for fear of antagonising the creature.

No. Slow and cautious, that's the way. His route won't take him especially close to the creature – within a few metres – but he's acutely aware of its reach. Up close he can see the layers upon layers of muscle built out along its shoulder and left arm. An observation that brings with it an involuntary image of those arms wrapping around his neck, or snapping his spine.

Before he knows it, he's next to Lucy, bending down to listen for breath sounds. She's unconscious, but still breathing, thank

God. Her face bloodied, a great rip through her coat where Pyotr hurled her across the camp. He tries to get his arms underneath her and immediately thinks better of it. She's not that heavy, but he's by no means strong enough either. He stares down at her for a moment, overwhelmed by dreadful possibilities and barely able to form a thought. Could he sling her over his shoulder? Drag her along the ground? At least it's mostly soft.

Then, to his surprise, he finds someone else at his side: Bjorn. He kneels down at Lucy's feet, not even looking at Pyotr. 'You take her arms,' he says to Rob, 'I'll get her legs.' His voice is gentle, unscared, and in that moment Rob's extremely grateful he's there.

The two of them pick Lucy up and carry her across the site. Rob can feel the creature's gaze boring into his back the whole way. He keeps his steps measured and cautious, wondering when it's going to change its mind.

And then, somehow, he's back with the others. He glances at Bjorn, who nods, and the two of them gently set her down. Cat and Kristian huddle around her as though to shield her from view, and the others quickly join them, forming a protective circle.

The whole time, the creature stays in place, watching them. There's an unsettling intelligence behind those eyes, some trace of Pyotr's humanity that no mutation could erase.

All of this is his fault. He's the reason Lucy came here. He doesn't know the exact scale of her injuries yet – he's still yelling at them to help her, to get her to safety – but he saw how hard she hit the ground. It must be bad.

MARGINAL

He brought her here. He let her convince him it was a good idea. All he'd really wanted was for this to be over: to say a proper goodbye to Marcus, and to grieve for the life his brother could have had. Now Bjorn's taken somebody else from him.

Elliot slides a sheet beneath Lucy's body, then lifts her onto a stretcher. It occurs to Rob that this might be the first time he's ever seen her looking so passive. It's so unlike her that he can barely process it. It's like they're lifting up a doll, a mannequin. Then her head lolls to the side and he sees her lacerated face, the blood at her temple, and he feels suddenly, violently unwell...

Cat directs them, muttering something about keeping Lucy flat, handling her gently, the kind of generic medical truisms that she could have pieced together from an episode of *ER*. She's not qualified for this, none of them are, and she must know it as well as Rob. They need an ambulance, proper medical help, and none is coming. That's on him too: he should have known this might happen, that one of them could get hurt and they'd not even be able to call for help.

'We need to get her out of here,' he hears himself say. 'Get her to a hospital.'

'Absolutely not,' says Cat. 'Not until we know how this thing spreads.'

'She needs some proper treatment, Cat. Otherwise her death is on us.'

Cat wheels on him. 'She's not going to die,' she snarls. 'I won't let her.'

'It's a bit late for that, isn't it?'

'Not at all,' Cat mutters. 'Not if I have anything to do with it.'

'How many people have to die here before you realise you can't go it alone?'

Cat's shaking her head. 'Right now, the main thing stopping me helping your friend is you,' she says. 'I won't waste time fighting this battle again, Rob. Now get the fuck out of my way or her blood's going to be on *your* hands.' She turns and stares Rob down, leaving him in no doubt she's won this battle. 'If you really want to help her, we're your best shot.'

She's right, and he knows it. He can see the bloom of Lucy's blood on the stretcher, the pallor of her skin. Pick your battles, his therapist would have told him if she were here. Remember who the real enemy is.

He does what he's told: takes one end of the stretcher and starts to carry Lucy to the infirmary. There'll be plenty of time for introspection later.

And yet, amid all the chaos, he sees something he can't explain: Bjorn peels away from the crowd and sneaks over to where Pyotr's standing; sees Bjorn lean in close to the creature and whisper something in his ear.

He needs to keep his hands on the stretcher, can't make out a single word Bjorn is saying, but all the same he's struck by the sight of the old man next to this great, hulking creature. Because there's no violence in Pyotr, not now: he seems almost peaceful.

39

Rob joins the rest of the Scriveners in the mess hall just after midnight. His eyes feel gritty and his head is spinning from tiredness. Cat and the others have set up a rudimentary barricade in front of one set of the doors: overturned tables, stacked chairs and logs. Kristian stands guard next to the other.

Rob's not sure how effectively their barricade could withstand the creature, but it seems to have lost all interest in attacking them, for now anyway. He can see it watching them through the open door, swaying slightly, but that's all it's doing.

All of which means, when Bjorn stands up on a table and begins to speak, he doesn't command his usual level of attention. They're thinking about Lucy, lying in the infirmary; they're thinking about Marcus, and how he exploded; they're thinking about whether they're going to last the night.

'Friends,' he says. 'You've heard the words of the Spirit: you know what has been asked of us. To trust in a greater plan; to trust that all this will bring about a better world.' He looks around at the grimy and battered faces and – Rob thinks – surely he must see they've lost faith. There's no way back, not now. But he's still talking. 'There are those among us who have grieved the Spirit. Those who thought to take matters into their own hands. And now we are reaping the consequences of that decision.'

He looks over at Cat, his eyes fierce. 'Cat,' he says, putting his hands together, 'I... I understand. I know, truly, that what's been asked of you is a terrible thing. But perhaps all of this has worked out for good: you can see now, each of you, the consequences of defiance. Can see what happens when we lose faith.'

He shakes his head. 'I thought we were ready for this—' he says, but Cat cuts him off.

'Help me understand, Bjorn,' she says, her voice hard. It's a challenge, not a plea. 'I don't see it. The beauty, the glory. All I see is a monstrosity.' There's a catch in her voice, and Rob realises she's on the edge of tears. 'So help me. I'm asking you sincerely. What am I supposed to see?'

Bjorn dabs at his eyes too. His expression seems to be one of utmost relief. 'Thank you, Cat,' he says. 'Thank you.' He swallows hard, sniffs. 'Think of who you each were when you came here,' he continues. 'Think of the love you had for knowledge, your belief that it could bring about a better world. That's why we're here, isn't it? That's why all of us are here.'

To Rob's surprise, they are nodding. They are smiling. Not all of them – Kristian still looks positively mutinous – but somehow, they're thawing. He looks over at the infirmary and he wants to scream.

'I know what this thing wants,' Bjorn says. 'It wants to learn, to share in your learning. That's all it's ever wanted. Just like you or I.' He shrugs. 'And so that's what it does. It sits there, quietly, inside of you, and it watches.' He pauses for emphasis, and then gives Cat a steely glare. 'Until we threaten it,' he says. 'That's when it takes everything it knows about us, and it tries to defend itself. Every mutation is a testament to how much it's learned about us. That's what happened with Reynaud, and with Pyotr, and... well, you know, Marcus. Marcus saw threats everywhere.' He gives a low chuckle, as though he's giving a homily. 'All that pressure he put on himself. I think in his case it reacted to that.'

He puts a hand to his forehead. 'Whatever this thing is, it's a pragmatist. It can use whatever it's learned, at least from what I've seen.' He seems suddenly sorrowful. 'But all this talk about fighting it is so... pointless. I'm convinced it doesn't have to be a threat to us. For all we know, it's what's given us our power for all these years.'

'I've said my piece,' he says. 'I don't expect you to agree.'

'You're goddamn right,' says Kristian, shaking his head. 'You're out of your fucking mind, man. I've humoured you enough, but I'm out of here, you understand?' He looks around. 'Who's coming with me?'

Bjorn bites his tongue, calms his breathing. Keeps his gaze level. 'Then we have to call the authorities,' he says, not just to Kristian but to the room, knowing exactly the reaction this will get. 'We've no other option.' He's not disappointed. To call it an uproar would be an understatement. They seem to all be yelling at him at once, and although Rob can't make out their words, he knows what they're saying. Bjorn's betraying them. He's lost his mind, forgotten everything he once held dear.

But then the door to the medical room creaks open, and from it emerges Lucy. Bandages across her arms, her chest, her head – more than one of them soaked with blood. She looks like she's been through a war, the kind of figure you'd see on the pages of *Time* magazine. She looks directly at Rob, speaking through cracked lips, her voice a pained thing.

'Bjorn's right,' Lucy croaks, nodding towards the darkness where Pyotr stands. 'It doesn't want a fight. We're the ones that are forcing its hand.'

Bjorn's triumph lasts approximately ten seconds, and then Lucy inhales and begins to cough into her fist: a harsh, hacking cough that goes on, and on, and on. When she's finally finished, her hand is covered in blood, and the whole atmosphere has changed. Elliot's kitchen team are on their feet, backing off towards the wall; Adam is still seated, his hand trembling atop a knife.

Miranda looks Bjorn dead in the eye and asks the question on everyone's mind. 'How do we know she's not going to end up like Pyotr?'

And then it's like something breaks, and all of a sudden everyone is shouting again.

40

When Lucy starts coughing, Rob knows he's in trouble. Both of them are, actually. There's a kernel of anger inside him that he doesn't much like. He swore he wouldn't do anything that left him at Bjorn's mercy, but then he let himself be talked into bringing Lucy along for the ride. Now look at the mess she's got him into.

Then comes a wave of compassion, and then panic. He wants to run to Lucy, to protect her. He wants to stand between her and the crowd, stop them from doing something reckless. But he also knows what will happen if he does.

He sees the look in her eyes, the mingled terror and defiance, and he opts for pragmatism. He moves across the room, conscious of everyone's eyes on him, and musters his loudest speaking voice.

He can see Adam fingering his knife; he can see the violence in Miranda's eyes. 'Stay away from her,' Rob says, straining to sound ferocious. 'You don't know if she's infected. Maybe she is. But if so, it's in your best interest to stay back, you hear?'

That seems to land. He senses a momentary reprieve, an opportunity to be seized. 'You're jumping to conclusions,' he says, a little less ferociously. That's the wrong thing to say. It triggers another wave of recriminations: now Kristian is shouting at him, Elliot, Ken. He looks over to Bjorn, unwisely expecting an ally, but Bjorn looks thoughtful.

'You know what we have to do,' he says. He pats the satchel at his side. Kristian audibly groans. Bjorn's gaze snaps up, meeting Kristian's defiance head on. 'You know I'm right.'

Cat has her head in her hands, and she's not the only one. But still Bjorn presses on. Opens the box, riffles through the cards, removes one and reads it aloud:

> 20160914/J: 'He who lets the world, or his own portion of it, choose his plan of life for him has no need for any other faculty than the apelike one of imitation.'
> A warning against haste, and against being unduly swayed by the crowd. We strive for higher things; how easily we are dragged back down to earth.

Bjorn's voice is hushed, almost awestruck. 'It works,' he says. 'You know it works.' He shakes his head. 'We're being too hasty, and you know it.'

'*No*, Bjorn.' Kristian is on his feet again. 'I'm done with this. I'm done, you hear? I can't live like this anymore. That's not even what that text means.'

'Kristian, sit down,' growls Bjorn. 'You're humiliating yourself.'

MARGINAL

'No!' Kristian says again. 'No, Bjorn. We are not doing this. We are going to have a rational conversation, like rational adults. We are beyond the System now.'

'We are never beyond the System!'

But Cat is on her feet as well, and Amy, and Margaret. 'He's right,' says Margaret. Her voice is quiet, but when she speaks there's a tangible expectation: *This is something worth considering.* 'You said it yourself, we know barely anything about this creature, or how it spreads. Until we know more, we owe it to ourselves – and to everyone else down the hill – to shut her away.'

It takes him a second or two to register what Margaret's said, and when it lands Rob feels a sinking feeling in his gut. 'You're talking about locking her up.'

'Yes. I am.'

'You said you weren't like this.' He feels like a small boy again.

She doesn't even look at him. 'There's a good reason, Rob.'

'There's always a good reason – that's how it starts – do you think I don't remember the reasons you lot gave my mum? Or Marcus?'

He waits for Margaret to answer, but Margaret says nothing. She's waiting for the room to digest this, to give him their tacit approval. It'll come, Rob can see that: they're halfway there already. He turns to look at Lucy, standing in the doorway of the medical room. She looks pale and exhausted, on the verge of collapse.

'No,' he says, desperate to stop this however he can. 'No, you can't do this.'

And then Margaret says something he doesn't expect. 'Do you want to go with her?'

In that moment, everything inside Rob screams. For years he's suffered panicked dreams in which he stumbles into a wood and finds himself entangled by thorns. Thrashing in the darkness, straining for an escape that never comes. His limbs constrained, the anxiety like drowning. He'd lie in bed, pinned mutely to the mattress with his eyes wide open, while elongated figures made from polished black marble stood watch over him in the reaches of the night. His therapist unpicked every one of those sensations, but she couldn't vanquish them, and now he knows why.

They weren't fears. They were prophesies. This was always how it was going to end. He was fated to die here, in this place. He thought he'd escaped: he was wrong.

Once more he looks at Lucy and imagines her locked away in one of these huts or left to die on the mountains. Shivering, starving, alone. He's seen the way they're looking at her. There's no compassion left in some of them. Only a blind and terrified desire to survive, whatever that takes. Maybe he could let them exile her, lock her away to die in grim isolation, but he couldn't live with himself if he did. Every night when he lay down to sleep he'd imagine himself in her position.

'I can't let her die alone,' he says helplessly, feeling his shoulders slump.

Bjorn gives him a tiny, respectful nod. 'And you've considered this decision?' Rob can see the flicker of doubt behind Bjorn's eyes. Even now Bjorn thinks he's reckless, impulsive, thinks Rob hasn't counted the cost. But fuck Bjorn. For all his studying, he hadn't seen any of this coming.

'It's the right thing to do,' he says. 'If you knew her better, you'd know that.'

From somewhere behind him comes Cat's voice. It's firm and commanding. Without remorse, although not without emotion. 'We should send them to the Pit.'

41

He's not sure whether Cat intends it to be so cruel. Perhaps she doesn't realise the scars that place inflicted. All the same, when he hears the name, he's that sixteen-year-old boy again, running for his life.

He can't do this. He just can't. He hears Marcus's words from that last night as clearly as though his brother were standing next to him. *Don't think I didn't see it in you, you worthless twat. The cowardice. The laziness. I lived with it every fucking night.*

And then he looks back at Lucy. Her face scraped raw, her arm in a sling. He thinks of his mother, living out her last days in darkness, all because of him. If he runs away now, he'll spend the rest of his life hearing Marcus's words, and Bjorn will have won. He can't do that. He won't.

'Do whatever you need to do to stop this thing,' he hears himself say.

He can see them splintering already. When the meeting's over, everyone ducks back into their huddles, the few people they know they can trust. He's left alone at his table, tainted by association with Lucy, until finally Cat sets herself down opposite him.

She's quiet for a moment, tense, as though waiting for him to tell her to piss off. When he doesn't, she seems to relax slightly, settles back into her seat. He thinks she probably wants to talk logistics, and right now the thought of it is unimaginable.

But she doesn't, not right away. Instead, she reaches over to him, puts a hand on his arm and says, 'You're a good man. You don't have to believe me when I say that, but I mean it.'

His head is in his hands, wondering what he's done. Imagining the walls closing in on him, the sound of his own voice playing endlessly in the dark. 'Don't,' he says. 'Please don't. I'd rather not think about it until I have to.'

'Sure.' Cat sits back in her chair again, allows him his silence. He starts to hate it after less than thirty seconds. His thoughts warp, twist, mutate into dreadful shapes.

'So how are we going to do this?' he asks her without looking up.

'What do you mean?'

'I mean, do we get food and supplies? Will you check on us?'

'We can knock on the door every morning,' says Cat with a shrug. 'You can knock back.' The unspoken words hang in the air: *for as long as you're still alive.*

'If Lucy dies…'

'You want to know if we'll let you out again?'

'Yeah.'

'I guess that depends on how things turn out in the next few days,' says Cat with a shrug. 'Whether we can keep this from the authorities. But I'd like to. We're not monsters.'

'No. You're just locking me away in a windowless cell.'

'For which you volunteered,' says Cat sharply. He probably deserved that.

'Sure. But, I mean, my options were pretty limited.'

Cat studies his face. 'You're a good man,' she says again. 'I know you'd rather I didn't say that. But I didn't really believe you had it in you.'

'Thanks,' he says. It's a backhanded compliment, but it's still a compliment. 'You didn't need to say that.'

'I'm sorry it all got so fucked up.'

'It's not your fault.'

She knows what he's saying. 'It's not Bjorn's either. Not really.'

'I guess.'

She's right, and he does know it. Bjorn didn't cause this madness, although God knows he's not helped it.

'You're worried about him too, though, aren't you?' he says. 'How he's reacted to all of this.'

'Course I am,' says Cat. 'But I've got it in hand. Trust me.' That word again: *Trust*. It hangs in the air between them like a bad smell. 'Let me go and get you some supplies,' she says after a moment. 'Enough to last you a week.'

'You think Lucy will last that long?'

'She's strong, Rob. You never know.'

'I hope you're right,' he says. He's tried not to think about what happens if she transforms when they're crammed together in that tiny space. Most likely he'll be crushed to death. It's a nasty death.

Cat's silent. He wonders if she's thinking the same thing, imagining another dead body on the infirmary table. And then she says something he's not expecting. 'I wish we had more time.'

'What would you do if we did?'

She takes a deep breath, like she's steeling herself for what she has to say. 'I helped bury your mother, Rob,' she says. 'After what happened.'

His mouth is dry, his heart pounding. He feels an incredible sense of relief, as though some part of him can finally untense – and yet somewhere, in the back of his mind, he feels rage breaking on the shore in swelling waves. 'Where?' he manages to croak.

'We buried her in a quiet spot in the woods,' Cat says softly. 'I'd show you if I could. She deserved some peace, after what she went through.'

'After what you put her through.'

'Yeah,' says Cat, her voice grim. She heaves a sigh. 'God, I'm sorry, Rob. She was in the Pit so long. I guess she wanted to give you the best possible chance to get away.'

'Why didn't you tell me?'

She looks at him with hollow eyes. 'You know why,' she says. 'How could you look at something like that – really, properly look – and still believe you were part of something good?' Her head is bowed, her voice low. 'So we chose to look away. Or at least I did.'

There's so much more he wants to ask, so much more he wants to know, but it's too late now. He can see the others eyeing them up from across the room, wondering if they're hatching a plan to spirit Lucy away from here.

'I'm glad you told me,' Rob says, although even he can't tell whether he means it. He wishes Lucy was sat here with them, wishes she had this whole thing on tape, but she's sitting alone at a table with her head in her hands. He needs to go to her, and soon. Any second now she's going to freak out, and that won't be good news for anyone.

'So am I,' says Cat. 'I'm really sorry.'

He makes his way over to her table. He can feel the others watching him as he crosses the room, but at least they're giving Lucy a wide berth. He can't tell if it's out of respect for her last free moments, or terror that she might mutate.

At the sight of her, his chest tightens: one side of her face is scraped red raw, her eye half closed, and her arm rests gingerly on the table in a makeshift sling. She's battered, for sure, but as she glances up at him he can still see some trace of the old defiance in her.

'Hey,' he says, pulling out a chair and sitting across from her. 'How are you feeling?'

'How am I feeling?' says Lucy, cocking her head and apparently regretting it. 'You mean, about being sealed into my tomb? Yeah, great. Just terrific.'

'I'm sorry,' he says, swallowing hard. 'I'm so sorry.'

She gives a one-armed shrug. 'You couldn't have known this was going to happen.' And then, again, that same disarming smile. 'You didn't, right?'

'God, no.' He sniffs. 'Cat says she'll give us a torch. So at least we won't be in the dark.'

'Well, great. I'll make sure to take a book.'

'I would. I'm not great company.'

She aims a playful punch, as best she can, at his arm. 'You're better company than you think,' she says. She leans forwards, lowering her voice.

'Oh, and one more thing,' she says. 'Can you grab my bag?'

'Okay,' he says, a little hesitant. He reaches down and pulls her rucksack up onto the table, conscious of the eyes on them. She nods for him to look inside and he opens it: it's densely packed with notebooks and index cards, plastic wallets stuffed with documentation.

'Consider it my way of saying thanks,' she says, nodding into the bag. 'If we can stash it somewhere, it might… well, it'll be something for people to remember us by when we're gone.' She sighs. 'Like you said, Rob. We need to destroy him.'

42

THE DOOR of the Pit closes, but at least this time they've left him with a lamp. He and Lucy sit on the floor with their legs stretched out as far as they can manage.

'Don't worry,' he says to her. 'I'll be here with you. Until the end.'

'You were locked up in here?' says Lucy. 'In the dark?'

'Mm-hmm.'

'It's tiny.'

'It is.'

'That's a dreadful thing.'

'Yeah.'

They're silent for a while.

'So this is where Bjorn made you listen to those… brainwashing tapes? As a kid?'

'Hardly the term he'd use, but yeah.'

'How did he get the recordings? Did he pressure you into making them?'

'We all made them. When we hit a certain age. I guess the adults did them when they joined up.'

Lucy thinks for a bit.

'So they must be out there somewhere,' she says. 'Proof.'

'Yeah,' says Rob with a sigh. 'Not that it would make any difference. He'd say we made them voluntarily. Who could argue with that?'

Lucy shakes her head. 'He doesn't seem like a monster,' she says dreamily.

Rob can't help himself. 'Yeah, but…'

'Let me finish,' she says, her tone suddenly sharp. 'That's what makes him so dangerous, isn't it? You can draw a line from everything he believes, straight to this room.'

'Exactly.'

She's quiet again. Rob keeps his eyes fixed on her face. Somehow that makes it easier not to panic.

'If I die here, do you think I'll become one of them?' she says eventually.

'I… I don't know.'

'If I do, I'll kill you. Without meaning to.'

'Yeah. Yeah, I figured that out.'

'Then why did you come with me? You need to tell people about what happened here. You need to survive, Rob. I need you to survive.'

Rob feels sorrow sweep over him like a wave. 'You really think it'll make any difference if I tell people? I tried that once and look at how it ended.'

'This is different. He can't hide this.'

He lets her words hang in the air. They feel like a judgement.

'Ask yourself this, Lucy,' he says after a minute or so. 'If I'd let them lock you in here all alone, would you really have thought I was doing something courageous?'

'I…'

'No. You'd have called me a coward. And you'd have been right. Because you know someone by their actions. I couldn't let you go through this by yourself. Not after what happened to me.'

She chews on the inside of her cheek. 'Thanks,' she says eventually, and rubs his shoulder affectionately.

'Don't mention it.'

They sit in silence for a while, her head against his shoulder. Somehow, with her here the terror is lessened, although he knows that doesn't make any sense. If anything, he's in more danger.

But for the moment, he doesn't feel it. Instead, he's almost giddy, a swelling happiness inside him that he only partly understands.

43

SHE AWAKES from sleep gradually, gently, her face pressed into Rob's shoulder. She can't recall having felt tired, but she must have been. When she lifts her head, she's startled by the change in Rob. His upper body shimmers as though in a heat haze, and he's surrounded by what appears to be a golden mist. Within it she can see distinctly humanoid shapes, as though someone's been roughly sketching Rob's outline and hasn't yet rubbed out their construction lines. A mass of shoulder blades, a mass of necks – Leonardo da Vinci's *Vitruvian Man*, as drawn in a breakdown.

Rob lifts a hand to his head, runs it through his hair.

And now the shapes move too, a shimmering mass of lines, but they're interconnected somehow, reaching off in strange directions.

Behind the Rob she knows, she sees a vast, distorted figure in shimmering gold, twisting away into angular shapes. His neck horribly misshapen, his mouth pulling open into a gaping leer…

She closes her eyes, and when she opens them again…

Bjorn.

Hunched over a desk, poring over his notes, surrounded, like Rob, by that same, shimmering golden haze…

That same set of lines, that same twisted pattern of musculature –

'What am I seeing?' she murmurs.

And then, to her surprise, something comes in reply.

The man that is, and the man that is to be.

Not a voice, not exactly. More like a thought. A thing she's known all along, but not realised until now. Surfaced from the depths of her unconscious for precisely this moment.

But that's impossible.

And yet, before she can pull on that thread, her mind draws her deeper into understanding.

I will not reason and compare, she hears the voice say. *My business is to create.*

She knows those lines from somewhere, but she can't place them.

Behold, I am making all things new.

At the desk, Bjorn moves, and his golden shadow moves with him.

Those who have ears to hear, let them hear.

She tries to shake it off, this patchwork of fragments, this voice inside her own head that's speaking in an ancient language – but it's insistent, and won't be denied.

Blessed is the one to whom all mysteries are revealed.

And then she sees it, with a clarity she'd thought impossible. This thing, whatever it is, wasn't trying to destroy them. It's trying to recreate them. To build a man of its own.

Somewhere in her guts she feels a swelling warmth, and it takes her a moment to recognise it for what it is.

Satisfaction.

And in that moment the part of her mind that's still her own, that hasn't already been colonised by this creature, thinks...

Shit.

44

Even with a lantern at his side, when the door opens the moonlight still takes him by surprise. It takes Rob a moment to recognise Bjorn, and as soon as he does, he's on his feet.

'What are you doing here?'

Lucy is behind him on the floor, rubbing her head. She looks paler than yesterday, and he doesn't like the look of her wounds.

'I've figured it out,' says Bjorn, and now Rob registers his expression. It's like he can barely suppress his delight, and that immediately puts Rob on the defensive. 'I know what it wants.'

Rob stares at him. 'And why do you want to tell me this all of a sudden?'

'Because I need Lucy,' he says, nodding over to her. 'I need to show them she's safe.'

Rob steps in front of her, blocking Bjorn's view. There's something possessive about his expression, like Lucy's a science experiment. 'No,' he says. 'The last time we did this, Pyotr ended up with a dozen arms. I won't let that happen to her.'

'It won't,' says Bjorn, with that same rapturous gaze.

'You can't know that,' says Rob fiercely.

Bjorn ignores him. 'It wants to replicate itself,' he says. 'That's why it exists. But it's not ready yet. It doesn't know how.' He takes a step to one side, speaks to Lucy. 'I'm right, aren't I?'

Lucy's voice is groggy. 'I…'

Rob thinks of his mother, locked in this room at Bjorn's behest until she finally lost her mind. He thinks of his brother, robbed of his future by this man's ideas.

'I said, stay away from her.'

Now Bjorn seems to see Rob for the first time, looking him over with an expression of hurt bewilderment. 'It's safe. I swear.'

'You heard me,' says Rob fiercely, seizing his opportunity. 'Back off.'

'She's safe, isn't she, Rob? You've been in here with her for hours and you have to see it. Because you're no threat to her.'

Rob can't follow Bjorn's logic: his mind is already two steps ahead. 'What?'

'Reynaud, Pyotr, Marcus… they only transformed when they were threatened. It's a defence mechanism! Whatever this thing is, it didn't want to kill them. All it wanted to do was stay alive, to keep learning – but we were the ones who forced its hand!'

'You're looking pretty threatening to me right now, Bjorn.'

Again Bjorn sidesteps him. 'But not to her.' He spoke to her. 'Isn't that right?'

Now Rob turns too. Lucy's getting to her feet, wincing. 'Lucy?'

'He's right,' she says. 'I'm not afraid of him.'

'That doesn't prove anything.'

Lucy rubs her temple. She looks woozy, dazed. 'I saw something while I was asleep,' she says flatly. 'A kind of... vision.'

Rob feels his stomach lurch. 'You saw what?' he says with mounting dread.

'I believe him, Rob. I think it was the contagion trying to... to show me something. About how it sees us, how it learns. And what it wants to do with that knowledge.' She swallows hard. 'He's right. It's not evil. It's just... curious.'

'No,' says Rob firmly. 'No, you can't.'

'If you try and escape,' says Bjorn, 'then they'll put the authorities on to her. I'm sure of it. What I have planned is her best chance...'

'You can't seriously expect me to trust you. After everything you've done.'

'No,' says Bjorn matter-of-factly. 'Not at all. But I'm not trying to hurt you.'

Rob frowns. 'That's not as reassuring as you think it is.'

Now Lucy cuts in. 'What's your plan?'

'I want to tell them what you just told me. To prove to them that you're safe. Show them how lucid you can be when you know I'm not dangerous.'

'And what if you're wrong?' says Rob.

'I'm not wrong.'

'Fuck's sake.'

'I need them to see this,' Bjorn says earnestly. 'To see it with their own eyes. I can't expect them to believe otherwise.'

Rob turns to Lucy. 'For the record, I think this is a bloody stupid decision.'

'I'm not saying you're wrong,' says Lucy after a deep breath. 'But I vote we do it.' She holds his gaze. 'I've got my eyes open, Rob. I know what I'm doing.'

'And what about me? How do you think I'll feel when this all goes to hell?'

He sees concern flicker across Lucy's face, but Bjorn answers for her. 'It's not on you,' he says. 'None of it is. It's her choice. That's how it's always been.'

45

As they round the bunkhouse there's the sound of screeching tyres and shouting, and Bjorn begins to run. Before them is a scene of chaos: Elliot sits in the driver's seat of the Range Rover, Kristian hanging out of the window with Cat's shotgun in his hand. On the bonnet is Pyotr, clinging on to the driver's side with several arms, and slamming the others into wherever he can manage. The windscreen, the side panels, the tyres: it's not random, Rob's sure of it, although it's frenzied. Elliot is fishtailing across the site, making for the road, apparently trying without much luck to shake Pyotr off.

'No,' murmurs Bjorn, his joy curdling into despair. 'No, what are they doing?'

And apparently he's not the only one to think that way, because from across the side comes the sound of another engine, accelerating rapidly. Cat is at the wheel of the Volvo, speeding through the gears at a pace Rob can hardly believe, and the ancient car is heading straight for the Range Rover.

'No!' Bjorn yells, but it's futile and surely he knows it. Cat's aim is true. The Volvo slams into the driver's side of the Range Rover, knocking it off course. Pyotr lets out a roar of pain but doesn't release his grip, doesn't stop battering on the windscreen. He shudders now, apparently growing even more limbs, enough of them to hammer away at the glass until it's impossible to see through, enough to survive being blasted to a bloody stump by the first round from Kristian's shotgun.

The Volvo skids into one of the vegetable patches, and its bonnet crumples. Rob sees Cat slumped over its dashboard, blood down her forehead. She's going nowhere fast. The Range Rover swerves violently and for a moment Rob thinks it's going to collide with her, but at the last moment Elliot manages to steer away. The door opens and Kristian hurls himself out, the shotgun skittering away across the gravel, as the Range Rover hurtles towards the fence.

The fence slows the vehicle's momentum a little, the jagged meshwork sticking into the bodywork. The impact is enough to dislodge Pyotr's grip: he tumbles to the ground in a tangle of limbs. Before he can regain his footing, the car's momentum carries it forward, the wheels rolling over his prone form with a hideous crunch. Far below, the village seems oblivious, the only signs of activity a few scattered lights in the houses.

The driver's side wheel sits across Pyotr's neck and several of those insectile arms, and his guttural groans are lost beneath the dying sounds of the engine. The air is heavy with the smell of blood and burnt rubber.

Bjorn looks stricken, split between chewing out Kristian and helping Cat, and he turns to Rob without thinking. 'Check on Cat,' he says. 'Get her out of there.'

He can do that. Hurries across the site to where the Volvo's come to rest and pulls open the door. Turns the key to kill the engine and unclips Cat from her seatbelt. Puts a hand on her shoulder. 'Hey,' he says, shaking her gently. 'Hey, can you hear me?'

Behind him he can hear Bjorn yelling, the kind of fury Rob remembers from all those years ago, although he's seen so little evidence of it since his return. He always knew it was there, no matter how well hidden.

'What the fuck are you doing?' Bjorn shouts. 'Look at what you've done! Who gave you the idea you could act unilaterally? You bloody fool! You stupid bloody fool!' A scatter of gravel, a crunch: did Bjorn kick him? 'Pyotr's still inside there!' Bjorn snarls. 'If you'd paused for a single goddamn second to talk to him you'd have realised that, but no…'

Rob turns back to Cat, shakes her shoulder again. 'Hey,' he says. 'I need you to get up, you hear me? We need you here.' This time the reaction is instantaneous: she jolts awake, grabs his arm and twists sharply.

'Jesus! What was that?' he says, pulling himself loose.

Cat's teeth are bared, her eyes wild. 'Don't touch me,' she growls. 'I don't like to be touched.'

He backs off, alarmed. 'Okay. Okay. I just needed to know you were alright, that's all.'

She blinks hard. Once, twice. Looks around. 'Did they get

away?' she asks, and then answers her own question. 'Fuck! That stupid bastard. He's fucked the lot of us...'

Beneath the Range Rover, Pyotr is still breathing, but his head is a bloody mess. Elliot stands next to him, panting, and it looks like there are tears in his eyes. He's pointing the shotgun straight into Pyotr's face.

'No!' Bjorn yells. 'You don't have to do this!'

Elliot stares at Bjorn like he's mad. 'We have to kill him,' Elliot says. 'He can't live like this.'

'You don't,' Bjorn says, a note of pleading in his voice. 'Listen to me. Whatever this is, it doesn't have to be our enemy.'

'Look at it!' he bellows. It's quite a sight. Kristian's shot has blasted a chunk of the skull away, shearing it off just above the eye socket. Rob suspects this was an accident: surely Kristian couldn't have aimed that well while moving. Beneath the creature's distorted grimace there's a look that's very much like sorrow.

Pyotr's body is fraying at the edges: there are great jagged rips along his arms like the seams holding him together can't take any more. Beneath it he can see muscle and sinew in impossible combinations, twisted and distorted beyond all belief. At the creature's collarbone he catches a fleeting glimpse of something black and rotten-looking, there for a moment and then gone.

'He's terrified,' Bjorn says. 'And who can blame him? After all this?'

Elliot takes a deep, shuddering breath. 'If that's what it does when it's afraid,' he says, 'I don't want anything to do with it.'

'Can't you see?' says Bjorn. 'Have you really learned so little?

We're talking about an organism that wants only to learn. Something like that could change the world.'

Elliot sounds exhausted. 'What on earth are you talking about?'

'It's using what it's learned to protect itself. It's been inside us for years. Watching us study, and watching us live our lives up here. Now it's using whatever it can from that to try and save itself. But it wouldn't need to do any of that if we didn't threaten it.'

It's at this point Elliot spots Lucy, and his whole demeanour changes. 'What in God's name is she doing here?' he says. 'You let her out?'

'Listen to me,' says Bjorn, suddenly on the defensive, but Elliot's shaking his head.

'I'm done listening,' he says. 'You're out of control.'

Rob sees the look of panic on Bjorn's face, knows this wasn't how he planned this at all. 'Okay,' Lucy says. 'If you're not going to listen to him, then listen to me.' Elliot gives her a look of pure malice. 'You don't understand this thing,' Lucy says. 'But I do. I've seen it, Elliot. It's inside of me. I know what it wants.'

'No,' says Elliot. 'These things have killed enough of us. I'm done trying to reason with them, you hear me?'

Again Elliot aims the shotgun at Pyotr's face.

'Elliot, no!' yells Bjorn.

'Doesn't seem like he's reacting now, eh?' says Elliot. 'And I think you'll agree I'm being pretty fucking threatening.'

Lucy tries a different tack. 'I'm begging you,' she says. 'Don't do this.'

But they're not alone now. There's headlights approaching the gate, the sound of engines straining on the hill, and she can see Elliot weigh up his options. 'Sorry,' he says to Lucy, and then to what's left of Pyotr. 'And to you too, buddy.'

And he pulls the trigger, and then suddenly everybody is shouting at once. Only Rob's not looking at them. He's looking at Pyotr, watching as the skin of his upper torso bursts open like a rotten banana. A flurry of wispy grey viscera, looking more like unprocessed cotton than human innards, flits into the sky and hangs gently on the breeze.

'Holy shit,' Rob says quietly, shaking his head. His whole body is trembling. 'Holy shit.' He stares out at the scraps, floating on the air. 'What just happened?'

'Listen, son,' says Elliot, laying a hand on his shoulder. 'That thing's dead, and we're not. And to my mind, at least, that's cause for celebration.' He looks over at Bjorn. 'Ain't that right, Bjorn?'

46

Up the hill come two cars, headlights cutting through the darkness. Lucy knows it's too much to hope that it might be help, the authorities riding in to save the day. They've come up from the village, and there's no way they're prepared for what they'll find up here. A part of her considers yelling to Bjorn to bar the gates.

She glances over at Rob, whose face is grim. 'You think we ought to tell them what's going on?' she says. 'Break ranks?'

He shakes his head, less in dismissal than despair. 'We have to de-escalate,' he says. 'I hate to say it. I really do. But if we choose now to pick a fight then a lot of innocent people are going to die.'

The cars come to a halt just outside the perimeter fence, and out steps a managerial type with a spreading paunch. He's quickly joined by a tall country gent, and several others in their early fifties. Francis tags along at the back of the group, looking suddenly very young. All of them look agitated, and Lucy spots at least one shotgun among the group.

'Shit,' mutters Cat, but Bjorn stares out at them, unruffled.

'Leave this to me,' he says, making his way over to them. He addresses the nearest villager, the imposing country gent who towers over him up close. 'Graeme,' he says, his voice tight. 'What brings you up to us so late?'

Graeme takes in the scene before him – the wrecked car, twisted fence and bloodied Scriveners. His eyes rest first on Lucy and then on the unrecognisable heap of flesh that was once Pyotr, and his expression twists into one of bewilderment. 'We heard a commotion,' he says, and she can hear a tremor in his voice. 'Rather a lot of commotion, actually. It sounded…' He swallows hard. 'It sounded like a warzone. We thought something dreadful had happened.'

'Like what?' says Bjorn, his eyes narrowing. Lucy glances over at Rob and she's certain he's thinking the same thing: why doesn't Bjorn just come out with it, tell Graeme everything. It sounds like Graeme knows most of it already.

Graeme shifts his weight from one foot to another. 'People talk, Bjorn,' he says. 'About what you're doing up here. We're not superstitious, not most of us. But all the same, I know some people have wondered if you've… taken it too far.'

Bjorn gives a low, resounding chuckle. 'I'm hardly Faustus,' he says. 'We're not summoning the devil up here.'

Rob grimaces. Graeme's smile suddenly looks pasted on, an impossible rictus grin. 'I'm not saying I believe it,' he says. 'Not that it matters either way. Because something's happened up here, anyone could see that, and it looks to me like you might be in need of some help.' He looks around for support. 'Is that right?'

From behind Bjorn there is a chorus of affirmation, but he doesn't turn. Instead he takes a step forwards, his voice oddly menacing now. 'You'd be best to walk away, Graeme,' he says, and then looks over the other villagers. 'All of you. You'd be better off if you went back to your beds and left us to sort this out ourselves. Trust me on that.'

Graeme's lips are a thin line. 'That sounds like a threat.'

'Not a threat,' says Bjorn, trying his best to sound affable. 'Just some neighbourly advice. We've knocked along fairly well next to each other the past few decades, after all. I'd hate to see something happen to you.'

A younger man steps forwards and puts a hand on Graeme's shoulder. 'Fuck's sake, Dad,' he says. 'You can't let him push you around like this. You remember the kid they found up here all those years back? Nothing ever came of that, and you always said that was because this lot swept it under the rug. You can't let them do it again.'

'No,' says Graeme, nodding slowly. 'No, Declan, I suppose you're right there.' He takes a deep breath, looks into Bjorn's face, seeming to gather his courage. 'I'd like you to tell me what's going on here.'

'And if I don't?' says Bjorn.

Declan looks him over like he's something he scraped off his shoe. 'Then somebody else will,' he says. He catches Lucy's eye, nods to her. 'Did he do this to you, love?' he says. She feels Rob flinch next to her. 'No need to worry about him anymore. We can protect you.'

Kristian snorts somewhere behind her. She can feel the big

man's dislike for Declan radiating off him in waves. Lucy stares at Cat, who gives her the faintest of nods, and then turns back to Declan. 'It's not him you need to worry about,' she says. 'It's this place. There's something up here, some kind of contagion. We don't know how it spreads, and we don't know who's infected, but it could be bad. Really bad.'

Graeme takes a step back, shoots Francis a look of alarm. Declan's expression is fierce. He speaks only to Bjorn. 'You wanted to hide this, didn't you?'

Rob puts a hand on her back, as though he's bracing to make a run for it. But Bjorn stays calm, speaks through gritted teeth. 'No,' he says. 'Not indefinitely. Just until we determined what it was, how it worked. So we could share in the process of discovery, rather than being... test subjects.'

Declan rolls his eyes. 'You said it was bad,' he says to Lucy. 'What kind of bad?'

'It's... it's hard to describe,' Lucy says. Declan cocks his head. Bjorn shoots Lucy a warning look, as if to ask, *Are you sure you want to do this?*

Lucy reaches painfully into her pocket, and winces. Declan recoils, and Rob too. When she looks up with her phone in hand, someone's pointing a shotgun at her. She ignores it, eyeing its owner with disdain. Holds the phone up to Declan.

'Jesus,' he says, lifting a hand to his mouth. 'Jesus Christ.' He looks up at Lucy, his eyes wide. 'That's what happened to your friend? What the hell could do that?' He turns to Bjorn, aghast. 'You were going to hide this?'

'No,' says Bjorn, but Lucy's already talking over him.

'It doesn't matter,' she says. 'What matters is that we get help. Proper help. We've got people injured here who need immediate medical treatment, and we need…' Bjorn's shaking his head, but Lucy says it anyway. 'We need the authorities. Someone who can contain this thing, who can hold it back.'

'You're making a mistake,' Bjorn says. 'If you bring the authorities here, they'll destroy it.'

'Good,' says Cat to her left, and Bjorn wheels round to face her.

'No,' he says. 'No, don't you understand? We'd not have any of this were it not for that contagion. It's the reason we've thrived up here, the reason we've made such breakthroughs. It's the heart of this place.'

Cat stares at him, uncomprehending, for several seconds. 'You're saying… you're saying you knew about this? All along?'

Bjorn closes his eyes. 'Not all along,' he says. 'But it didn't take me long to realise there was something special about Craigdhu. I've always been able to work with a supernatural focus here. For years I thought it was because I was growing my own vegetables up here, eating from the land.'

Cat's staring at Bjorn in disbelief, her hand to her mouth. 'Bjorn,' she says, and he turns to her. 'No. You're telling me you knew about this and said nothing? For all these years?'

She can't read Rob's expression. He looks aghast, and yet something else keeps breaking through: a horrible, manic smile, a kind of swelling delight at what Bjorn's done.

Bjorn holds his hands up. 'I didn't know,' he says vaguely. 'I only ever suspected.'

Some part of Lucy wishes she had all this recorded, although she's not even sure if her recorder survived the battering Pyotr gave it. It would make for a hell of a series finale. There's a visible ripple of disquiet among the Scriveners: heads shaking, fists clenched. Declan and his friends, on the other hand, are horrified. Graeme's gone white; Francis looks like he might collapse.

'I've heard enough,' says Declan. 'If there's some contagion in Craigdhu – if there's even the faintest likelihood that we could be infected too – then we need to figure out how the hell we stop it turning us into one of those things.' He glances uneasily at Lucy's phone, then back to Bjorn. 'And you've seen these fucking things in action, so we need your help.'

Bjorn starts to protest, and Graeme cuts him off. 'This isn't a negotiation,' he says. 'You're coming with us.'

'You're making a mistake,' says Bjorn. 'This contagion... it reacts to threats. I'm certain of it. If you threaten us – if we even *feel* threatened – then any one of us could transform into one of those things.'

Now Declan wears a nasty smile. 'Look around you,' he says, nodding to the other Scriveners. Rob follows his gaze. 'It's not us they're afraid of, Bjorn. It's *you*.'

And it's true. Cat's face is pale, her eyes darting between Bjorn and the others. Kristian's arms are crossed tightly across his chest as if trying to shield himself. Amy looks like she might be about to vomit. Whatever trust they had in Bjorn is rapidly eroding, and even Bjorn can see it now.

His shoulders slump. 'Very well,' he says to Declan. 'I don't suppose there's much sense in arguing.'

'Good man,' says Declan. He leaps into action, directing the injured towards some of the waiting vehicles – those who can walk, anyway. The others get reluctant support from the older villagers, although it's pretty clear they'd rather be almost anywhere else than here. Bjorn watches them go with a hangdog look.

'Take 'em to the pub,' Declan calls over when the first car is filled. 'Plenty of space in there.' Then he turns to Francis. 'Frankie boy!' He pats Francis hard on the shoulder. Francis flinches. 'Okay, okay,' he says, rolling his eyes. 'Just wondered if you could help us with some medical supplies, that's all.'

'Sure,' says Francis, although he doesn't look happy about it. 'Can I borrow Cat and Lucy for a second? Talk me through what they need?'

'Aye, if you need,' says Declan. 'But don't be long. This place gives me the heebies…'

The moment the glass door of Francis's shop closes, his calm façade disappears. The fluorescent lights flick on and reveal high shelves stocked with medical supplies, stretching in narrow aisles to the counter at the back. Francis is resting his arm on one of the shelves like he might collapse, his movements agitated, his eyes full of panicked intensity.

'What the hell happened up there?' he asks them. 'Is this because of the antifungals?'

Lucy takes a deep breath. 'We had no idea that would happen. Like you said, you can buy that stuff over the counter.'

'Jesus Christ!' says Francis, putting a hand to his forehead.

He pushes himself up from the shelf, begins pacing up and down the aisle. 'Bjorn makes it sound like he's known about this for years.' He glares at Cat. 'Are you really saying he never mentioned it to you?'

'Absolutely not,' says Cat, her face grave. 'Believe me, Francis, if I'd known—'

'Yeah, yeah,' he says, waving his hand airily as though unwilling to waste even a moment. 'The bigger question is, what do we do now? If you're expecting me to give you penicillin for people's injuries, you can think again.'

'No,' says Cat. 'All we need is basic medical supplies. The more basic the better. Bandages, cotton wool, splints.' She scans the shelves behind the counter, her eyes flicking over the bottles and boxes. 'I don't even want to risk antiseptics.'

'No way we can risk it,' says Lucy. 'Although I doubt anyone would let us get near them with a bottle of TCP anyway.'

'Fuck,' says Francis with a low whistle. 'You need to keep my name out of this, you hear? I'm not going to prison as an accessory to murder.'

Cat rolls her eyes. 'I think we're a little beyond that,' she says. 'When the authorities arrive, we tell them everything.'

'That's easy for you to say. You're not the one responsible for that man's death.'

'Bjorn's the one responsible for this,' says Cat, her jaw set. 'I'll make sure they know that.'

'Fucking hell,' says Francis. He swallows hard, still shaking his head. 'You'll go down in history for this. You'll be… legendary.'

'You mean infamous,' says Cat grimly.

'Aye,' says Francis. 'Aye, I guess that's more accurate.' He shoves his hands in his pockets, seems momentarily lost for words. After a few seconds he seems to settle on safe conversational ground. 'Right then,' he says. 'Let me pull out anything you can use to wrap up wounds.' He removes a key from his pocket, and opens a door opposite. Inside is a small storeroom, the walls inside lined with pill boxes. 'Just give me a sec,' he says, the door swinging shut behind him.

Cat's head is bowed, her eyes hooded. 'Are you okay?' says Lucy to Cat.

'Not at all,' says Cat. 'I swear, Lucy. I had no idea.'

'What would you have done if you'd known?'

'God knows,' says Cat wearily. 'Mostly I just feel cheated. And dirty.'

From the storeroom she hears a crash, the sound of boxes scattering across linoleum. 'Shit,' mutters Francis.

'Everything okay in there?' calls Cat.

'Yeah,' he shouts back. 'Butterfingers.'

'You need some help?'

'No,' he says, but Lucy can hear him muttering 'shit, shit' under his breath.

'Let me go check on him,' Cat says. 'I don't want to hang around here any longer than we have to, not if they're going to come after us with pitchforks.'

'Good plan.'

Lucy follows her. Francis is stood on his tiptoes, with a stack of boxes pressed up against his chest. He flashes what she assumes is meant to be a charming grin. It's distracting enough that she doesn't notice what's wrong right away.

Then she spots it, beneath the white coat: a strange, malformed growth, making him look more like a hunchback. A bulge in his neck, like he's straining to reach something. A rippling across the tendons in his arms, as though his whole body is pushing against its boundaries. He turns to see her and there's a flicker across the surface of his eyeball, like a wave on the sea.

'Take a picture,' he says. 'It'll last longer.'

She swallows hard. 'Hey,' she says, as casually as she can. 'You want me to help carry that?' She nods down at the supplies he's loading into a basket.

'Sure,' he says, lifting it over to her. There's something unsteady in his gait, an unexpected spasm as he hands the thing across, and he frowns, shakes his head. 'Weird.'

47

Rob's funnelled through the heavy wooden door into the gloom of the pub. The smell of woodsmoke, spilled beer and, somewhere, the astringent tang of antiseptic.

From the moment he enters he feels like he's at a nightmarish school disco. To the left, the Scriveners, leaning against the bar and nursing their injuries. A few of the villagers have ventured over to tend to their wounds, setting up makeshift splints and tourniquets. Beatrice is pressing a pad against her bicep to staunch the bleeding; Hazel's forearm is ringed with cloth bandages. Bjorn sits at the far end of the bar, head in his hands. Even the Scriveners are giving him a wide berth, and Rob's not surprised.

He can't understand why the Scriveners didn't mutate when Pyotr attacked. At first he thought it proved they weren't infected. But the past few hours have taught him a harsh lesson: don't assume anything about the contagion. Don't assume you understand it.

The remaining villagers sit in small groups on the right of

the room, watching the Scriveners. Some of the older gents are eyeing them up like a jury, weighing up their verdicts. The village's strongest men line one wall: not blocking the door, exactly, but ready to do so if it comes to it. Nobody here even saw Pyotr at his worst, only that heap of flesh beneath the Range Rover's wheels. Maybe they'd be treating the Scriveners like this if it was a normal day.

In the centre of the pub, a set of wooden tables have been pushed together to create a kind of triage area. There's a couple of first-aid kits, a small pile of bandages and a spool of blue roll. It's pretty unimpressive, but that's probably for the best after what happened to Pyotr. The more advanced the technology, the more threat it presumably poses this thing.

God, he's going to have to explain what happened up there, isn't he? Already he can't find the words. If he doesn't, and someone jabs antibiotics into their arms… it doesn't bear thinking about.

He scans the room. Spots Declan, huddled in a corner booth with his dad and a few other prominent villagers. Makes his way over, but before he gets there Declan's on his feet, as though afraid Rob might launch himself across the table and attack.

'Everything okay?' he says tersely.

'Uh… well, no,' Rob says, running a hand through his hair. 'There's something you need to know. About the Scriveners. And about the infection.'

He's stopped by a hand on his shoulder. Kristian's suddenly next to him, but to Rob's surprise he doesn't look angry: his expression is sober, pensive. 'It's okay, buddy,' he says, and Rob flinches at the term. 'They know it all already.'

Rob stares at Kristian, bewildered. 'They do?' he says. 'How the hell did that happen?'

Declan sucks on his teeth. 'Hate to break it to you,' he says, 'but your friend here's been sending us updates for a while now.' He holds up his smartphone, waggles it from side to side. 'Thank God for WhatsApp, eh?'

Some part of Rob feels obscurely furious, an anger that goes entirely beyond reason, as if Kristian has betrayed him personally. Old habits die hard, clearly. 'How long?' he says, turning to Kristian. 'What do they know?'

'Maybe six months?' says Kristian with a shrug. 'Ever since I started wondering about Bjorn.'

'So we know plenty,' says Declan, ignoring the drama playing out in front of him. 'Enough to alert the authorities, and enough to know how to handle this.'

'I assume Bjorn isn't aware of this,' Rob says, still speaking to Kristian.

'It doesn't matter,' says Declan. 'It's over. The grown-ups are in charge now.'

'Listen,' says Kristian, his tone conciliatory. 'We've been living in a former military base, that the Army abandoned without any apparent reason. Whatever they were doing up there, all this has to be connected to it, whether Bjorn can see it or not. There must be records of what they did somewhere, and some kind of antidote.' He looks at Rob as though he's expecting an encouraging smile, but Rob's face is ashen. Kristian's expression twists into one of exasperation, and he folds his arms tightly across his chest. 'They'll recognise what's going on here,' he says. 'I'm certain of it. And then they can begin setting things right.'

There's the scrape of glass on wood. In the booth, Graeme is fidgeting with the empty glasses, obsessively arranging and rearranging them into various configurations.

'Dad,' says Declan, frowning. 'Dad, would you stop that?'

But Graeme doesn't seem to hear him. He continues frantically rearranging the glasses, his breathing heavy and uneven. Declan reaches out, places a hand gently on his father's arm. Graeme startles at his touch.

'It's okay,' Declan says. 'Just take a deep breath.'

Graeme closes his eyes and inhales shakily. When he opens them again, he looks at Declan like he's never seen him before. 'I'm sorry,' he whispers, his voice hoarse. 'I just… I can't stop thinking about it.'

He puts a trembling hand to his forehead. There's a sheen of sweat across his skin. 'This infection,' he says, the words tumbling out in a rush. 'It's spreading. I can feel it. We need to act fast, before it takes hold. Before it's too late.'

Declan nods effusively. A little too effusively, perhaps. He reaches for his drink, knocking it with the back of his hand as he does and sending dark beer splashing across the table. 'Exactly,' he says, apparently reassuring himself. 'So that's what we've done. Protected ourselves. Kept ourselves separate from… your lot.'

There's a look of faint alarm in Kristian's eyes now. 'What about me?' he says. Declan gives him a cold stare.

'You were up there,' says Declan, 'with the rest of them. And you said yourself, you don't know how this thing spreads.'

'Come on, man,' says Kristian, and Rob can hear a note of pleading in his voice. 'I'm on your side. You must be able to see that.'

'That's not really relevant, though, is it?' says Declan, louder and more aggressively than perhaps he intends to. The Scriveners are watching now, and Bjorn's got to his feet. 'If you were up there, you're infected. Bjorn said as much.'

'You bastard,' says Kristian. 'You'd throw me to the wolves?'

Graeme's hands are clenching and unclenching on the table, apparently involuntarily. There's a strange ripple across his skin. Next to him an older man, perhaps in his late seventies, has his eyes closed and is banging his head gently against the back of the booth, over and over…

'Kristian,' Rob says, laying a hand on his arm, but before he can explain, Bjorn's there.

'Declan's right,' Bjorn says. 'It's in all of us. Anyone who's drunk the water up here, or eaten anything grown in this soil. But that's the power of this place: that's where the blessing comes from. I've felt it since that first week I stayed here.'

Declan cocks his head. 'What are you telling me?' he says slowly. 'That whatever this thing is, it's… it's in us too?' He blinks hard once, twice, then seems to sway a little. 'We export fruit and veg. Our cows eat the grass. Fuck, we've been selling cheese for the past fifteen years.' He looks like he might vomit. Looks from Rob, to Kristian, to Bjorn. 'You knew about this all along?' he says, beginning to shudder all over. 'And you never thought to tell anyone down here? You've doomed the lot of us, man. You've killed us all.'

MARGINAL

'I…' Bjorn swallows. 'I thought it was a blessing. I still do.'

Declan stares at Bjorn like he's lost his mind. 'A blessing?' he sputters, his voice rising. 'Kristian told me this thing turns people inside out. You think it's a fucking blessing?'

Bjorn starts to answer, but Declan doesn't give him the chance: he launches himself across the table and flies at Bjorn with a guttural roar. But Kristian is faster. He grabs Declan around the waist and hauls him backwards, sending the two men crashing to the floor in a tangle of limbs.

Kristian presses Declan's head into the floor, but even that can't stop Declan talking. 'You'll burn in hell for this,' he snarls at Bjorn. In the booth, his friends are scrambling over each other to join the fray, shouting curses. Only Graeme is still seated, rocking back and forth, lost in his own world.

One of Declan's companions, a heavyset man in his mid-sixties, manages to break free of the tangle of bodies and launches himself at Kristian. Rob tries to shove him out of the way, but the man comes back at Rob with surprising strength. Rob sees his fist too late. The next thing he knows he's on the ground, his head spinning, and Kristian is under a pile of bodies.

Rob can see the panic in Kristian's eyes, can hear the sound of fists pounding flesh. And then Kristian's eyes harden, focusing on something Rob can't see. Rob follows his gaze and there it is: a steak knife, lying discarded on someone's plate. With a desperate lunge, Kristian breaks free of his attackers and knocks the knife to the ground. His fingers close around the handle and, with a grunt, he swings the serrated blade into the neck of his nearest assailant.

Declan reels backwards, letting out a wet choking sound. His hand goes to the knife, pressing against it as if he can't quite believe it's real. One by one, Kristian's attackers fall away, their fury replaced by disbelief. 'What the fuck have you done?' Rob hears one of them murmur, and he's wondering the very same thing.

Only instead of collapsing to the ground, Declan begins to shudder. The flesh surrounding the knife begins to pulsate, rippling with tumorous growths. His head is wrenched to one side by an unseen force, his mouth stretching into a leer. Then, with a hideous crack, his skull begins to elongate, the bone warping. His jaw unhinges with a wet pop, and seems to split itself into two. A second tongue emerges from his throat, the skin of his neck splitting as it does.

In the booth, Graeme cries out. Rob can see his muscles convulsing beneath his skin, his right arm twitches, the biceps and forearm swelling, the skin beginning to split with the rapid growth of muscle tissue. There's a pop, and Graeme's shoulder takes on a new, jagged shape, a new set of shoulder blades. His head is twitching, his neck muscles straining, and as Rob watches his left eye begins to swell, the eyelid splitting open as a second eyeball pushes through the bloody tissue.

Graeme's flung forwards onto the table as his torso begins to contort. His whole body warps out of shape, his spine twisting like undulating waves. Within seconds he's a grotesque asymmetry, barely recognisable as human at all, he slides off the table and then begins hauling his way across the floor towards Rob.

The Scriveners are screaming, running for the door. Behind

the bar Rob glimpses the bartender, her face split vertically, the two halves peeling apart to reveal a pulsating mass of tissue that might be a new brain. Her jaw has distended, and two sets of teeth push their way out of her gums at baffling angles. There are old men writhing on the floor, their backs arching impossibly as new legs burst from their spines with a series of wet snaps.

Declan emits a gurgling, inhuman shriek from what used to be his mouth, his misshapen head raised, his two tongues lolling obscenely. He staggers towards Kristian on limbs that are still rapidly mutating, the bones snapping and reforming as he moves.

Kristian is paralysed, watching Declan approach in a kind of blank incomprehension. Bjorn grabs him by the shoulder and tries to haul him to the door. 'Move, you fool!' he shouts, struggling to shift Kristian's bulk. 'Can't you see what you've done?'

Finally, after an eternity, Kristian seems to rouse himself, and begins stumbling towards the door like a man half-awake. But out in the street, Rob can see other villagers starting to twitch, and he can't shake the sense that this horrible night is nowhere near done.

48

Lucy steps out of the pharmacy with the basket of medical supplies in hand, Cat by her side, only to discover they've got an audience. In the small square outside is a little crowd of villagers in T-shirts and jogging bottoms, hiking fleeces pulled hurriedly over pyjamas. Some hold hands, while others stand alone.

Most of them look away when Lucy and Cat approach, but a few meet their gaze with grim stares. She can see the fear in their eyes, the unspoken accusations, and it's unbearable. She tries to look past them, but can't help catching the eye of a young blonde woman with her hair pulled back into a ragged ponytail. The thing inside Lucy thrums with recognition, and a wave of nausea washes over her.

She wants to vomit. She wants to run. She wants to end it all, right there in the middle of the square. But she does none of these things. She swallows the terror. She pastes a smile across her face and fixes her eyes forwards.

The shuffling of her feet sounds unusually loud. As she and

MARGINAL

Cat pass the villagers she can make out hushed whispers, the occasional sob, but nothing specific. There's a heaviness in the air now, an expectation she can't explain.

Maybe they know already. Maybe they can feel it like she can, pulsing in her veins, bristling at the corner of her vision. Surely their bodies know, even if their minds have yet to register the change. They've sensed something's different, a shift at molecular level, and perhaps immune systems and antibodies are being rallied to combat it.

For several seconds, they just stare. And their hard, frightened gazes might be alarming enough on their own, but then they begin moving towards Lucy and Cat, pressing in on them. They're firing off questions in angry, staccato bursts, their voices a cacophony of fear and confusion.

But Lucy's not listening, in fact, she can hardly hear them at all. Because opposite the pub, standing silently at the roadside like sentinels, are a group of older villagers. They're dressed in shabby woollen jumpers and beanie hats, a symphony of muted tones, their eyes are sunken into their heads. It's not their faces that scare her, it's that she can see something under them, something moving beneath the skin.

They're beginning to shudder. Strange convulsions going through them, the odd twitch here and there, which they try to shake off. They are starting to bulge and stretch in strange places, in ways that they shouldn't, she can see a shimmer in this one's tendon, that one's calf…

49

As he bursts out of the pub, Rob's conscious of a strange ripple passing through the crowd, like something is passing from person to person, some strange, interconnected process unfolding before him. He spots Lucy, across the square, and wants to scream for her to look away, to run as far as she can from this place.

There is something horribly, terribly familiar about what's happening here. A tremor across one man's biceps, a sudden and unprompted shiver like a spot of violent cold is localised in a single area of his body. A spasm in the tendon, the skin pulsating where it made contact.

A woman's leg begins to shake and she flinches, like she is shaking off a fly. For a moment it stops – and then it comes again, even stronger. Now she is unsteady on her feet, staggering, looking as though she might fall to her knees.

And he knows what is coming. People have started looking around, suddenly aware they're not alone in these sensations. They're leaning into their partners, placing hands upon their shoulders. He can see people swallowing hard, trying to remain calm, can see the panic that's just below these attempts at calm.

And… oh God…

There are children here too.

At the front of the crowd stand a couple, watching him, with their little boy in front of them. And Rob can see it.

The tremor running across the boy's shoulder and down his arm.

The look of panic on his face as he turns to his mother for reassurance.

And then it erupts.

Rob sees the boy's head begin to bend backwards as his trapezius begins to multiply, sees the collar bone press against the skin, sharper and sharper, his face contorted into agony.

And then with a great gout of blood, bone breaks skin, and he is still being bent backwards, his eyes blank now, rolled back in his head, his parents screaming.

He is an impossible shape.

Rob hears the boy's ribs crack, sees the jagged mass emerge from what used to be his chest like a thicket of thorn and briar.

His parents are bent over this strange and twisted thing that just a moment ago was their boy, weeping, the crowd is running to them.

But now it's spreading – even as the boy's parents bend over to cradle his body, he can see them transforming too…

50

A<small>ND YET</small> they're not moving. Every one of the creatures is watching them, their gazes intense and unflinching, exerting a tangible pressure. Many of them are still twitching, but that doesn't break their concentration, nor the sense of *expectancy*.

It's an explosion of arms, legs and internal organs, sticking out at wild angles. Every one of them looks to be in agony: their lips contorted, their teeth bared. Every one of them training what they have left of their eyes on Rob and the others. Swaying slightly, many of them threatening to overbalance if they haven't already done so. Alive with the stench of blood and sweat and shit.

They look just like Pyotr did, standing out there on the edge of the camp. They're on the outskirts of the village, blocking the road back up the mountain, but they're just waiting. He's sure he can detect an air of malice to them, although how he knows this he can't say. Perhaps that's just what he would have felt in their position.

And yet they haven't entirely forgotten themselves: families are grouped together, parents resting deformed arms on their children's bloodied spines. Rob wants to vomit, keeps reliving the moment where their bones burst through their skin. Manages, somehow, to hold it down, although only by looking away altogether. None of this would have happened without Bjorn. The world would have been a better place if he'd never been born.

'What do we do?' Rob hears Miranda ask from beside him. The Scriveners seem transfixed, unable to tear their eyes away from this new creation that Bjorn had spoken about so often. Even Rob feels it. There's something haunting about being watched so intently, like seeing yourself in a funhouse mirror. 'What do they want from us?'

'They want to see how we'll react,' Bjorn says to Miranda. 'That's all this thing has ever been doing. Watching us.'

'There's so many of them,' mutters Miranda. 'We'll never fight them off.'

'Don't you understand?' Bjorn says, turning to her. There's a real irritation in his voice, an exasperation verging on aggression. 'We don't need to. We've never needed to. They're no threat.'

'Are you fucking kidding me?' says Kristian. He stands to one side of the pub's doorway, resting his hand on a discarded shovel wedged into the flowerbed, his hiking fleece spattered with blood. 'Declan just tried to strangle me, and that was before he turned into one of… them.' He takes a step towards Bjorn, then another, shaking his head. 'No threat. Just try telling that to Pyotr. To Reynaud.'

'They reacted like that because we threatened them. It was self-protection, nothing more.' He fixes Kristian with a steely glare. 'Look at Lucy, if you need any more convincing. She knows we're no threat to her, and she's no threat to us. It's practically harmonious.'

It's an absurdly optimistic assessment of the situation, and it takes all Rob's strength to hold his tongue. This isn't the time to point out how wide a berth people are giving Lucy. He sees Lucy glance at him, sees that strange shimmer across her skin that's so slight he wonders if he imagined it. He wants to recoil too. It's instinct, human nature. It feels like something is wearing her as a costume.

'And how do we know what she perceives as a threat?' says Kristian. 'We can't co-exist with them, not when we've no idea how they think.'

'Then ask us!' Lucy yells. Rob's not the only one who flinches at that collective pronoun. 'You want to understand, just ask.'

Kristian makes a valiant effort to keep himself from losing it, but his anger is volcanic and cracks are starting to appear on his surface. 'You're one… person,' he says through gritted teeth. 'At least you still look human. But what about them?' He throws his hand out in the direction of the villagers. Still motionless, the only signs of movement are their eyes following Kristian's hand and the slow rise and fall of their breathing. Rob tries not to look at the man whose lungs have burst through his chest.

Lucy sighs. 'If they wanted to kill us, they'd have done it by now,' she says wearily. 'We'd not stand much of a chance if they did. But they haven't done anything like that. Use your head,

Kristian. Think rationally. That's not what they want from us.'

Rob wants to believe that's not the parasite talking. Surely it can't have that level of control over her. But all that time it's been looking through her eyes, hearing with her ears. It's impossible not to wonder.

'They bloody well want to kill me,' says Kristian.

'That's because they're still more human than you realise,' says Bjorn, with a note of pleading. 'They're emotional. That's what Declan reacted to in the pub, those emotions. All that fear, that anger. But look at them now…'

And he's right: the creatures are just standing, their aggression stilled, watching this drama play out. Kristian surveys the scene, scowls. Looks back to Lucy.

'Okay, Lucy,' says Kristian, his jaw set. 'Assume they don't want to kill us – then what they want is to replace us. To worm their way inside us and learn what we're made of so they can do away with us once and for all.' His arms are folded, his manner that of a man who's won a decisive victory. 'So ask yourself this: what's to stop them doing that? How long before every person on this planet has one of those things inside them?'

'Kristian. If I may.' Bjorn takes a couple of steps forwards, turns his back to the villagers, and looks Kristian straight in the eye. Kristian struggles to contain his irritation. 'You're scared. I can see that. But I beg you. Try to understand. What we're witnessing here is something glorious. The beginning of a new world. A new humanity. A people who hunger and thirst for knowledge with their very being. Just think of what we could achieve as a species. We'd be… unstoppable.'

Kristian's eyes are wide, as he looks from Bjorn to the villagers. His jaw hangs open, his face aghast. He seems to be struggling to speak. 'I... I...' he looks to the others. 'You're seeing this, right?' he says to them, looking from Cat to Elliot, from Rob to Lucy. 'They're monstrosities. I can't be the only one who sees that.' He leans forwards, hunched over his shovel, dazed. 'Jesus Christ,' he mutters. 'Jesus fucking Christ.'

And then he seems to gain strength. Straightens his spine, looks Bjorn full in the face.

And, before anyone can stop him, he lifts the shovel up in a graceful arc.

And its blade slices through the air, glinting in the moonlight.

And then it comes down, straight into the side of Bjorn's head.

That's when all hell breaks loose.

51

THE SHOVEL hits Bjorn in the side of the head, hard enough that it sticks. The force of it knocks him to the ground, and Rob watches his body to see if he transforms. But no, he just lies there, bleeding out, his eyes closed. A gash at his temple, his teeth bared.

Some part of Rob can't believe it. He won't be able to believe it for some time. This monolith, this golem he'd built from his experience, is flesh and blood after all. It shouldn't be this easy. There should have been a battle.

He almost feels sorry for Bjorn. He supposes that is some kind of victory: it's not hatred he feels, nor contempt, only pity.

It occurs to him a second later that he's in the minority. Cat has already hurled herself at Kristian, yelling 'Kristian, what the *fuck?!*' and he's rolling around in the dust trying to stop her from smashing his head into the ground. Amy and Miranda are running towards Bjorn, kneeling at his side, assessing the wound in his head.

Nobody is looking at the villagers, not at first. At first there's only weeping and panic. That quickly changes, though. They twitch and contort as their bodies generate new limbs, as their rib cages twist themselves into great angular claws, as they start growing taller and stronger.

And then suddenly they're coming for Kristian, lumbering and scuttling and dragging themselves towards him, and he's the first to notice. Rob hears him call 'Cat – Cat, stop!' and she turns and leaps off him and now everyone is staring, wondering what the hell they're supposed to do now.

And then Cat's screaming, 'Run, for God's sake, run!' and then, like all the others, Rob is running through the village, hardly thinking of where they'll end up. He's dragging Lucy behind him, stumbling and tripping, and as he glances back over his shoulder, he sees the creatures following after, a dozen of them, maybe more.

There are cries of terror in the air, punctuated by the crack of bones, the wet squelch of flesh reshaping itself. There's nothing up ahead but the distant form of the quarry, its floodlights just barely visible through an avenue of trees. Rob pushes blindly on, Cat close behind. His lungs burning, his legs screaming in protest.

Behind him, he hears Kristian's desperate shout. 'Cat! Cat, wait!' Over his shoulder he sees Kristian sprinting towards him, speckled by the moonlight falling through the trees. Looming over Kristian is a grotesque fusion of human and… something else entirely. The creature's torso is a mass of twisted, elongated ribs. They jut out at unnatural angles, forming what looks like a cage; what's left of its arms are jagged, bony spikes.

It lunges for Kristian, and he tries to duck out of its way. But the path is narrow, lined by trees, and he misjudges how steep the banks are. As he scrambles for purchase, the creature lunges forwards, impaling him. He lets out a wet grunt, as though winded, and then the creature hoists him aloft and he's screaming, his blood splattering across the dirt.

'Kristian!' Cat yells, and then Rob shoves her forwards.

'There's no time!' he says. The creature turns its gaze on him, its eyes shining with a malevolent intelligence. They're next: he's certain of it. But then, to his surprise, the creature hesitates, its eyes lingering on Lucy for several seconds before it turns its attention back to Kristian's body.

Rob's already running when he hears the crack of branches behind him, and the sound of something heavy being hurled into the trees, thinking, *I'm going to die like that, and it will all be Bjorn's fault*.

Now and then he looks over at Lucy next to him, the parasite nestled up against her spine. Remembers how the creature looked at her, and asks himself, *Why am I not dead already?*

A little way ahead of them Rob can see Amy, her initial pace slowed by what looks like a sprained ankle. She's moving unevenly, a few steps followed by an ungainly hobble. As they catch up to her, he can see she's in bad shape and her foot is already swelling up. 'Come on,' he hears Cat say. 'Not much further.'

Amy makes a valiant effort to follow them, but she's going to slow them down and he can see from Cat's face that she knows it too. He can hear heavy, lumbering footsteps behind them, growing closer with each passing second. Despite their misshapen limbs, the creatures are relentless, and they don't seem to be tiring or slowing in their pursuit. When he looks back he can see a nightmare of bulging eyes and grotesquely elongated limbs.

And then Amy falls. Cat does her best to help her to her feet, but she's not going anywhere. 'Don't leave me,' she says, looking up at Cat with shining eyes. 'Please. I'm begging you.'

Cat closes her eyes. 'Amy, I—' Her breath catches in her throat. 'Try again. Please.' She turns to Rob. 'Get her other arm,' she says fiercely. 'We can do this.'

Rob doesn't move. 'We can't,' he says. 'You must be able to see that.'

'Fuck you!' howls Cat. 'Get her up!' She tries her best to lift Amy single-handedly, but only succeeds in lifting her a short way from the ground.

'We have to go, Cat,' says Rob. He can't let himself look at Amy, can't bear to. 'I'm sorry.' And then he starts running again, and he hears Amy sobbing 'No, please God, no,' behind them, and suddenly Cat is at his side. There are tears streaming down her face, and at the sound of Amy's dying gasps Cat visibly flinches.

By some miracle, they are nearly at the quarry. He glances to his left and sees Miranda, her face streaked with tears and her eyes wide with terror. To his right, Danny stumbles and nearly falls, his breath coming in short, sharp bursts. They're all exhausted, all running on pure adrenaline. He can't believe he's still alive, nor that Lucy is still standing, despite her injuries. It all feels a little too easy.

There's no time to dwell on it now, though. The half-a-dozen survivors pile in through the quarry's service entrance. Discarded machinery waiting for the Monday morning shift, the control booth a squat concrete block to their right. The slate walls tower above them and he wonders why he listened to Cat when this is so obviously a stupid idea. They're trapped, of course they are, and every one of them is going to die here.

Cat has other ideas. 'We've still got time,' she says. 'Not much, but enough.'

And it's true, they're faster than the creatures, who are weighed down by their additional bulk. He tries not to think about Tommy, who was overtaken by one of those insectile creations on the path and of whose final moments Rob heard only a set of dreadful, choking gasps.

'Anyone who can still run, get to one of the vehicles,' yells Cat. 'Anyone who can't, come with me to the control room. Those things are still flesh and blood. They might be strong, but they're not immortal.'

There's no time to argue, although his mind – his stupid goddamn mind, still running away from him after all those years in therapy – can't help asking if this really solves anything. Surely the first poor idiot to stumble across one of the bodies will become the creature's next host. But the others are already in motion, heading for the bright yellow machinery, the excavators and bulldozers and dump trucks like children's toys beneath those great walls. Rob follows them, because he can hear the creatures coming, can hear their snarling and groaning and screaming and squelching, and knows they are close…

And then he's inside the cockpit of a bulldozer, his heart pounding in his chest, searching the interior with shaking hands. 'Come on, come on,' he mutters, checking the doorframes, the cup holder, the floor mat. Nothing. Outside he can hear panicked screams.

He runs his hand under the dashboard, praying for a miracle. His fingers brush something metal, and to his surprise it comes loose. It's a small magnetic box: inside is a key. He wants to sob with relief.

He jams it into the ignition, but the engine just sputters. 'No, no, no,' Rob pleads, turning the key again. There's a whine from the starter motor, but the engine still refuses to catch.

Finally, on the third try, the engine roars into life. Rob scans the controls. A daunting array of levers and pedals, bearing only a scant resemblance to his car. He takes a deep breath, tries to calm his nerves. Pushes one of the levers forwards.

The bulldozer lurches forwards, nearly stalling. 'Fuck,' Rob mutters. Steadies his hands, tries again. He pushes the lever forwards again, more gently this time, and the vehicle strains against the uneven ground. Through the grimy windscreen he sees the creatures surge forwards, their misshapen bodies twisting and contorting as they lunge at the survivors.

And then he spots Lucy.

Standing in the centre of the quarry, dead still. Her eyes fixed on him.

And he feels a little shudder run down his spine as he watches the creatures lumber towards the others, and he sees Elliot and Danny manoeuvring their vehicles to try and pin the creatures against the rock face, and he can read the question in Lucy's eyes:

Are you a threat?

And there's something in her expression that's so vulnerable, so human, that it makes him take his hand off the lever. He can't take this on faith: he needs to be sure.

He's paralysed, then, watching the chaos unfolding through the windscreen. Unable to make himself hit the gas, unable to bear the thought of being buried alive, unable to finally put an end to this thing.

He's a coward. He's always been.

52

INSIDE THE control booth, sealed behind glass, Cat pushes a button that activates the hydraulic wedges. Unseen machinery whirs to life, driving wedges deep into the pre-drilled holes along the quarry wall. As the pressure builds, the slate begins to fracture and calve off in massive sheets. Rob hears himself shout *no*, but his voice is lost beneath the noise.

The slate falls away in great sheets, cascading down on the creatures – he sees them try to run, sees the look of panic on their faces before they disappear beneath a cloud of dust. He prays that any humans beneath those sheets of rock were dead long before they fell, and tries not to let himself think about how recently the creatures were human too.

For a moment he lets himself believe they might have won, that, when the dust clears, the creatures will be buried and the nightmare will be over. But he knows it's a comforting fiction. Before the debris has even settled, they are clawing their way out of it, hurling themselves towards the control booth in a great frenzy of snarling flesh.

He could run to Cat, try and help her, but he no longer understands what the point would be. She knew what would happen, knew how the creatures would respond to aggression, and chose to push the button anyway. He's done fighting. He's been done fighting, he thinks, for some time. He can't recall the last time it did him any good.

When Lucy emerges, he's unsure how to feel. Somehow, she still looks like herself. Something about her must know he's no threat to her. It's true he can't imagine turning on her, even if it came to it: the idea of putting a hammer through her skull, a bullet in her face, is literally unimaginable. He can't think of it without a throb of visceral revulsion. But if she'd somehow perished… maybe he could have lived with that.

'You're alive,' he murmurs.

She cocks her head. 'You sound surprised.'

'Cat…' he tails off. 'I swear, I didn't know she was going to do it.' He shakes his head, trying to clear it. 'Did anyone else make it out?'

Lucy's eyes narrow, and again he'd swear he can see some alien intelligence behind them. 'You don't need to convince me,' she says. 'I'm on your side.'

He knows he shouldn't ask, but it comes out anyway. 'Are you?'

He can see the hurt on her face. 'Is there anything I could say that would convince you?'

'No, I guess not.'

'Well, shit.'

He laughs despite himself.

'I'm still the person I always was,' she says. 'I've just got this thing inside me. Watching what I do. That's all.'

'It's more than that, though, isn't it? We both know that. It's in your head. How the hell am I supposed to know when *it's* speaking, and when *you* are?'

Her fists clench at her side, and he flinches involuntarily. That only seems to make her angrier. 'So this is how it's going to be, then?' she says. 'I'm going to spend the rest of my life with people terrified of me? Wondering if I'm going to sprout arms out of my back like Dr Octopus?'

He doesn't answer that. He doesn't need to. He sees it dawning on her, the realisation that there is no rest of her life. This has to end here. She can't live like this, and nor can anyone around her.

'No,' she says, her face crumpling. 'No, you can't. I won't let you.'

'It's the only way.'

There's the sound of shifting rubble, slabs of slate being hurled aside by impossibly strong arms. Something is climbing out of the debris, covered in dust. It's one of the villagers, his clothes torn and his skin split. His right shoulder is a single, sheer mass of muscle, pulling his neck out of joint; his facial features have been dragged along by the force of it. Even with his strength, he struggles to move the stones, but once he's finally hauled himself out of the rubble he turns, trying with all his might to shift the slabs nearest to him.

Lucy turns to Rob. 'I feel like we ought to help,' she says.

'You're kidding.'

'You heard what Bjorn said. They're not a threat to us. Or they don't have to be.'

'That was before Cat tried to bury them alive!' he hisses. 'How do you think they'll feel about that?'

She shakes her head. 'I don't think they're angry,' she says. 'They're scared. And sad.'

Rob stares at her, trying to ascertain how she knows all this, what the nature of her connection is with these things. Sure, he's pissed that she's repeating Bjorn's words to him too, but right now he's not sure what to think.

'What use are we going to be?' he says, gesturing to the creature digging through the pile of shattered stones. 'We can't shift any of this, not without a vehicle.'

Lucy doesn't look impressed. 'It's not about that,' she says. 'It's about showing willing.'

For a moment he can't get his feet to move. He's certain the moment he gets within reach of that villager he'll be ripped apart. But Lucy's already walking over, her footsteps only slightly tentative, and as much as he wants to run for his life, he knows he has to end this somehow. He can't leave her here, infected with whatever she caught up at the camp. He did that once, letting Bjorn's toxic ideology grow stronger and stronger, and now this. They need to be destroyed, every trace of them wiped out. He's certain Lucy will see that.

She's already getting stuck in, pulling aside what she can of the debris to search for survivors, and as Rob gets closer he can hear the villager emitting a sound very much like a sob from what's left of his mangled throat. He's hunched over, his vast right hand bloody from where he's tried to rescue his neighbours, his friends, his children. He glances up at Lucy when she sets to work, but seems to ascertain no threat.

All that changes when Rob approaches. It takes the man a second or two to register Rob's face, to recognise him as one of the commune, but as soon as he does he breaks off from digging and hurls himself towards Rob as fast as he can manage.

Shit. The villager is huge and unwieldy, which is in Rob's favour, but he's also got a hell of a long reach, and that's assuming he doesn't pull a similar trick to Pyotr. Rob takes off across the quarry, stumbling over his own feet. He can hear the sound of dragging footsteps, the creature's hoarse, laboured breathing. And then another sound. Lucy, shouting 'Stop!'

This can't possibly work. And yet, somehow, it does. The creature first slows, then stops altogether, turning its head as best it can towards Lucy with a quizzical expression. Lucy shoots Rob a look that doesn't fill him with confidence. There's more panic in it than he might have expected, an indication that she's not entirely planned this out.

'He's not a threat,' she says. 'Look at him. He's trying to help.'

Rob can't take his eyes off the villager. His heart's pounding in his ears, and he's still braced to run. On the edge of his vision he can see movement: the creatures that killed Cat stagger towards him, and there are others emerging from the debris. Lucy looks around at all this movement, and then back at the villager before them. She raises her voice, aware that her audience has grown. 'Do you hear me?' she says to all of them, and every one stops to listen. 'This man doesn't want you dead.

He understands what you're looking for. He's willing to leave you in peace.'

Now she turns to Rob. 'Tell me I'm right,' she says, and he feels half a dozen pairs of eyes on him, the crushing weight of expectation.

I don't know what to think, he wants to say. *I don't know who to trust anymore. My judgement's all shot to hell. If you say they're not a threat, then who am I to argue?*

He's seven, kneeling beside his mother in the vegetable garden, the smell of freshly turned earth in his nostrils. Sun on his back, soil cool and damp on his fingers. He places a carrot seed into the divot she's made for him, scoops dirt over the top of it, pats it down. Turns to see her smiling.

'Good job,' she says gently, and then turns her face upwards to enjoy the sun, closing her eyes and breathing deeply. 'God, I love it out here,' she says, half to herself. 'The potential of it all. All of this life, just waiting to burst out of these shells.'

He nods, not really understanding, but glad to be next to her anyway. Glad to be outside, rather than stuck in the vault poring over a book.

A shadow falls over him. He looks round to see Bjorn towering over him. The sun reflecting on his glasses makes his eyes unreadable. 'Hello, Rob,' he says, and Rob sees his mother's face tense slightly. 'What have you been learning today?'

Rob swallows, his mind racing. 'I… I learned about the promise of seeds,' he says. 'About the knowledge inside of them. The secret code that makes them grow.'

Bjorn smiles, but Rob's not sure that it reaches his eyes.

'Very good,' he says, with a slight little nod. He glances up at Rob's mother. 'Well done, Nora.'

He's thirteen, approaching Bjorn's table in the mess hall with a stack of pages in hand. His heart pounding, his stomach roiling. 'Bjorn,' he says, 'can I, uh, ask you about something?'

Bjorn looks up from his reading, nods wordlessly.

'I've been, uh, thinking about… about how we might let people know about the Scriveners. Everything we're doing. I thought we could, uh, create a website, maybe? Or a Facebook page. And there are discussion forums, now. And this site called, uh, YouTube. It's for sharing… like, short video clips. You can record anything you want and they'll put it up there. People can even leave comments.' He takes a deep breath, feels sweat run down his back. 'I'd love to try?' he says, holding out his palms. 'If that's okay?'

Bjorn looks up, and all Rob sees in his face is displeasure. 'What makes you think I'd want that?' he says. 'And, now we're at it, who on earth gave you the impression that it was your responsibility?'

Rob feels himself deflate. 'Of course,' he says. 'And I'm sorry… I didn't mean to suggest…' He heaves a sigh. 'It just felt like an… uh, an opportunity.'

'You want me to praise you for your initiative,' says Bjorn sharply, 'but I won't. I can't. Not when you know so little, when you've no idea what you're proposing. The impact of it. How easily it could distract us, or expose us to risk.' He shakes his head. 'It's idiocy, Rob. Pure foolishness.' And, without another word, he goes back to his writing. Conversation over.

MARGINAL

Rob lowers his head, mumbles an apology. His cheeks are burning. From the corner of his eye, he sees Marcus watching him, a smirk playing over his lips.

He's fifteen, watching Bjorn place a hand on Marcus's shoulder, and Bjorn leaning in to whisper something in his brother's ear. Marcus is sweaty from a day digging the vegetable patch, his T-shirt streaked with dirt where he's wiped his hands. He looks worn out, but when Bjorn places his hand on him Marcus stands up straighter, his face rapt with attention. Hanging on Bjorn's every word.

Rob strains to hear what Bjorn's saying, but he can't make it out. Not that he needs to: he knows what this means. He feels a faint twist of jealousy in his gut at the thought Marcus is being groomed, marked out as a future leader. A chosen one.

He wants to grab Marcus, rip him out of Bjorn's grasp. Only Marcus would never forgive him if he did. It's already too late.

Rob's in the Pit, the darkness thick enough that he can almost taste it. His voice a ceaseless, echoing chant, the words losing their meaning with each repetition, hollowing out everything he's ever believed in…

He is being hugged by Bjorn, who tells him he's the inheritor of a sacred gift: a forerunner, a pilgrim on the shores of a new world. That he's restored…

And right then he knows, beyond question, that the evil here isn't the contagion. It's Bjorn. What he built, what he promised. It warped these people out of shape long before the contagion ever did, taught them a new way to think, so when it finally found them, and nestled itself cosily alongside their spinal columns, it discovered fertile soil.

Maybe if they'd been less scared, less angry, it might never have become so monstrous. Might even have been something beautiful. But they never stood a chance, just like Marcus. It was all Bjorn's fault.

Lucy stands in front of him now. The only person who understands him, the only one he can trust, who'd listened to his story and said, 'We'll make him pay, Rob. We'll make him pay for what he did to you, to all of them.'

God, his head hurts. There's a strange corona effect around the quarry lights, and he's beginning to see double.

Lucy's staring at him, waiting for an answer. 'Rob? Tell them. Tell them you're not a threat.' There's something insistent in her voice, a pressure he'd not heard before. Is she scared of them? Or is she threatening him? He no longer knows the difference.

He looks round at the creatures: bloodied, grotesque, caked in dust. There's still so many of them. 'Listen to me,' he says, his voice trembling as he tries to raise it to a shout. His whole body is shaking, and he can't tell why. Shock or fear, it doesn't much matter which. 'You're not monsters,' Rob says, 'or at least you don't have to be. You're victims. Same as me, same as Marcus. Victims of Bjorn. He thought he'd uncovered a new way to live, but it didn't make any of us better, did it? It just made us angry and scared.' He shakes his head. 'And now look at this mess. Look at what he did to us.' He can see teeth bared, eyes bloodshot and furious, but can't tell if that means anything in their case. 'The authorities are coming,' he says. 'Let me tell them what he did. Let me tell them who you are. Because it doesn't have to end here, I swear.'

Lucy's nodding slowly, but there's a blankness behind her eyes, a slackness in her face. She speaks in a voice that doesn't sound quite like her own: something synthetic about it, as though it has been run through a computer. 'You'd do this for us?' she says.

'Of course,' Rob says, although in his head now there are images of soldiers pulling into the quarry, helicopters descending, great sheets of plastic and sterile medical tents, and he can't shake the sense of something being superimposed over his experience, some part of him that's being manipulated. If only he could determine what was truly his own.

'Oh, Rob,' says Lucy, nodding slowly. 'At last you understand.' She gave a deep sigh. 'I can't begin to tell you how grateful we are.'

She's walking towards him now, her arms open wide. Something so welcoming about her embrace, like coming home. Her arms wrapping around him, her head on his shoulder.

She holds him tightly, so tightly, for the longest time. Tightly enough that he can't move when her torso begins to split, when it forms itself into two enormous jaws. Tightly enough that he can't scream when she drags him into her. Tightly enough that, by the time he loses consciousness in the blackness of her insides, he feels no terror, only familiarity.

53

Subject: THK-▮▮▮: Redacted After-Action Report and Threat Assessment–URGENT

Classification: EYES ONLY – TOP SECRET

Mission: Investigate and neutralise replicative biological threat originating from Craigdhu Quarry (Operation: Silent Purge).

Executive Summary:

Operation Silent Purge resulted in the partial containment of a previously unknown, highly contagious, and rapidly replicating biological entity designated THK-▮▮▮ (hereafter 'Wormwood'). While initial assessment indicated localised replication within specific human organs, subsequent mutations exhibited unpredictable and uncontrollable characteristics, posing a significant and evolving threat to national security.

Current Situation:

The full extent of infiltration remains unclear. Initial estimates suggest widespread societal penetration,

MARGINAL

potentially exceeding containment protocols. Mandatory blood testing and genetic screening programs are currently underway, revealing numerous confirmed cases across major population centres.

Initial observations at Craigdhu confirmed at least four distinct mutation pathways, each resulting in highly destructive physical alterations. These mutations appear to have been triggered by perceived threats or stress, posing a significant risk during containment and neutralisation efforts. Further research is essential to understand the triggers and potential for more aggressive mutations.

Public awareness of the threat posed by Wormwood has triggered widespread panic and social unrest. Major disruptions to infrastructure, communication networks and supply chains are ongoing. Martial law has been declared in key regions to maintain order and facilitate containment efforts.

There was one human survivor found in the quarry, a twenty-six-year-old male answering to Rob. He was unconscious when retrieved. Upon awakening he was lucid, but seemed to be suffering from memory loss, and recalled nothing of how he came to the quarry nor how he survived the events at Site 248.

The body of Bjorn Thrissell, leader of the sect known as the Scriveners, was retrieved from Craigdhu: from notes retrieved from the journalist Lucy Hawthorne's car, we can ascertain that Thrissell appears to have viewed Wormwood as a form of divine gift. Advise that we should suppress this detail in any media reporting, to avoid the belief spreading further.

Recommendations:

1. Accelerate research efforts to understand Wormwood's biology, focusing on replicative

mechanisms, mutation triggers and potential vulnerabilities. Develop rapid and reliable field-testing methods for identifying hosts.
2. Expand mandatory testing and implement stricter quarantine protocols. Develop and deploy specialised containment units equipped with non-lethal neutralisation tactics to minimise mutation risk.
3. Implement a comprehensive media blackout and distribute strictly controlled information to maintain public order and prevent mass panic. Prioritise disinformation campaigns emphasising the efficacy of containment efforts.
4. Elevate military alert levels and prepare for potential large-scale operations to contain and neutralise Wormwood outbreaks. Prioritise development of specialised weaponry and tactics effective against mutated hosts.
5. Continue with observation of subject Rob at a secure facility, to determine whether he possesses any biological immunity.

Conclusion:

Wormwood poses a clear and present danger to national security and global stability. Swift and decisive action is required to contain the threat before widespread societal collapse and catastrophic mutation events occur. This report remains classified to the highest level to prevent public panic and maintain operational security. Further updates will be provided as the situation evolves.

JN354167A/1

ACKNOWLEDGEMENTS

Writing a book is a team sport. There's no way I could have done this without the support of family, friends and the incredible team at Titan Books.

Among others, I'd like to thank Daniel Carpenter, my editor, for his continuing insight and clear love of the genre. It's great to be edited by someone who sees what you're aiming for and can help you realise it – and who understands your most esoteric cultural references.

Thanks to Jordan Lees, my agent, who's been a huge source of support (both emotional and literary), and who encouraged me to pursue this idea back when it was mostly set on a train in Norway.

To Joe Barnes, who did such a great job copyediting this, and for whose encyclopaedic knowledge of British cars I'll be forever grateful.

To Olivia Cooke, whose skilled eye for publicity and marketing finally persuaded me to join Instagram. I'll make it to one of those festivals one day, I promise.

To the team at Titan who pulled together such a great cover. Sorry we made you work up so many options, but the end result is spectacular.

To Miranda, Martin, Milly, Sarah, Lynne, Andrea, Liz, Nicola and Sian who have been an invaluable source of support and encouragement while I've tried to wrestle this thing into shape.

And finally, and most of all, to Mel and Ellen. For their limitless patience while I sneak off to the office to write, for listening while I recount the details of yet another cult or note-taking system, and for reading the very scrappiest of first drafts. I couldn't do it without either of you: shame this book is probably too gory for you both.

ABOUT THE AUTHOR

Tom Carlisle is interested in horror centred on folklore and religious belief. In 2017 he graduated with distinction from Bath Spa's Creative Writing MA, also winning the Bath Spa Writer's Award for outstanding writing. Originally from the north of England, he now lives in Bristol with his family. His debut novel *Blight* was published in October 2023.

For more fantastic fiction, author events,
exclusive excerpts, competitions, limited editions and more

VISIT OUR WEBSITE
titanbooks.com

LIKE US ON FACEBOOK
facebook.com/titanbooks

FOLLOW US ON TWITTER AND INSTAGRAM
@TitanBooks

EMAIL US
readerfeedback@titanemail.com